OUR IMMORTAL BIND

Copyright © 2026 Christopher Hartland

www.tinyghostpress.com

All rights reserved.

The characters and events portrayed in this book are fictitious. Any similarity to real persons, living or dead, is coincidental and not intended by the author.

No part of this book may be reproduced, or stored in a retrieval system, or transmitted in any form or by any means, electronic, mechanical, photocopying, recording, or otherwise, without express written permission of the publisher.

ISBN:
E-book 978-1-915585-38-7
Paperback 978-1-915585-39-4
Hardback 978-1-915585-40-0

Cover Art by: S.J. Gautreaux

OUR IMMORTAL BAND

Christopher Hartland

Tiny Ghost Press

*actual size

To the ones who don't belong.

"A door, once opened, may be stepped through in either direction."
- Doctor Who: "The Girl in the Fireplace"
by Steven Moffat

Chapter One
Orpheus

The blue door is my favourite. It always has been. I'm not sure what it is that sets it apart from the rest. Perhaps it's the pattern of cracks along the wooden surface which I love to run my fingers over. Or maybe it's the particular shine of the brass handle in the hallway's ethereal glow, or even the way you can see the brush strokes in the paint (despite the fact that it was never actually painted). In any case, it's the door I come to when I'm feeling overwhelmed or need a moment of peace.

That's what I desperately need right now: peace. The man's screams still echo through the labyrinthine network of corridors. I sit in front of the blue door with my eyes closed and my wings wrapped around me, a feathered barrier against the noise. My breaths keep coming, thick and fast, as I try to calm myself. I reach out and place my hands against the wood, focusing on ripples and natural warping, searching for the cracks.

Mother's still out there somewhere with the screaming man; of that I am certain. Last I saw, she was holding him to her chest, enveloping him in her winged embrace. I hope that's enough to calm him. His hysterics could lead to corruption, and that's not a fate I'd wish on anybody. Sometimes I wish I could be more like Mother, stoic in the face of terror. But that's not me. When the screaming started, I ran. I turned down corridors, weaving in every direction, until I reached the blue door.

Calling it "the blue door" is an overgeneralization, of course. After all, there are infinite blue doors, just as there are infinite doors of every colour in the Halls of Styx. The labyrinth stretches and twists on and on forever, without a blank stretch of wall in sight. Instead, the walls are adorned with countless doors. Some are plain, some are colourful, some are cracked and worn, some are elaborately decorated. All are wooden, and all have a keyhole, but every door is unique. Just as unique as the people who live behind them. Not that they have any idea – at least, not as long as they're alive.

I often ask people what went through their mind when they saw their door opening. The answer, more often than not, is pure confusion. I suppose that makes sense. The humans of the mortal world are used to the laws of physics, as Mother once explained. They aren't accustomed to seeing a door appear out of thin air, nor do they expect a previously invisible space to be revealed when the door opens. And yet it's an experience that every human goes through.

I can't blame them, therefore, when they react the way the screaming man did.

It was all going so smoothly. Mother had just finished with one of the most peaceful souls I'd ever seen, so I was all too happy to join her in guiding the next one. I followed her to a crimson red door, which she unlocked with one of her many keys, and the man was stood behind it. Dark-skinned and broad-shouldered, he seemed perfectly calm upon seeing my mother, even when his gaze fell upon his own dead body at his feet.

Mother was in one of her most common forms – not the cloaked skeleton of her predecessor, but a tall blonde woman in a long white dress. Her white wings were stretched out behind her, and she was bathed in light. It's a form a great many humans picture when they imagine an angel, and thus it is the one she often chooses.

She stepped over the threshold, held out her hand to the man and led him back through the door before closing and locking it. Her ring of keys remained tightly clasped in her spare hand.

"Hello," I said to him.

And then the screaming started.

An hour passes before the echoes abate – a mortal hour, that is. Time is a funny thing in the Halls of Styx: it doesn't work the same way as in the human world. It couldn't, otherwise how would Mother be able to open the doors of every human at the moment of their death? Much like the Halls themselves, time here twists and turns in all sorts of directions. But mortal time still matters, especially for me.

Still, I keep my hands on the door, drawing comfort from its surface. I sometimes wonder what it'll be like on the day that this door opens. Will the person on the other side come calmly, or will they scream? The calm ones are far more common. In fact, of all the psychopomps so far, Mother has the most successful record. By and large, the humans follow her willingly all the way to the afterlife. I help where I can, or at least, I like to think I do. I talk to the humans about their lives: where they're from, who they loved, what their dreams were, whether they were happy. It comforts them, I think, and Mother has never stopped me. But that's not the only reason I do it. I find humans fascinating – their cultures, the rules of their world. It's all so unfamiliar to me.

Most of the time, they tell their stories with a hint of sadness. They'll shed a tear or two, but they'll stay calm and collected. There are some, however, who don't. Some will lose control of themselves completely. They won't stop asking what's happened to them, and Mother's calming aura won't affect them. Sometimes they get aggressive. They scream and lash out. I hate what happens next, so I never stay to see.

The fact that the screams have gone now is a good sign, though. Hopefully, Mother managed to bring the man to his senses rather than lose him to corruption.

"Orpheus!" Mother calls, snapping me out of my reverie.

Her voice is close, and a moment later, she turns the nearest corner to see me sat beside the blue door. Her wings are folded in now, and she's no longer gleaming with light.

She smiles. Well, she gives the hint of a smile. Hers are never the beaming variety I've seen on the occasional human. It's a smile of acknowledgement, not of joy.

"I thought I'd find you here," she says.

"Is he okay?" I ask, my memory flooding with the man's screams.

"Yes. It took some time, but he followed."

I breathe a sigh of relief. I hadn't realised how tense my body had become.

In the reigns of previous psychopomps, when corrupted sprits were far more common, many would find their way back to the human world. The spirits would slip through the cracks at the very edges of the psychopomp's realm and find their way home, but they'd no longer be themselves. The humans found their own words for the corrupted spirits: ghosts, wraiths, poltergeists, and all manner of other phantoms. The Halls of Styx aren't so easy to escape from, however, not with Mother's complex design.

One of the keys in her hand begins to glow, an old, rusty-looking thing, bright and hot as though set alight. Mother glances down at it, then back at me.

"Are you joining?" she asks, her voice its usual absent tone. There's no emotion behind the question. She simply wishes to know.

I pause. I don't want to go through what just happened again. I feel like my heartbeat has only just returned to normal. But reactions like the man's are a rare thing, and if

I only have the chance to speak to one more human today, I'd like to end on a high.

I nod, and without a second thought, she turns and walks away, leaving me to follow.

The door Mother opens has a natural dark-brown colour. It's dotted with knots, and the edges are warped, but the brass handle is ornately decorated with curled flourishes. When it opens, the scene behind it is one I've witnessed many times. The decor may vary, but the machinery to either side of the single bed always gives away that I'm looking at a hospital. Stood to the side of the bed, where her body still remains, is an elderly lady. Her white skin is lightly tanned and adorned with wrinkles. Her hair is silver and falls in short curls. She turns to face Mother and smiles.

"I'm ready," she says.

This happens a lot with older people: they don't often protest. Mother reaches out her hand, and the woman takes it, following her back through the door into our domain.

"Hello," I say. "What's your name?"

She looks surprised to see me, but happily replies, "Elodie. And you?" Her language is different to the man from earlier – French, I think – but it comes as naturally to my tongue as any other.

"Orpheus."

We're already walking down the corridor, Elodie's hand still in Mother's. We move slowly but with purpose. This will be Elodie's final journey.

"Do you mind if I ask you about your life?" I say.

Elodie chuckles. "What do you want to know?"

I resist the urge to say "everything". Human lives are complex. They need a starting point to talk from, or they won't be able to decide. But there are so many elements to the mortal world that it's hard for me to know what to ask. So I start where I usually do: vague but focused.

"Were you happy?"

Elodie's lips curl into a gentle smile – a smile that, over my time hearing the stories of humans, I've come to learn implies contentment.

"In the end," she says, "yes, I was. Happier than ever, in fact." She looks ahead, down the endless corridor, staring off in thought. "But I wasn't always. For a long time, I wasn't living as my authentic self. I was hiding."

"What do you mean?"

She turns back to me. Her brown eyes glisten, brimming with tears, but her smile remains. "When I was a child, my mother used to tell me that one day I'd meet a man who would sweep me off my feet and make me the happiest person alive. She said I'd love him, and he'd love me, and we'd have children who we'd love even more." She sighs. "But I didn't understand her. I'd never been even slightly attracted to boys, and I told her as much.

"'That's just because you're a child,' she'd say. 'You'll change your mind one day.' And she was almost right. I did meet a man, and he did sweep me off my feet, and I did love him. But not in the way he loved me. I loved him as a friend and nothing more. We had children together, and the love I had for them was greater than anything else, just as my mother had predicted. But still, I was not in love with my husband."

We turn a corner into a curved corridor, Mother still leading the way. I can tell she's listening to the story, even if she won't ask questions.

Elodie continues. "I knew, deep down, the reason why. While I had never felt an attraction towards men, I definitely had towards women – many times. But I had never acted on those feelings. I wanted to be faithful to my husband and couldn't bear the thought of breaking his heart." She sighs again. "But then, when our children were grown and having families of their own, my husband died."

"I'm sorry to hear that," I say. Death can be quite upsetting for humans, so I hear.

"Thank you, dear. It was hard, but in a way, it was also freeing. For the first time in my life, my feelings for women didn't bring me shame. In fact, I found myself rather excited by them. And that's what led me to meet Camille." Her face lights up as she speaks the name.

"Camille?"

"The most beautiful woman I ever met. I came to love her deeply, and she loved me in return, all the way to the end of my life."

The tears fall now, but I know they're not tears of sorrow; they're tears of joy. Elodie reached the end of her life genuinely happy as her true, authentic self.

She tells me more about her time with Camille: the days they spent in Paris, their trips to the beach, the night Elodie invited her children to meet her, the joyful meal they all shared together. I listen to her stories with absolute focus, picturing it all in my mind, only stopping her to ask for more detail, but eventually, her story comes to an end. We've reached the gate.

The corridor stretches out before us. There are no doors here, just vacant walls that give way to a vast white nothingness. The three of us stop.

"This is where you leave us," Mother says, looking at Elodie but reaching out a hand to the void.

"Where does it lead?" She looks nervous. I imagine the gate is quite intimidating for humans. Much like the doors, it defies the laws of their world. "Nowhere and nothingness" is a difficult concept for them to grasp.

Mother replies with one word: "*On.*"

Elodie nods. She looks from Mother to me, thanks us both, then walks forward, into the void. Much like the floor, walls and ceiling, she fades away. Gone forever.

Another key starts to glow.

"Are you joining?" Mother asks again, not leaving any time to dwell on Elodie's departure.

I continue to stare at the gate. "No. I think I'll go to bed, if that's okay."

She leaves without a word.

Since the Halls of Styx are infinite, they don't truly have a centre, but that's where I imagine my house is. Before Father came here, the house didn't even exist. Mother has no need for such a human space, after all. But she created it for him, the same way she created the Halls themselves, crafting a structure out of thin air.

Mother doesn't speak about Father much, and I don't know whether it's because it hurts for her to remember him or because she's ashamed. It's probably a bit of both. According to every rule of the Angelic Order, I shouldn't exist. The only humans allowed in the Halls of Styx are dead, but when Father was here, he was completely alive. Mother has never told me the full story, so all I know is that he somehow managed to pass through a door alive and fell in love with Mother, and together, they had me.

I also know that he looked like me. Same dark hair, gangly frame and pale skin. Same wide blue eyes.

"Like the ocean," Mother used to say, "or that door you love so much."

I enjoyed the first comparison. I've never seen the ocean up close, but it's one of the many things I long to visit in the mortal world.

The house, so I'm told, looks like what humans would refer to as a cabin – all wooden and cosy, filled with blankets and cushions and an ever-burning fire. It sits in the centre of a circular room made to look like woodland. The trees are sparse but tall, stretching up to the illusory ceiling. They're based on one of the previous psychopomp's realms, the Styx Forest. This is the one place in the Halls of Styx that is intended to replicate the human world. It even has a day and night cycle, despite the lack of an actual sun. The ceiling takes the form of an eternally cloud-filled sky. It helps me keep track of the biological clock I'm bound to thanks to my human half.

Unlike Mother, who can change her form at will, the only thing separating me from a basic human appearance is my wings. And that means I age. In mortal terms, I'm around sixteen years old – almost an adult, at least in a lot of the cultures that I've come across when speaking to the humans.

My room is upstairs, and aside from the bed, it is filled mainly with stacks and stacks of my diaries. Well, I call them my diaries. In a way, it would be more truthful to call them other people's. I may write in them, but the words belong to the humans. I grab the one nearest my bed, along with a pen, and turn to the first blank page.

The diaries are where I write the stories the humans tell me. It's my way of remembering them. I often look back at my oldest ones and try to recall their voices as I read them. I title the new page *Elodie* and start to write her tale. I wonder how long it will be before I forget her voice. It gets harder to remember the more time passes. Still, the stories remain, even if the voices don't.

I once asked Mother why she doesn't ask the humans about their lives the way I do.

"I used to," she said. "But I found, after a while, that all the stories started to sound the same. Humans often fall into predictable patterns."

I didn't ask how long the "while" was, but I hope I never experience the same feeling. Sure, there can be some similarities between their stories, but even if the beats are the same, each human's rhythm is unique.

I finish writing Elodie's story with a full heart and a tired mind.

That's when the bells start ringing.

Chapter Two
Evan

Something's wrong with Dad. Or maybe it's more accurate to say something's not wrong enough. He was dying. He flatlined. His heart completely stopped, and that was supposed to be that. And yet here he is, smiling at me and Mum as if nothing strange is happening at all.

I should probably be smiling too. That's how normal people react when their dying dad gets to live a little longer. But I'm not. The first thing I feel isn't joy – it's anger. It might be messed up to say, but I was ready for him to die. In fact, I *wanted* it. Still do. Not that I'd ever admit that to anyone.

"I don't understand," Mum says from my left, wiping the tears from her eyes. We're both standing at the foot of the hospital bed while a doctor fiddles with the machines around Dad. The expression on his face does nothing to explain the situation.

"Anna?" Dad says, eyes fixed on Mum. He still looks just as sick, just as "dying". His skin is pasty, and his ginger hair lies limp on his head. The heart monitor continues blaring its single note, but Dad keeps breathing.

"Doctor?" Mum says. "What's happening?"

The doctor doesn't reply, which says a lot. What says even more is the fact that another doctor bursts in seconds later, parting the thin green drapes to reveal a face of wide-eyed confusion.

"You too?" she asks, voice shaking.

The first doctor stops messing with the machines and looks up. "What do you mean?"

The second gestures for him to follow her, which he does, leaving the three of us alone. It feels like a punishment. I never wanted to be here in the first place, and I thought it would all be over quickly. Yet now here I am, cut off from the rest of the world by vomit-green curtains, with a teary mother and a man I despise.

Mum rushes to Dad's side, taking his hand in hers and gushing about how she thought he was gone and that she "wasn't ready". Dad attempts to comfort her in whispered words, but I know full well it doesn't come naturally to him. Kindness never has, except in very rare moments when it's directed only at Mum. Never at me.

I clear my throat. "I'm gonna go ask around, see what's going on."

Just as I expected, neither of them acknowledges me.

The scene I open the curtains to is like something out of a movie. Doctors and nurses are darting around, either looking stressed out of their minds or shaking their heads in disbelief.

"Excuse me?" I call out to one of the only nurses who doesn't seem completely freaked out. I've seen him around a few times when visiting Dad. He has light brown skin and a short beard, and he's the kind of handsome that makes you spend your time stealing discreet glances instead of focussing on what you're supposed to be doing.

"Hm?" he says, looking up from his clipboard.

But then a hijabi nurse steps between us and mutters something to him that transforms his face into the same crazed look as everyone else.

"How is that possible?" he says before running off with her to another ward.

I look around at the other patients – at least those who aren't hidden behind curtains – and they're all starting to look anxious. I'm feeling it too. What could be so bad that it's got every doctor and nurse acting so strangely? Are we about to learn of a zombie virus outbreak?

My phone buzzes in my pocket. It's a text from Wren.

Have you seen this???? it says, with a link pasted below.

I open it.

Holy shit.

For the last few hours, across the entire world, there hasn't been a single death. Not one. People have been injured. People have been ill. Hearts have stopped, and spines have snapped. By all accounts, many people *should* have died. But they simply haven't. Somehow, it seems, the human race has become immortal.

It's all over every news site and social media platform. Some are calling it a government hoax, some a scientific experiment, some an act of God. But most are stating the only thing that could be true: magic.

All too often, magic gets the blame for global crises. Most recently, it was claimed to be the cause of COVID-19. I remember the conspiracy theorists suggesting that witches were trying to wipe out all mundane folk, demonstrating as usual how little they understand about how magic actually works. But this time? This time, magic is the only logical answer. How could it be anything else?

And yet . . . I'm baffled. Turning the entire human race immortal would take an immensely complex spell. I can't even begin to imagine how many witches it would require to pull it off, and the preparation alone would be impossible to keep hidden.

"So, your dad's still alive, then?" Wren asks over the phone.

"Yeah." I'm a few streets away from the hospital now. I couldn't stay there, not with all the news unfolding. The staff were getting more and more manic, and I get why – not only has their entire understanding of human biology been torn apart in front of them, but they're also starting to realise what the impact on the hospital will be. If those who were supposed to die keep living, then pretty soon, the hospital beds will be overflowing.

"You don't sound too happy about that," Wren says.

I sigh. "Does that make me a terrible person?" I cross the road to avoid a group of drunk middle-aged men huddled outside a pub. "He flatlined, and Mum was crying, but I just watched. I was ready. I . . ." I don't finish the sentence, but I'm sure Wren knows where I was going. They know my dad and I don't get along (and that's putting it lightly).

"*He's* the terrible person, not you."

I turn up a narrow street and silently curse myself for not having brought my hoodie. The sun has fully set, and it's getting pretty chilly. Plus from the look of the clouds, I think it might be about to rain.

"And anyway," Wren continues, "it doesn't matter. He's alive. You've got nothing to feel guilty about."

"Maybe this is the universe's way of punishing me for wishing him dead."

Wren laughs. "Turning everyone immortal seems a bit extreme for that. And I'm not sure I'd call it a punishment."

"You might not be saying that in a few days."

I recall the last thing I read before leaving the hospital. It was a Reddit post talking about how quickly things could go downhill if this whole immortality thing keeps going. Without people dying, hospitals are going to become overrun, and the world population will skyrocket like never before. As far as resources are concerned, no one is prepared for something like that. This has the potential to be a global catastrophe a million times worse than anything we've seen before.

"Listen," I say as I turn onto my street, "I'm home now. I'll call you later, okay?"

"Okay."

The rain starts as soon as I put the key in the door. I dart inside and lock it behind me, taking a deep breath and trying not to dwell on the fact that the whole world has completely changed.

I dump my shoes at the foot of the stairs and head up to my room. It's just as I left it before I rushed out with Mum – school bag and uniform tossed carelessly on the floor, laptop still open on my desk, half-finished homework still awaiting my return beside it. I ignore all of that and open the drawer in my bedside table instead. Under a few sheets of paper torn from one of my schoolbooks is my grimoire, and on top of that is a thin, short rod of brass-like metal with a hooked top. To the untrained eye, it could easily be mistaken for a crochet hook, but it is my wand. Passed down to me by my grandma, these are my most prized possessions, and as far as my parents are concerned, they don't exist.

I pick up the wand, pocketing it, before running my hand across the worn leather cover of the grimoire. The pages within are yellow with age and barely held together at the spine, but Gran's work remains as clear as ever as I flick through the pages. Drawings of wands hooking and stitching different coloured threads together sit beside descriptions of the effects of the various spells. The patterns are made clear, with a described order in which each coloured thread must be added to the row of stitches. They bring memories to mind of Gran teaching me the basics of witchcraft, her hands guiding mine as I used my wand to form stitches in the fabric of the universe.

I find the page I need and head back downstairs and through the living room to the locked door of Dad's office. With the grimoire propped open on a nearby side table, I take a deep breath and close my eyes. When I open them again, the world looks different. Now across my field of vision, on top of the mundane world that any sighted person can see, there is a near-infinite set of thin, dull, golden threads.

The threads stretch out in every direction, intersecting every object in sight, each one corresponding to a different property of the object it's connected to. I focus on those that touch the door in front of me – specifically those in and around the keyhole. I keep my mind on the goal at hand and watch as certain threads turn from a dull gold to various vibrant colours. I still hear Gran's guiding words even now.

"Think about the spell you want to cast," she used to say. "Hold the desired effect in your mind. The colours will show you which threads to use."

The door's density, the flow of the air through the lock, the temperature of the lock's metal . . . I spot the red, green and blue corresponding threads. I reach out, curling my fingers around the threads that define each property, gently manoeuvring my hand so that they become nicely taut. I glance at the open page of the grimoire. I've done this spell many times, but it's fiddly, and I want to make sure I get it right.

Matching the sketch in the grimoire, I bring my wand into view with my spare hand, reaching out to pull on the taut threads, looping them around the hook at the wand's tip, adding each colour in a different order and interlocking them to form a row of stitches. I close my eyes again and focus on the vibrations that are ever-present within the threads, letting them move through my body, feeling them trigger a spark somewhere deep within myself – the spark of magic. I open my eyes to see my wand now glowing, and as a new vibration emanates outwards from within me, that glow passes from the wand into the threads. Their colours become one combined shining light as my magic travels out from the metal of the wand, along the threads and into the keyhole.

The lock clicks, the threads vanish, and the door swings open.

I can't help but smile. It gets easier every time.

The lights in Dad's office are always dim, as though he thrives in darkness. Bookshelves and chests of drawers line the walls, and in the centre is an ornate mahogany desk that used to belong to Gran. I know for a fact that she'd hate seeing it used by Dad. I never saw her will, but I like to believe she left the desk to me, no matter what my parents might claim.

Stacks of files cover the desk, all stamped with the same obnoxious seal by the witchfinders. I've been known to sneak in here and take a peek at those files, no matter how "top secret" they are, but that's not why I'm here now. I move to the other side of the desk, sit myself in the stiff old swivel chair and turn on the computer.

Here's my theory: if the sudden mass immortality was caused by a spell (which is surely the only logical cause), then that spell would have to be very powerful – the most powerful spell ever cast, even. I can't begin to imagine the complex rows of stitches or the number of different threads involved. And if that's the case, then there's no way it has gone unnoticed by the witchfinders. With any luck, there'll be an email sitting in Dad's inbox right now detailing exactly what's gone on.

One password (which hasn't changed in years – thanks, Dad) and a few clicks later, the latest emails are on screen. There are plenty of them, and all about the events of today, but it seems the witchfinders are as much in the dark as the rest of us. Somehow, that makes me even more worried.

Mum calls a while later to update me on Dad (still breathing) and check how I am (as lost as the rest of the world). She's going to spend the night at the hospital, but I warn her that pretty soon, there might not be enough room for that.

I'm on the living room sofa, blanket draped over me while I watch the news. The Prime Minister's making a statement. It's a load of waffle about how all the "best people" are trying to work out exactly what caused the immortality, a thank you to the hospital staff working tirelessly as the bizarre event unfolds, and a plea for people not to panic. Like that will make a difference. I suppose you can't blame her, really. What the hell *should* she say at a time like this?

I get a text from Mum: **Your dad's boss is making a statement on ITV.** I can't help but scowl when I switch the channel to see her.

Eloise Morgan is a tall, slender white woman in her late sixties, with grey hair tied back in a tight bun. The permanently sour expression on her face sums up exactly how I feel about her and perfectly matches her utterly self-indulgent job title: Witchfinder General. Rather oddly, however, the screen displays a static image of her smoking a cigar with her "statement" plastered across her in bold lettering rather than a live interview.

I remember when Gran first explained to me who Eloise is and what the witchfinders do. At the time, I was too young to fully understand the context of it all, but I know now why I needed to be told. Gran was keeping me safe. Everyone knew that she was a witch, but only she knew that I was a warlock, and she intended to keep it that way.

"Magic scares people," she told me. "It always has. People fear what they don't understand, and fear makes them do terrible things."

It didn't take long for me to see those terrible things in action, especially with a father like mine. A man who would turn against his own mother.

I shake my head, not wanting to dwell on those memories. I turn my attention to the TV.

The world is facing an unprecedented supernatural event, Eloise's statement reads. It's unusual for her to miss an opportunity to spout her rhetoric on TV, though I suppose she might be too busy to face the cameras. **The mass immortality is quite clearly an act of perversion against the natural order of our world, brought about through the unlawful use of magic.**

I scoff. If Eloise had her way, any use of magic at all would be unlawful, and she has campaigned for such a rule many times. As it stands, the use of magic is legal if it is performed in the privacy of a witch or warlock's own home and doesn't impact the lives of the mundane. Obviously, whoever has caused the immortality has broken that rule.

But who could have that power?

I can assure you all that the witchfinders will be working tirelessly alongside the police to bring the perpetrator of this act to justice.

I roll my eyes and turn off the TV.

Chapter Three
Orpheus

I've only heard the bells once before, when a coven of necromancers managed to stop a spirit passing through his door. Mother dealt with that quickly, though. They only rang for a matter of minutes before she successfully brought the spirit across, not that he was too pleased. I know that the bells also rang when Mother first met Father. The presence of a living human in the Halls of Styx was bound to set them off.

Aside from those occasions, however, the bells have remained silent throughout Mother's time as psychopomp. Until now. The dolorous echoing thrum captures the meaning perfectly: something is wrong.

I drop Elodie's diary and run out of my room. The wooden walls and floor vibrate with each ring, so loud in volume I worry the house might collapse. Even the trees outside seem to shudder.

"Mother!" I call, but to no response. It's unsurprising – she's very rarely near the house and even less likely to be inside it. Instead of shouting for her again, I follow my instincts. The Halls may be infinite, but it's impossible to get lost in them. Well, impossible for anyone with angel blood. It's like a map of the Halls is woven into my body. I don't need to think about where to go; I just know.

I leave the forest, pass doors and turn corners, all the while surrounded by the ringing of the bells. The further I move, the clearer it becomes that there's a problem. The ethereal glow that always fills the Halls is faltering. It flickers, almost like the electric lights of the human world, which I've only ever seen through the doors. And there's a chill in the air, a draught. I often feel a gust of wind from the human world when a door is opened, but it never lasts this long.

I turn once more and finally see Mother. Her hair is darker than before, and she's shrouded in a black cloak, one of many appearances she often dons. But her face is unlike anything I've ever seen – not in form, but in expression. In front of her, a green door hangs open, and she's staring at it with wide eyes and her mouth hanging open. She's horrified. I might even say scared.

"Mother?" I say, voice quiet.

She says nothing.

I step closer, rapidly filling with nerves, sidling up to her so that I can see whatever she's seeing through the door. Whatever it is that has her reacting so extremely.

But it's just a room. A normal room in a house like any other. Dimly lit and decorated with framed photos. Worn sofas angled to face a television. The corpse of an old man sat in a chair. It's no different to what we see through the doors every day, except the old man's spirit is nowhere to be seen.

"Did you take him to the gate already?" I ask, turning to face Mother.

She retains her horrified expression and stays silent, but she nods.

"Okay . . ." I look back at the door. It shouldn't still be open. Mother always locks the doors as soon as she brings the spirits through. Is that what the apparent crisis is? Did she just forget to lock this door? That would be a dangerous thing to do, and very unlike her, so I'm sure a reaction like this would be her natural response.

I hesitate, but when Mother continues to say nothing, I step forward and close the door myself, shutting off the draught. I hold out my hand to Mother. "Can I have the keys?"

Still nothing.

"Mother?" I make a point of waving my hand. "The keys?"

She shakes her head. "The keys are gone."

The ringing of the bells grows louder.

"Gone?" I say, blinking in disbelief. "What do you mean 'gone'? How can they be gone?"

Mother looks to the hand in which she normally carries the ring of keys, now empty. "Stolen," she says. Her voice carries no emotion, but the weight of her horror hits me all the same.

Without the keys, no door can be opened. And if no door can be opened, then . . . oh gods.

"What do we do?" I ask.

It takes a moment, but Mother's eyes come into focus, her jaw clenches, and she closes her empty hand. Without a word, but with absolute purpose, she turns and walks away.

I follow Mother through the corridors, all the way back to the forest beneath a dark sky. She walks right up to the house, but rather than entering, she goes to the back, where the well-trodden earth gives way to a descending spiral staircase. It's never been hidden from me, but I've never gone down. Mother made it clear to me from a young age that the lower floor was for her only, and even then, it's rare to see her entering it.

Now, though, I follow her descent, and she doesn't stop me. The Halls' ethereal glow returns here, but it continues to flicker. I'm faced with a vast cavern with stone walls. It reminds me of one spirit's description of the caves they loved to explore before they died. From the ceiling hang five bells in a pentagon, each the size of my entire house, their surface the same brass colour as the handle of my favourite door.

The cave seems to stretch out as infinitely as the Halls above, but rather than doors, it is instead filled with glowing orbs. They're small enough that they could be held comfortably in a person's palm, and their colours vary as much as the doors. They float in the air, some moving slowly while others remain still.

Mother waves a hand, and the bells cease their oscillations, plunging us into a deep silence. The orbs move aside as she walks along the stone floor, letting her pass without obstruction. I follow, and the orbs move for me too. As I pass them, I hear whispers. The quietest whispers I've ever heard, too quiet to make out their words, but whispers all the same. From this distance, it becomes clear that the orbs aren't just solid balls of colour but are instead made of an incredibly thin fibre rolled into a ball, almost like a glowing ball of colourful wool. It brings to mind the few stories I've heard from witches over the years, how they cast their spells by manipulating the fabric of the universe. Are these orbs made of that same fabric? I'd say I can't believe this has been hidden beneath me all my life, but I learned a long time ago not to question the work of angels and the gods.

Mother finally comes to a stop in the centre of the pentagon formed by the bells. Lines carved into the stone floor form the shape. I stay at the edge, cautious, and Mother's eyes meet mine.

"Only a witch could have stolen the keys," she says. The fear in her face is gone now. She's back to her usual matter-of-fact self, yet I can't help but feel scared.

"How?"

"I can't be certain. But with the right spell, they could have kept the door open after I brought a spirit through."

"And then they could have entered the Halls?"

"Indeed."

It wouldn't be unprecedented. Father was alive when he managed to get in, after all. But to enter the Halls *and* steal Mother's keys? That would take a true master of magic.

"My memories of the moments after opening the door are hazy," Mother continues. "Whatever the witch did, it's possible they caused me to leave the keys in the door, making them easy to steal."

I gulp. The idea of a human so bold as to attempt something like this baffles me. The repercussions of such an act will be catastrophic.

"So, what happens now?" I ask. "Will you chase after the witch? Enter the human world?"

Mother shakes her head. "Would that I could, but I must remain here. The unlocked door is already causing damage to this realm."

The light flickers again.

"As long as it remains unlocked, the laws of the mortal universe will continue to seep into the Halls of Styx. If I leave, I won't be able to slow the effects. Entropy will take hold, and everything will fall apart."

I try to imagine what she's describing. The doors crumbling. The cabin falling to pieces. Everything I've ever known, gone. It's a terrifying image. I wonder if that's what was going through Mother's mind when I found her at the open door.

"Then how do we get the keys back?" I ask, trying to sound as emotionless as her but failing with a voice crack.

Mother hesitates. "Believe me when I say this is a last resort, but as I cannot leave, I'm afraid you will have to go in my place."

"Me?"

She nods.

Now I'm the open-mouthed one. "But . . . I don't . . . I can't . . ." I never even considered this possibility. She wants *me* to get the keys back?

"I wouldn't ask this of you if there were another choice."

An orb floats past my right ear, its whispers permeating my confusion. Mother's suggestion is ludicrous. Completely impossible. I've never left the Halls of Styx. All I know of the human world is what I've heard from the spirits of the dead. To take on a task as important as this is the most terrifying thing I've ever imagined. And yet in the back of my mind, there's a spark of excitement. The one thing I've wanted to do since the moment I first learned of its existence is travel to the human world.

"You're scared," Mother says in her absent tone. "I understand that. But such a human emotion is exactly what will help you in their world."

I shake my head. "I wouldn't even know where to start."

"You're not as naïve as you think. Their world is different to ours, yes, but it has its systems. It has its rules. They will not be so hard to learn. And besides, I don't intend for you to do this alone."

She holds out her hand, and suddenly, a green orb comes hurtling across the cavern to land in her palm.

"What do you mean?"

The edges of the pentagon in the stone floor begin to glow the same green as the orb. Mother releases it, allowing it to hover in place at the pentagon's centre. At that same moment, more orbs make their way towards her, entering the pentagon and floating in various positions around it.

"A witch stole the keys," Mother says, "so you need an expert in tracking witches."

She starts to inspect the nearby orbs, some more intently than others. When she reaches the sixth one, she taps it. It spins in place and glows a little brighter, emitting orange light. The thread that forms it unravels slightly so that the orb grows in size. Apparently satisfied, she clasps her hand around it, and the rest of the orbs float away, the green one included, and the glowing lines on the ground fade.

She looks at me and holds up the orange orb. "This represents a human who would have been one of the next to die had the keys not been stolen. Geographically, he is close to the open door. And he's a witchfinder."

She stares at me as though I'm supposed to have understood. I've heard the term "witchfinder" before, from a dead warlock. He didn't say much – he preferred to focus on happier memories – but he said he'd always been scared that the witchfinders would catch him. They didn't sound like the type of people I'd want to make friends with.

"So . . . ?" I say to Mother, confused.

"So you must enter the human world through the open door, seek out this witchfinder and ask him to assist you in finding the keys."

I chew my lip. She makes it sound so easy, yet I'm certain it will be anything but.

"And there's one other thing." She approaches me, leaving the pentagon. With her spare hand, she reaches into her black robes and pulls out an object that I've never seen before. She hands it to me.

It reminds me of a pocket watch carried by a spirit I met a few years ago. It has a brass back and is small enough that I could easily close my hand around it and hide it from view. There are no hands or numbers, but instead a circle of exposed, complex clockwork that seems to go on forever if you look close enough. The cogs turn and click against each other in no discernible pattern, and from the centre emits the familiar ethereal glow of the Halls of Styx. The whole device is attached to a long chain loop, like a necklace.

"What is this?"

"A gift from the gods," Mother says.

I look at her with an inquiring eye.

"Come," she says before walking back to the staircase.

The leaves of the forest look different. In the dim light, it's hard to tell, but they're not as green as usual. They've never been alive, not truly, but right now, they're looking less alive than ever. In fact, a few look to be turning shades of orange and red. This must be the onset of entropy that Mother mentioned.

We head out of the forest and back into the Halls. I keep a tight grip on the clockwork pendant.

"You are a child of two worlds, as you well know," Mother says, eyes on the path ahead, "and your birth was an unprecedented event. The gods had not been happy with your father's presence in this domain, but they allowed it. Your existence, however, posed a new question: where did you belong?"

I've never heard this story before, but I suppose it makes sense. A half-angel child can't have been what the gods expected when they appointed Mother as psychopomp.

"Your father had no intention of leaving the Halls, and so for your childhood, it made sense that you would remain here with us, even after your father's death."

I catch up to Mother's side and notice a familiar glint of sadness in her eye when she mentions Father. If he'd chosen to return to the human world, he would have lived for many more years. I wonder if it was his love for Mother that prevented him from choosing a longer life. Or perhaps it was his desire to raise me with her, even if he wouldn't be around for much of my life.

"But," Mother continues, "as a half-human, it was decided that you have the right to live in the human world, should you so choose. That is a choice I would have presented to you on your eighteenth birthday. And the choice would have come with this." She points at the clockwork device still in my hand. "You see, by the laws of the mortal world, your existence is impossible. If you were to step through the door right now, your angelic form would begin to tear your human body apart. You would have an hour at most to live before your human body would be destroyed completely, and your angel half would disintegrate in turn. You wouldn't just die; you'd cease to exist."

Quite how this story is supposed to make me any less scared, I don't know. We turn left, and the ethereal glow flickers again.

"That's why the gods created the anchor. If you wear it, your angelic form will be kept safely in your human body, unable to break free. As far as the laws of the universe are concerned, you will be just like any other human."

I stop in my tracks. "So, when I go to the human world, I need to wear this . . . or I'll die?" I shake my head. "Sorry, 'cease to exist'?"

Mother stops too. "Well, you could last an hour at most, but essentially, yes."

I stare at the anchor. This device was made by the gods themselves to give me a chance at a human life. It's hard to believe that not so long ago, I was sat in bed, adding to my collection of diaries just as I would any other day.

I take a deep breath and face Mother again. "You really want me to do this?"

"It's not about what I want. It's about what the world needs. Humanity is not built for immortality; it is imperative that you return the keys to me. You must find the witchfinder, ask for his help, and not tell anyone else what you're doing. Anyone could be the thief."

My heart is racing, but again I feel that twinge of excitement, and I nod.

We start walking again, and after one final turn of a corner, we're faced with the unlocked door.

"How do I find the witchfinder?" I ask.

"That's what this is for." Mother holds out the orange orb again. "Place your hand on its surface."

I do as she says, and my mind is suddenly awash with images. I'm looking into a mirror and seeing the face of a man in his forties with ginger hair and sallow skin. *Flash.* I'm exiting a car to see a large cement block of a building with hundreds of windows. There's a sign to the right of me declaring it *Elmwood Vale Hospital. Flash.* I'm in a hospital bed with doctors swarming around me as a single note blares on and on. *Flash.* I'm looking at a short woman with curly golden hair, her eyes red with tears, and a broad-shouldered boy a similar age to me with a mop of strawberry blond hair stood to her left. He doesn't look sad at all. In fact, he looks angry. *Flash.*

I'm back in the Halls of Styx. Mother retracts the orb while I reorient myself, breathless.

"Was that him?" I ask, picturing the dying man. "The witchfinder?"

"Yes. His name is Arthur Weaver. And you have a location?"

"Elmwood Vale Hospital."

"Excellent."

We face the door. This is it. This is the moment my quest begins. It's all happened so fast, and there's nothing I can do to stop it. Whether I like it or not, I have to do this.

Mother reaches out and opens the door, revealing the same living room I saw earlier.

"Oh, and one more thing," Mother says.

I force my face to stay calm. How can there be more?

"As long as this door remains unlocked," she says, "time in the Halls of Styx will be synchronous with time in the human world. Every moment I don't have the keys is a moment the humans cannot die. Their world isn't prepared for that. You must find the keys as quickly as possible."

I close my eyes, searching for the courage I desperately need.

"Understood?"

I take a deep breath and open my eyes again. "Understood."

Mother smiles at me. A genuine smile. Now I know this is serious.

"Good luck, Orpheus."

I smile back, place the chain of the anchor around my neck, and step through the door.

Chapter Four
Evan

For a moment, when I wake up, I forget what happened yesterday. As I reach over to turn off my alarm, the world feels blissfully normal. Then I remember.

There's a text from Mum on my phone sent late last night, well after I fell asleep, telling me that Dad seems stable and that there's talk of discharging him even with the lack of a heartbeat.

I don't reply, instead tossing my phone onto my mattress and stretching myself awake. It's a Friday, which means school, which seems absolutely ridiculous given the circumstances. And yet I don't know what else there is to do. My overzealous attempt at doing something about the crisis last night proved pointless. As if I could make a difference anyway. If I don't go to school, all I'll be doing is sitting alone with my thoughts, and that's never a good idea.

I pull on my uniform, which has been a lot tighter recently. I think I've missed my chance at an upwards growth spurt, but after joining the swimming team, my shoulders have broadened, and nothing quite fits like it used to. I could do with a new blazer, really, but what with Dad's illness, there's not been time to do a uniform shop. Besides, I've only got the rest of year eleven, and then I won't need it anymore.

I down some cereal and pack my bag before heading out but stop myself at the door. Usually, I'd leave my grimoire and wand at home, safely tucked away in my bedside drawer, but given yesterday's events, I'm not sure it's wise to be so unprepared. I run back upstairs, grab the grimoire and wand and slip both into my bag. I can only imagine the look on Mum and Dad's faces if they could see me.

Wren is already waiting at the bus stop when I get there, rocking on the balls of their feet while listening to music through their headphones.

"Morning," I say.

They don't hear me.

I wave my hand in front of their face, and they stumble back, startled, pushing their headphones down around their neck. Now I can hear the music too. It's the usual mellow sound of an indie band I've never heard anyone talk about except Wren.

"Are you trying to kill me?" they blurt out.

"Maybe not the best choice of phrase at the minute," I say, smirking.

Their dark eyes widen, and their freckled face, usually a light brown, takes on a rosy hue. "Oh, God. Sorry. I didn't think. I—"

I laugh, patting the side of their arm. "I'm just messing with you."

They force out a breathy laugh and shove their headphones into their bag. "So, how are things?"

"Oh, you know, Dad's still impossibly alive, and Mum's still with him."

"Normal Friday, then?"

"Pretty much."

Wren fidgets with a strand of their dark mullet and smiles weakly. They're always pretty good at finding the humour in a bad situation, but it's clear they're not quite sure how to handle this one. I doubt anyone is.

The bus pulls up, and we head to our usual seats near the back of the bottom deck. We used to sit up top way back in year seven, until Wren fell down the stairs and everyone teased them about it for weeks. It still gets brought up occasionally by the laziest of bullies, but they're usually met with an eye roll.

I rest my bag on my lap, gripping it more tightly than usual thanks to the presence of my grimoire and wand. The last time I took them anywhere public was the nearby forest, and even then, I was a ball of anxiety, worried that I might lose them. I was casting some very basic spells, encouraging flowers to bloom in a clearing. It'd have been too risky to do anything stronger thanks to my dad being one of the witchfinders. As far as he and the other witchfinders are aware, I'm completely mundane.

"Hey," Wren says, "it's okay. She doesn't catch the bus anymore."

"Huh?" I raise an eyebrow.

"You've never looked more tense. I know it's because of Zara. But you're barely going to see her."

"Oh." I chuckle.

I can't blame Wren for misunderstanding – they have no idea I'm a warlock. If the events of last night hadn't happened, I probably *would* be worrying about seeing Zara. But right now, she's the least of my priorities.

All around us, talk is turning to the topic of immortality. A year nine girl at the back of the bus loudly proclaims that it *has* to have been caused by a witch. There are a few mutters of agreement, but then a year ten boy across the aisle rolls his eyes.

"Oh please," he says. "It's obviously all fake."

Another year ten boy scowls at him. "Mate, what are you talking about? My dad's a doctor, and he says—"

"I don't care what your dad says. It's just another hoax, like all that COVID crap."

I bite my tongue. There's no getting through to some people, even when clear evidence stares them right in the face. But all these theories turn my mind to a new question:

if the immortality was caused by magic – which it must have been – then how is the magical community ever going to recover?

Witches have been hated for centuries, but the extent of that hatred has varied. From a complete ban to an age restriction to our current state of keeping it private and discreet, the laws around the use of magic have changed many times. Our history has been erased, countless grimoires destroyed or confiscated, wands melted, and thanks to the witchfinders, some of us have lost our magic entirely, but there have always been those with hope for a better future. There are people who campaign for better magical rights, and every so often, they gain a bit of traction. If a global catastrophe gets blamed on us, though? I'm not sure any more progress will be made.

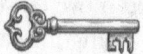

Elmwood Vale High School is one of the oldest buildings in the area. Decades ago, it was a fancy private school exclusively for boys who no doubt spent their free time laughing at the plights of the poor. These days, it's open to everyone, even if the building itself still gives off an elitist aura. Tall arched windows cover the front of the building, each surrounded by ivy which is some of the only greenery still around this far into October.

I follow Wren to our form room, but as we move through the corridors, I notice that the hordes of students we usually have to wade through aren't as dense as usual. In form, too, there are fewer people. I realise as I take my seat that some parents must have decided to keep their kids home after the events of last night.

"Morning, everyone," says Mr Khan.

There's an unusual edge to his voice. Normally, he's the more put-together, serious-all-the-time type of teacher, but right now he seems . . . nervous. Uncertain.

He speeds through the register and puts the usual morning announcement slides on the board, but then his attention snaps to a raised hand at the back of the class.

"Sir?" says Laura. "Could you put the news on?"

"Oh," he says. "Um, I'm not sure if—"

"Please, sir," says another voice – Haroon, who I'm not sure has ever said the word "please" before in his life.

There are murmurs of agreement across the room. Usually, form time would involve half the class listening to Mr Khan's notices while the other half doodle in their planners or go on their phones under the tables. Today, though? Everyone just wants to know if there have been updates to the immortality situation – including Mr Khan.

Sure enough, he abandons his PowerPoint and loads up a live feed of the news.

There are only fifteen minutes left of form, but in that time, we learn that the immortality shows no sign of stopping, that the world's top scientists are working tirelessly but are no closer to understanding what happened, and that religious leaders are divided over whether this is a gift from God or a sign of the end times. When the bell goes, the image on the screen is a graphic depicting a worst-case scenario in which a population boom will cause us to run out of food.

"I'm pretty sure form is supposed to be a *positive* start to the day," says Wren as we leave the room.

I laugh weakly, replaying the news report in my mind.

"But the thing I don't get is, why do it?"

"Hmm?"

"Whichever witches did the spell," Wren says. "Why do it? What's the goal?"

I shrug. I never know how to respond when Wren talks about magic, which, given that it's their autistic special interest, happens a lot. Sometimes, I think it would be easier for me to just confess that I'm a warlock. I know they wouldn't out me, and my God, would they be delighted to find out they have a warlock as a best friend. But I can't. No one can know. I promised Gran.

"I was reading this Reddit thread last night, and this one guy was saying it'd take every witch in the world to do a spell that big. But that can't be right, can it? I mean, some artefacts could have been involved, couldn't they?"

"No idea." I'm not lying. Sure, I'm a warlock, but in this world of magical suppression, it's pretty hard to be particularly knowledgeable about magic. I've only ever had Gran and the grimoire she left to teach me. And as far as artefacts are concerned, I've never even held one. I've only ever had my wand. I wouldn't be surprised if Wren knows more about magic than me, even though they're mundane.

"Maybe it's some sort of protest? Like, 'Hey, if you keep screwing us over, we're going to change the entire world.' I mean, all power to them if so. I guess they'd probably have made some sort of statement by now, though."

"Probably." I could do it right now. I could grab them by the arms and tell them I'm a warlock, thank them for being so supportive of witch rights. They'd hug me, and we'd be closer than ever. But I can't. If there's even the slightest chance that my parents would find out the truth of who – of what – I am, my life would be over.

"You've got history now, right?" Wren asks as we reach the end of the corridor.

"Yeah."

"I've got music. See you at break?"

I nod, letting them run off in the opposite direction.

As if I couldn't feel worse, there's a new seating plan in history, and I've been placed next to Zara. She sits first and then resolutely ignores me as I sit by her side. She fixes her eyes on the teacher and sweeps her long, dark hair over the shoulder closest to me, as though forming a barrier. I catch the familiar scent of her shampoo – green apple – and try my hardest not to drown in memories of running my hand through her hair.

I turn my eyes to the worksheet on the desk, but even then, Zara remains in my periphery. She writes on her worksheet with the fountain pen I bought her for her fifteenth birthday back in year ten, when we were nothing more than friends. I hate that part of me wishes it were my hand in hers rather than the pen.

Mr Holden clears his throat and starts rambling about how our mock exams are in a few weeks. I don't listen – I can't – because now Zara is doodling on the back of her hand, creating jet black swirls against her dark brown skin, and I can't think about anything else. And there was me thinking I wouldn't care about seeing her today.

There's a spark in my mind. An itch. A desire to reach out. Not physically, but mentally. One of the last things Gran taught me was how to use magic to make a psychic connection with someone, a bond between minds so that information can pass between them. It's harder to perform on an unwilling subject, but a strong emotional connection can bypass that difficulty. If Zara is thinking about me, it would be all too easy to enter her mind. It would only take one gentle pull of a thread, one simple stitch around the hook of my wand. And oh, would I love to know what she's thinking right now. To know if she regrets what she did.

But I snuff the spark. Gran was always very clear about the morals of magic, and invading a person's mind for personal gain definitely goes against those. Such abuse of power is exactly what turns people against witches. It's what fuels the hatred that people like Eloise Morgan harbour. I refuse to ever fan that flame.

It doesn't matter what Zara thinks. Whether she regrets it or not, she still cheated on me. And I still broke up with her. And right now, that shouldn't be anywhere near as important to me as a worldwide supernatural event.

There's a knock at the classroom door, halting the monotonous drawl of Mr Holden.

"Sorry to interrupt," says Ms Scott, the head of year eleven, poking her head into the classroom. "Could I please borrow Evan?"

I pretend not to notice that Zara is now staring right at me.

Mr Holden nods, and I follow Ms Scott out into the corridor.

"Evan," she says plainly, "we just got a call from your mum."

"Oh?"

"About your dad."

Chapter Five
Orpheus

There is no noise as my feet touch the ground. I'm used to the echoing that accompanies my every step in the Halls of Styx, but here the floor is carpeted. It dulls the sound.

I flex my fingers. My body feels different, more solid. And, most noticeably, there's a distinct lack of wings on my back.

I hear the door close behind me and turn to see it standing there, translucent. To humans, it will be completely invisible.

I breathe in the air, cold and strange smelling. Not unpleasant, just odd. There's no dead body here anymore; the old man's chair is empty. I know from stories of humans that it is customary to delay the natural decay of their corpses and hold events known as funerals, so I assume the man's family must have collected his body already.

The funerary traditions of humans have always seemed odd to me – the body, after all, is just a vessel for the real person within, and that real person leaves their world as soon as their door is opened. But I suppose the body becomes a symbol of who the person was, and the funeral is a transition between a world with the person in it and a world without. It's like the spirit's journey through the Halls, in a way.

The room is dimly lit, with daylight seeping through the thin drapes from outside. I crouch down and run my hand along the carpet, laughing gently at the sensation of the fibres against my skin. At the edge of the room is a cabinet filled with trinkets that twinkle in the gentle glow. I move over to them and tap each one lightly. There are painted plates and ceramic animals, glass goblets of various shapes and a collection of framed photos.

It's hard to make out in the darkness, but the photos are mostly of what I assume is the old man's family. A wife and daughter. Smiling faces. Stories captured in images, like a more visual version of my diaries. It's a shame I wasn't with Mother when she guided the old man through the Halls. I could have heard his tale, and perhaps my presence would have foiled the key thief's plan.

I shake my head. I can't waste time exploring the home of a dead man. I'm here for one reason only: to catch the thief.

Outside, the distractions continue. First, it's the noise of the world itself – the singing of the birds, the distant blasting of what must be a car horn, the rustling of leaves in the nearby trees as a soft wind blows. But what catches my attention most is the people. I'm used to only ever seeing one human at a time, but now here I am, stood in the doorway of a human's house, seeing others walking past farther houses. A mother pushes her baby along in some sort of wheeled contraption. A father berates his two sons for being incredibly late for school. The baby pusher notices me and gives me an odd look that I can't read before continuing on her way.

Here I am, finally in the world of mortal humans, seeing the stories I might one day have heard from spirits. I take further steps along the sturdy ground, eyes darting to everything they can. I look through the windows of other people's houses, catching more odd looks as I do, and I find myself giggling at the sight of drinks cans and small pieces of rubbish that roll beside me, carried by the wind.

I soon come across a gate that leads to a vast field. I wander in, hands stretched out to feel the touch of the longest blades of grass, gazing up into the blindingly bright sky. It's such a clear and vibrant blue, though not as deep a shade as my favourite door. The sun hangs there too, but it becomes clear very quickly that I shouldn't be looking at that. I flinch at the pain it brings to my eyes and shield them instantly. But there's something thrilling about the experience, something so incredibly human.

Something tickles my hand. I lift it up in front of my face, into the light of the sun. It's a small, winged creature, barely larger than the tip of my thumb. I turn my hand so I can see it from every angle. The creature looks so delicate; it would barely take a touch to end its life. As I lower my hand, it flutters away, off to continue its simple existence.

I've never really asked Mother about the non-human creatures of this world. I don't know whether or not they have souls, but perhaps there are other afterlives and other versions of the Halls of Styx for them. Perhaps there are other worlds out there in the sky, too, amongst the stars that I can't yet see, with creatures and afterlives of their own. The Halls of Styx may be infinite, but this world is easily more complex.

I continue into the field, which gradually slopes up a hill. When I reach the top, I find myself breathless for the first time in my life. My legs ache, and I want nothing more than to stop and sit down. I can hear the faint ticking of the anchor around my neck, keeping me safely in this human form while also condemning me to experience the downsides of a mortal body. It amazes me that humans can get so much done if this is how they feel after just walking up a hill.

I turn and gaze down at the village below. Seeing so many houses together is a bizarre experience. All those people, constantly able to find others to talk to. It's the complete opposite of what I'm used to. It must be stressful, surely, to walk those streets when they're at their busiest. You'd never have your own space. You'd never be truly alone. But maybe that's a good thing.

I'm not sure why, but I'd assumed navigation would be easier than this. I know where I need to get to, and I know it's nearby, but I don't know how I'm supposed to find it. Beyond the hill, I find myself beside what I believe is called a road. Cars speed past, bringing to mind the many diary entries I've made about deaths caused by their crashes. Their noise is immense, an unending rumble.

I know from the glimpses I've had through various doors that where I am right now would be considered quite remote, and yet it seems so loud – the engine of every passing car, the wind that blows far stronger up here than it did in the village below. How could anybody cope in a city?

A larger vehicle passes, this one much taller than the cars and more rectangular. It comes to a stop just ahead of me, beside a sign that says *Bus Stop*, and its doors swing open. Curious, I poke my head in. A large man who I assume is the driver raises his eyebrow at me from behind a transparent screen.

"Are you getting on?" he asks.

I hesitate. "I don't know." I glance to the right to see the many empty chairs. There are two passengers who both stare at me with the same expression as the driver.

"Where are you heading?" the driver asks.

"Elmwood Vale Hospital."

"That'll be two pounds."

I hesitate again. "That's money, isn't it?"

The man chuckles. "Yes, mate."

I've heard plenty about money. It seems to be a very important aspect of human life – a bit too important, if you ask me. As far as I can tell from the stories I've heard, it's not worth all the harm it seems to cause.

"I don't have any money," I say plainly.

The man heaves a heavy sigh. "Then what are you wasting my time for?"

I'm forced back as the doors swing closed. The roar of the engine starts up, and just like that, the bus drives off. I watch as it heads off on its journey, the red lights on its back shrinking as it gets farther away.

At least now I know the right direction.

Walking is utterly exhausting. I try my best to keep going but have to stop over and over again. And gods, am I thirsty. It's not a completely new sensation. As far as I know, I experienced all the usual human bodily functions in the Halls of Styx. The cupboards in the cabin were always stocked with food and water, but I never felt hunger or thirst to this degree.

I take a moment to rest on a bench beside the road, and across the other side, I notice something behind the stone wall that separates the pavement from a collection of fields. It's a patch of land different from the grassy fields around it. There are rows of plants and a couple of small glass buildings set amongst them, containing even more plants. Not just any plants – food.

I clamber over the wall, falling straight into the mud on the other side and finding the grass wet with tiny droplets of water, but I get to my feet and stumble over to the glass house. Inside it are the red fruits I know to be called tomatoes. As I tear one from its stem, I silently thank my mother for giving me human food. I'm sure she could just as easily have fed me on something that didn't remotely match the food of this world; then I'd have no idea about what's edible and what isn't.

My first watery bite brings instant relief, but it also brings surprise and somehow also disgust. The flavour is unlike anything I've tasted before, and it's utterly bizarre, all wet and intense and unfamiliar. I'm sure my body is grateful for the food and hydration, but I realise that just because the food Mother provided me with *looked* like human food, perhaps it didn't taste of it. It never really tasted of much at all.

I remember one spirit who used to be a chef, and they spoke so passionately about their expert palate and how much they adored certain flavour combinations. I nodded along and enjoyed their enthusiasm, but I didn't really understand them. Food and water, for me, had always served one simple purpose: to stop me being hungry or thirsty. I had never experienced actual flavour. Not until now.

I grimace as I swallow the last bite of the tomato, hoping that the chef wasn't lying and that some food does in fact taste amazing.

By the time I reach Elmwood Vale, I am well and truly exhausted. I've forced down a couple more tomatoes and taken many more rests, but I breathe a sigh of relief when I see a sign welcoming me to the town. The ground here is slightly damp, which must be due to rain. I chuckle at the sight. There's something so baffling about the idea that it could have been raining here but not where I entered this world. Weather is not something I'm used to.

There are more people here, too, and they continue to stare at me in that unusual way I keep encountering. Their eyes follow me as I walk past, and their mouths make this odd shape I believe is called a smirk. I find myself glancing down at my clothes – the simple white robes I've always worn at home, now stained in various places with mud thanks to my fall into the plants. It's the first time in my life I've ever felt conscious of my appearance. I suppose no one else is wearing anything like this. Perhaps that's why they seem so fascinated.

Still, I continue on, following the directions of the occasional signs that read *Hospital*. Soon enough, a familiar sight comes into view: a large, many-windowed cement block with an ageing sign beside it. Elmwood Vale Hospital. Two large automatic doors part as I approach the entrance. The people walking in and out give me the same strange looks as everyone else, but I try to pay them no mind.

It's very busy inside, and the noise is overwhelming. It's like the air itself is shouting directly into my ears. People are arguing with each other, and others in matching blue clothes are trying to calm them down. Within the entrance is a desk with three open windows above it, behind which sit one man and two women, all of whom are red-faced, wild-haired and either typing frantically on their computer keyboards or having heated discussions with the people stood in front of them.

People are queuing in front of each of these desk workers, so I do the same. This seems to be how things are done. An age passes between each movement of the queue, but I take the opportunity to observe the chaos around me.

I can't say I enjoy it, what with the noise, but it's interesting all the same. I wonder if it's like this all the time, or if the theft of Mother's keys has had an impact. I think back on all the spirits whose doors opened in hospitals. So many humans die in places like this every day. What must it be like now that nobody is dying? Where will all those people go?

"Hello?" comes an urgent voice.

I turn to see one of the red-faced women at the desk, who is now right in front of me.

"Oh," I say, surprised by the sudden speed of the queue. "Hello." Every conversation I've ever had with the spirits flashes through my mind as I try to recall how to sound like a normal human. "Could you please direct me to Arthur Weaver?"

The woman raises an eyebrow. I'm not sure what that means.

"He's a patient here." I add.

"And are you a relative?"

"No," I say instinctively. It's only after the word leaves my mouth that I realise being a relative might be a prerequisite for finding out Arthur's location. "I mean yes."

The woman's face twists into the smirk that's becoming all-too-common a sight. "Young man, I don't have time to deal with jokes. Please stop wasting my time."

Even though I'm still in front of her, she shifts her eyes to look at the person behind me.

"Next," she says.

I don't have to be an expert in human social interaction to know our conversation is done. I step aside, feeling lost in the sea of noise. What am I supposed to do now? Can I find Arthur myself? Are people allowed to just walk anywhere they want in this building? I have a strong feeling the answer is no.

I sigh, turning back to the entrance, when another familiar sight comes into view: a broad-shouldered boy no older than sixteen, with strawberry blond hair falling in subtle curls.

Chapter Six
Evan

I'm sick to death of this place (if that phrase even makes sense in this strange new world). When Mum contacted the school, I expected some huge update, like that death had come back to the world and Dad had passed away. But no, he's still here, along with every other walking corpse. Turns out the hospital is letting him go home, despite the non-functional heart. Got to make space for new patients, I suppose. And what does Mum want from me? A change of clothes for Dad, because she couldn't possibly leave his side to go home and get the clothes herself.

The hospital is heaving, and I'm glad I don't need to go to the front desk. The workers look like they're ready to slap someone. I start toward the corridor that leads to Dad's ward when a boy stumbles into my path, blocking the way. The way he moves, it's like he's not used to his own body. He's too tall for his own good, his hair is an unkempt brown mop, and he's dressed in what I can only describe as a robe – a filthy robe, at that. The white fabric is stained all over with dirt and a couple of pale red splatters as well.

"Hello," he says, staring at me with wide blue eyes. He's smiling, but it's odd. It looks forced, uncomfortable.

"Um . . . hi?"

"You're Arthur Weaver's son." He says it so matter-of-factly, as if it's the most ordinary thing in the world that he knows who I am without ever having met me. He must be about my age, but I don't recognise him from school. Is he a patient?

"Who are you?"

"Oh. Yes, of course." He shakes his head. "I'm Orpheus." He waves his hand as though greeting a friend from afar.

I stare back, deeply confused. "Can't say I've met an Orpheus before."

His eyes flit between his waving hand and me. "Sorry, I thought . . ." He drops his hand and nervously bites at his lower lip. "Was that not right?"

I ignore the question. "How do you know my dad?"

He looks taken aback. It's very bizarre. I get the strange sense that he didn't expect me to question him at all.

"I . . . can't say," he replies.

I almost laugh. "Look, I don't really have time for this." I try to walk past him.

He remains in my way. "Wait! Please. I need to meet your dad."

A disgruntled nurse sidles past, giving us both dirty looks.

I roll my eyes. "You want to meet my dad? Who even are you?"

"I told you. I'm Orpheus." He pulls that uncomfortable smile again, and I do my best not to laugh at how ridiculous this conversation is.

Another pair of nurses walk past, huffing, and I become very aware of the fact we're blocking half the corridor. I step to the side to stand by a poster on the wall that's encouraging the elderly to get regular health checkups. Orpheus remains in the middle of the corridor, watching me with a curious raised eyebrow.

"Mate," I say, growing ever more frustrated, "you're in the way."

I reach out and grab his arm, ready to pull him to the side, but the instant I make contact, I feel him tense as though a bolt of electricity has flowed through him. His bright eyes linger on the spot where I touched his arm for a moment before widening and meeting my gaze. And then he says the words I never want to hear in public.

"You're a warlock."

I stand, frozen in place. Every ounce of frustration I felt towards this boy turns instantly to panic and fear. He's here to meet my dad, the witchfinder, and somehow, through a single touch, he knows that I'm a warlock. Is he a witchfinder too? Is that why he's here? To assist in the ever-growing hunt against magic users?

I glance around, making sure nobody else heard, as my breaths come thick and fast. I feel the distant pulse of magic deep within me. If I wanted, I could bring it forward, pull out my wand and stitch rows of threads to create some sort of distraction and run away. But doing magic in public is never a good idea.

"What's wrong?" Orpheus asks.

And I'm perplexed, because he sounds genuinely concerned, and not in the least aware that his words are incredibly dangerous to be spoken in public. I look at him, his bright eyes unblinking, and struggle to imagine how someone like him could be working with the witchfinders. But that's the thing – no matter how friendly someone seems, you never know what secret bigotry they're harbouring. Hatred is an insidious thing; it seeps into every corner of the world.

"Is it something I said?"

I don't know what I'm supposed to say. He just unveiled my biggest secret as if it were as unthreatening as a comment on the weather, and now here he is questioning why I'm so scared. It doesn't make sense. If he were a witchfinder, or at least in cahoots with them, surely he wouldn't just be standing here waiting for my response. And how can he know what I am from a single touch? I look around again, still anxious that someone might be listening.

Orpheus studies me and after a moment asks, "Do you want to speak somewhere else?"

I'm still unable to speak, so I just nod. I wait a moment, just to see if he'll make some sort of surprise move, but when he doesn't, I slowly turn and head back down the corridor to the hospital entrance. Orpheus follows me all the way out, across the car park and to a nearby treeline. It's not a particularly dense set of trees, and I know that just a short way through there's a clearing with a children's playpark, but I think just behind the first couple of trees is as private a place as we're going to get.

I stop and lean against a tree, taking a deep breath as I face Orpheus. He isn't forcing a smile anymore. In fact, he's looking around in what appears to be wonder. It's as if he's never seen trees before.

"Who are you?" I ask, feigning confidence.

"I'm—"

"And *don't* just say your name. Where did you come from? How do you . . . how do you know I'm . . ."

"A warlock?"

There's no one around, but I shush him anyway. Even hearing the word spoken aloud makes me feel sick with fear. This isn't a conversation I ever thought I'd have to have, and it damn sure isn't one I want to have with a stranger. The only person I've ever imagined telling my secret to is Wren.

He blinks in confusion and continues to speak in a whisper. "That's the right word, isn't it? Warlock? A male witch?"

Is he seriously asking about semantics right now?

"Sorry," he continues, "I think I've made you uncomfortable. I didn't mean to. I just need to speak to your dad."

"*Why?*" I ask for what feels like the thousandth time.

He bites his lip as he figures out his next words. "I need a witchfinder."

My heart sinks, and my mind cycles through all the spells I know, searching for one that could get me out of this situation. If I could stun him and run away, that would be perfect, but that's not the sort of thing Gran ever taught me. Harming people is not what magic is for, she'd say.

"I can't tell you why," Orpheus adds.

I shake my head, unsure whether to laugh, cry or throw up. All these years, I've been hiding who I am from my father, and now he's finally going to find out the truth. I was so close to being free of that fear yesterday. A lump rises in my throat, and I feel the beginning droplets of tears.

Orpheus steps towards me, face gentle. Concerned. "You're upset."

This time, I do laugh. "What do you expect? You're about to out me to the witchfinders."

"What?" He looks genuinely puzzled.

"You can drop the act. That's obviously why you want to meet my dad. Just answer me one thing before you do." I take a breath, steadying my voice. If this is how everything comes crashing down, I'm going to face it with bravery. "Why do you hate witches so much? What is it that makes us so detestable?"

"Hate witches?" he says, taken aback. "I don't hate witches."

I'm not sure I've ever been more confused in my life. "But you want to speak to a witchfinder . . ."

"Yes."

"A person whose life revolves around hating witches. A person who seeks them out and forces them to have their magic stripped away." I feel the tears ready themselves again as Gran's face flashes in my mind. The vacant expression she wore towards the end.

"That's what they do?" Orpheus says, and the defeated tone in his voice makes me think his words might actually be genuine.

I pause. "You don't know?"

He shakes his head and glances back at the treeline, towards the hospital. "But Mother said . . ." he mutters before turning back to me. He fixes me with a worried look. "The witchfinders are bad people?"

It's a question that I'd laugh at any other day. It sounds so childish, so innocent. But he says it seriously, so I reply with the truth. "Yes."

He nods, and his gaze travels around me, as though making some sort of assessment. "But you're a warlock, so you understand the workings of witches, yes?"

"I guess."

"Then I need your help instead of your father's."

I stare, bemused. "My help with what?"

"Bringing death back to the world."

I was seven when Gran told me I was a warlock, but I remember it as clearly as yesterday. I was spending the night at her house while my parents travelled down to London for work. We watched an old film, devouring popcorn until we felt we might burst, and then as the credits rolled, she turned to me.

"Evan," she said, "have you noticed anything strange happening around you recently?"

I stayed quiet at first, nervous because it was the sort of question you instinctively want to say "no" to, and yet I couldn't. Things *had* been strange. It was hard to verbalise, but I'd been feeling what I now understand to be the buzz of magic within me, especially in moments of intense emotion.

"What do you mean?" I asked.

She smiled reassuringly, no doubt sensing my nerves. "Well, do you remember when I came to your house for tea last week?"

I nodded.

"And your dad said some . . . unpleasant things . . . and you got awfully upset?"

I wished I didn't remember, but I nodded again.

"And then the lights flickered . . ."

I almost gasped. I recalled the lights flickering, just as she'd said, but it had only happened for the briefest moment. Most people wouldn't have noticed, myself included, were it not for the fact that the flickering had come at the same moment as that strange buzz in the pit of my stomach.

As always, Gran read me like a book.

"You felt something odd then, didn't you?" she asked. "A spark?" She placed her hand on her stomach. "Right here?"

I'd been trying to ignore it whenever it happened, because of course I knew what it might mean. Everyone knows about the telltale signs of being a witch, especially when your grandma is one. But I couldn't possibly be one, could I? Not when my dad said such awful things about them every chance he got. Not when he was considering getting a job with the witchfinders, who I didn't know much about, but from Gran's reaction to the mention of their name, I knew they couldn't be good.

And yet, despite the fear and doubt and anxiety that had built up inside me, I told Gran, "Yes. That's what I felt."

And with her gentle smile and the touch of her hands on my shoulders, she made me feel as safe as she always did.

"Evan," she said, "I think you might be a warlock."

There's a feeling of bewilderment that consumes you when you hear those words, of knowing that what you're being told is true yet finding it utterly impossible to believe. It's a feeling that's never been replicated for me.

Until now.

"Yesterday," Orpheus says, his back against the treeline that separates us from the hospital, "the keys to the afterlife were stolen by a witch. As long as the keys are missing, no human will be able to die. I have been sent here to find the thief and retrieve the keys."

I can only imagine how comical my open-mouthed face must be right now.

"Okay . . ." I say, brain slowly catching up to the words I just heard. "I have maybe one thousand questions? First one, is this a joke? Second, the afterlife has keys?"

Orpheus doesn't even blink. "It's not a joke, and yes, it has keys. Well, technically, the keys are for the liminal space between the mortal world and the afterlife, but as far as I know, you mortals aren't fully caught up on the structure of the spirit realms. Not even the witches. Except maybe the thief? They must have had some knowledge, I suppose. What do you think?"

His words hit me at a hundred miles an hour, and it feels like every single one of them raises a new question. I'm about to ask another when my phone buzzes in my pocket.

"Shit," I say when I see the name lighting up the screen.
Mum.

Chapter Seven
Orpheus

I think I may have revealed too much too quickly. The warlock is frozen to the spot, staring at his phone in one hand while holding a bag in the other. Perhaps this is the sort of reaction Mother would get when telling people they're dead if it weren't for her calming aura. I wonder if I could exude such an aura if I weren't wearing the anchor.

The phone in the warlock's hand continues to buzz, but he does nothing.

I step forward.

"Stay there!" he says. So his mouth works, at the very least. "Just . . . stay there until I figure out what the hell is going on."

Did I not just explain what's going on? Maybe he needs more information. I open my mouth to speak—

"Don't say another word!" At long last, his arm moves, and he holds the phone to his ear, swiping the screen with a thumb on the way. "Hey," he says, voice not as loud as before.

I can't make out the words, but another voice emits from the phone.

"Yeah, sorry, I got held up," he says. "I'll be there in five minutes though, promise."

More words from the phone.

"Okay, bye." His body almost deflates as he returns the phone to his pocket with a loud sigh. He shakes his head, eyes on his shoes, and I remain silent. Waiting.

Another sigh and he's looking at me. "Right, here's what's gonna happen." His voice has a new tone now. It's clearer, less shaky. "You're going to stay here. I'm going to go give this bag to my parents. Then I'll come back, and you're going to start from the beginning. With me asking the questions." He nods, as though to confirm his own words to himself. "Understood?"

"Yes, but—"

He raises a hand. "No. You wait. I'll be back in ten minutes, max. Just . . . stay here."

It's only once he's walked away that I realise I've failed at one of the most basic steps of human interaction: I never asked his name.

As I wait, I replay our conversation in my mind. I can't stop thinking about one part in particular – when he told me what the witchfinders do. That they hate witches. That they "strip away" their magic. I met a few witches in my time in the Halls of Styx. They were interesting to speak to, as they were usually a lot less baffled than their mundane peers, even if they weren't pre-warned of all the specifics. But they rarely spoke much about their magic. Perhaps I should have asked, but it was the more mundane parts of their human lives that always fascinated me. Witchcraft seemed far closer to the world I already experienced, a world beyond the confines of human scientific laws. When the supernatural is all you've ever known, the natural becomes far more interesting.

I had never considered that being a witch could be dangerous, and yet this unnamed warlock seemed scared to talk about his identity. One word in particular stood out when he spoke of the witchfinders: *hate*. In my many conversations with humans, hatred is perhaps the thing that baffled me the most. Of course, people usually spoke of the things they loved. What else would you want to spend your dying moments recalling? But I've found it's rare that a life hasn't been shaped in some way by hatred.

It's like Elodie, the last human I spoke to before leaving the Halls. Her life would have been so different if her mother hadn't convinced her she had to fall in love with a man. Her mother's hatred for Elodie's capacity to love a woman meant she spent years of her life unfulfilled. She had a happy ending, but there are many who haven't.

I've heard of hatred in many forms, but I've never understood it. I like to believe that humans are driven by love, be it of another person or a passion. That's what the stories in my diaries usually boil down to. And yet it seems that some are driven by hatred. I can't help but wonder if those people feel unfulfilled when their lives come to an end. There are those who refuse to follow Mother when they enter the Halls, those who run and lose themselves in the labyrinth, drifting into the void on its edges as a corrupted spirit. Perhaps that's the destiny of those who have lived to hate.

When the warlock returns, bag no longer in tow, I'm studying the crisp leaves of the trees, watching the ever-changing dappled light in the canopy.

"Right," he says, running a hand through his blond curls. "I have about a million questions."

"What's your name?" I ask before he has chance to continue.

He blinks, startled, but answers. "Evan."

I mentally riffle through the diaries I can remember. "I'm not sure I've ever met an Evan."

He shrugs. "It's not that rare. Not like yours. I can only think of one other Orpheus."

"Oh?"

He smirks. "The one from the myth? Greek, I think? The guy who goes down to the underworld to save his girlfriend but ends up losing her in the end?"

I laugh. I hadn't considered that stories of the old afterlife – from Charon's time as psychopomp, no less – would have trickled down through this many generations. "That's who my mother named me after."

Mother told me the story of Orpheus when I was about five years old, how he defied all the rules to save Eurydice, travelling all the way to the underworld without dying and brokering a deal with Hades. He could leave with her, but she'd have to walk behind him, and if he turned to look before they were back in the mortal world, she'd be lost to him forever. Which is exactly what happened.

Mother said that Father reminded her of Orpheus, with him breaking the rules for the sake of love. I suppose his tale ended in tragedy too. I've always liked that my name connects me to him, though I'd gladly claim another if it meant I could meet him.

"Your mother?" Evan says. "Is that who sent you to . . . find the keys?" He sounds like he can't quite believe what he's asking.

"Yes. She's the current psychopomp; the keys belong to her."

"Psychopomp?"

"The person who leads the dead from this world to the afterlife." I bite my lip, wondering how to explain this more easily. "You know the myth of Orpheus, so you must know about the River Styx, yes?"

"I . . . think so? There was a ferryman, right? Who you had to pay a coin to to get to the afterlife?"

"Exactly. Charon. He was the psychopomp at the time – the very first psychopomp, actually. But what with his weird charging system and the fact that people like Orpheus bypassed it, he got replaced by someone else. It happens every few hundred years or so. My mother is the current one."

Evan runs both hands through his hair, interlocks his fingers and shakes his head. "Sorry, are you saying that the Greek myths are real?"

Ah. So that's what happens when the stories trickle down through the generations. I did wonder why he kept saying "myth".

"Yes."

He laughs, though I don't think it's because he finds it funny. "So out of all the religions, it's the ancient Greeks who had it right all along?"

I raise an eyebrow, confused. "That's not what I said."

"Well, the others can't be right too, can they?" He drops his hands to his side, leaving his hair in chaos.

"Why not?"

"Because they contradict each other."

Ah. There's that major difference between our worlds.

"Only according to the rules of your world," I say. "Outside the mortal realm, the rules are different. Two contradictory things can both be true."

"So, what? All the religions are right?"

I nod. "All. And none. The gods change with the times. Their forms are unrestricted. That's why they're gods."

He looks down, laughing again, and paces between two trees. But I still don't think he's finding it funny.

"Okay," he says, opting to lean against one of the trees and face me. "So, what, your mum ferries people across a river?"

"No. Each psychopomp gets to design the passage between this world and the afterlife. Charon had the River Styx; my mother has the Halls of Styx."

"And what's that when it's at home?"

"At home?"

He studies my face as though trying to solve a puzzle. "I mean what is it? What does it look like?"

"Oh. Well—"

"Actually . . ." he steps forward but seems hesitant. He pulls a bag off his back and reaches in, then looks back at me. "Could . . . could I see?"

"See?"

"I know a spell . . . a way of looking in someone's mind. If you let me, I could see your memories. Only the ones you want to share, I mean. But . . . you could show me the Halls. And these missing keys you want to find."

I've never seen human magic in action before. I can't pretend I'm not intrigued. And perhaps if I show him, he'll understand exactly what's happening.

I nod. "Okay."

He takes another step forward. "You'll feel me in your mind. Just picture the memories you want me to see."

He pulls a metal stick out of his bag. It's about half the length of his forearm, with a hooked end, and it's the same brass-like shade as the anchor. He closes his eyes and takes a deep breath. When he opens them again, there's a strange haze to them, as though they're slightly out of focus. He brings up his spare hand and begins to move his fingers as though grabbing things in the air and bringing them to the hooked end of the metal stick. I recall the spirit of a witch who told me about stitching threads together to cast spells; this must be what Evan is doing. He manoeuvres the stick and his fingers like he's tying something together.

With his right hand, he reaches out towards me, closing his fingers right in front of my face and pulling them back to him. In an instant, I feel a sense of dizziness come over me and the urge to *remember*. I give in to the feeling, closing my eyes and picturing home. The Halls of Styx. The doors, including my favourite. Mother, her wings outstretched, her ring of keys. The night of the bells. Mother's horror. The room of glowing orbs. The anchor and the quest Mother set me on. The moment I stepped through the door. The old man's house. My journey to the hospital. Seeing Evan for the first time.

But it's strange. It's not like I'm remembering things as they were. It's like there's something extra there now. A presence, almost like a pulse of energy, whose source is just out of sight. And there's a spark to it that I recall from the moment Evan first touched me. A spark I knew from encountering witch spirits to be a sign that he was a warlock.

Evan is here, among my memories. Observing. Learning. But also leaving his mark. And it's not just a magical spark that I feel, but the emotions hidden beneath it too. There's confusion and fear, but also amazement. Evan's mind is in mine, and I can feel what he feels.

There's a cold rush, I feel a release and my eyes snap open. Evan falls to his knees in front of me, panting, hands pressed to the sides of his head. The metal stick has fallen to the ground beside him. I kneel down as soon as I see him.

"Are you okay?" I ask.

He looks at me, open-mouthed. "Your mother . . ." he says between breaths, "she's . . . the wings . . . she's an angel?"

"Yes."

"So you're . . . ?"

"Half angel, half human."

"And that . . ." He points at the anchor hanging from my neck.

"Keeps me in human form. You know, maybe we should have done this to begin with; we could have saved a lot of time."

Evan's laughter returns, but this time, it's different. I can see it in his eyes, and I can feel the remnants of his emotions in my mind as they fade away. He was scared, but now it's changed. There's a sense of wonder. This time, he thinks my words are genuinely funny. I find myself laughing too.

"This is ridiculous," Evan says. "You know that, right?"

"By mortal standards, I imagine it is."

After a final chuckle, Evan grabs the metal stick and

clambers to his feet. I follow suit.

"Well," he says, brushing the dirt from his knees, "I guess it's time we find these keys."

Chapter Eight
Evan

I gaze at Orpheus beneath the trees, this half-angel boy who has barrelled into my life on a day that was already strange enough. I'd forgotten how intimate connecting with someone's mind can be. I didn't just see his memories; I felt them too. That intense longing he had to enter this world, mixed with the nerves at being handed such a burden by his mother – it's all still there at the edge of my mind, ebbing slowly away like the tide.

But I won't forget it. The images of the Halls of Styx, of Orpheus' winged mother, of the glowing orbs and the doors, all remain burned into my memory. And with them is a certainty I never expected to have when I met this bizarre boy – I have to help Orpheus. If I hadn't bumped into him, he'd have found my dad, and it'd be down to the witchfinders to solve this global crisis. God only knows the damage it would do to witches if the witchfinders caught the culprit and plastered their face across the media. I have no doubt that Eloise Morgan would relish the chance to blame all of witchkind for the actions of one.

If Orpheus and I can find the culprit first, we can return the keys to his mother, and the crisis will be over. Everyone can go back to their normal lives, and witches can avoid being hated even more than they already are.

"So, where do we start?" Orpheus asks, looking to me as though I'm the expert now.

Already, I feel out of my depth. Are we looking for a single witch or a group? Are they local? If so, have they fled? What spell did they use? I suppose it must have been some form of necromancy, which isn't a very common form of magic. I bet Wren would know if there were rumours of local necromancy, but they'll be in school for a few more hours.

"Do you know anything about the man who died?" I ask. "The one whose door you came through?"

Orpheus shakes his head. "I didn't get the chance to speak to him before Mother led him through the gate. And she won't have asked him much. She never does."

"Well, whoever snuck through the door must have planned it, right?"

"I suppose so."

"So maybe his death wasn't random." It's an awful thought, that a witch might have killed a man to gain access to the Halls of Styx, but we can't ignore any possibility. "I think we should start at his house."

"Okay," says Orpheus, though he sounds unsure. "It's a long walk."

"Or a short bus ride," I add. "It looked like Blackwell Hill in your memory. The bus goes from near here." I nod my head towards the road. "Come on."

Orpheus' uncertainty drops as he grins.

"I assume you've not ridden a bus before?"

"Never." He's practically bouncing with excitement.

"Prepare to be underwhelmed."

The bus stop is mercifully free of other people, but I still check around to make sure no one can overhear us.

"Have you never left the Halls before?"

"No."

"You know some things about this world though, right? Like, you knew what a hospital was?"

Orpheus nods, but he's not looking at me as he does. Instead, his eyes flit about our surroundings like he's trying to cram every cloud, every passing car, every distant bird or rustling tree into his memory.

"I've spoken to lots of humans," he says. "Mother doesn't like to ask about their lives, but I do. I write their life stories down in diaries."

"Why?"

"So that I don't forget them." He watches a set of orange leaves whirl past, sent into the air by a speeding car.

I smile at him out of sight. I wonder what the dead think when they arrive in the Halls of Styx, greeted by an angel to guide them to the afterlife and then confronted by her half-human son asking for their life story. It's a funny image, but it's also sweet. He might be a bit abrasive at first, but I can't pretend there isn't a sort of charm to Orpheus. His curiosity is endearing.

The bus approaches, and I stick out my arm to make it stop.

"I almost got on one of these earlier," Orpheus says, "but I didn't have money."

The doors slide open, and I bite my tongue. Of course he doesn't have money. This is going to be a little bit pricier than I expected.

"Two day riders, please." I hand over the money, grab the printed tickets and head to the stairs.

Orpheus follows, looking puzzled as ever.

The bus is pretty empty, especially the top deck. That's the benefit of it being the middle of a school day, I suppose. Especially one where the whole world is scared of what its sudden immortality might mean. I let Orpheus take the window seat and sit beside him, figuring he's going to enjoy the view of this boring town far more than I am.

As soon as the bus moves, his face lights up. I, on the other hand, pull out my phone and check the latest news. It's mostly what I expect to see – world leaders urging people not to panic and anti-magic bigots blaming witches - but there's also an American witch and warlock couple who have gone on national television asking people not to assume all witches are the same. I've seen them on the news before.

Chantelle Adeyemi has made multiple posts about it too. She's probably the most well-known of the few openly magical influencers out there. As expected, her videos are expressing her anger at the public's response. I'm sure Wren will be reposting the videos when they see them. They've always been a big fan of her.

There aren't many witches willing to put themselves in the public eye like Chantelle or the American couple, but some do. Not that it makes much difference, at least not as far as I can see. You only have to look at the comments to see that the support is almost non-existent.

Unnatural scum!
Devil worshippers!
Stay away from our kids!

"Why do people hate you?" Orpheus asks, making me jump as I realise he's looking at the comments on my phone screen.

I check behind me, confirming that the only other person up here is a middle-aged man with a hefty pair of headphones on.

"They've hated us for centuries," I say in a hushed tone. "Magic is seen as something deeply wrong. Unnatural. A perversion."

"For centuries?" Orpheus says, matching my volume. "But not forever?"

"No. Not forever. My gran used to tell me stories of how the world once was, long before she or I were alive. How magic could be freely talked about, how covens grew to vast sizes and knowledge could be shared. Then the witch hunts started, and everything changed."

"Your gran sounds nice."

"She was." I smile as I imagine what she would have said if she knew what I was doing today. She'd have been proud to see me go against my father; I have no doubt.

"Did she teach you how to cast spells?"

I nod. "She used to say that magic was the music of the universe and we witches were the conductors."

Orpheus' eyes meet mine, their deep blue almost seeming to swirl like water.

"Do you think . . ." I start. "Do you think you might have met her? In the Halls? She died three years ago."

"It's possible," he says, smiling softly. "Time is a funny thing, though. It doesn't really line up between the worlds – at least not when everything is working as it's supposed to. Three years here isn't necessarily three years there."

I nod. Probability wise, it must be unlikely that he'd have met her. So many people die every day, after all. And when you throw in messy timelines, the odds aren't in my favour. Still, it's nice to imagine Gran would have seen a friendly face when she passed on.

"Why did your mum choose the Halls?" I ask. "As her design, I mean. You said she chose what it looked like, right?"

"Yes."

"So why corridors full of doors?"

Orpheus looks out of the window again. "It gives humans the illusion of choice. Stepping through a door is a lot less intimidating than paying a man to ferry you down a dark river."

The bus pulls to a stop, and a couple get on, joining us on the top deck. I lean back in my seat, not probing Orpheus further. Now's not the time. Not while there are other ears so near.

It's not long before we're in Blackwell Hill, with its cobbled roads and vast fields. I press the stop button, and Orpheus follows me off the bus.

"This is the right area, isn't it?" I ask him.

"Yes." He spins on his heel and points down a nearby road. "The house is that way."

"You're sure?"

"I can feel it." He starts walking, more confident than I've ever seen him.

I speed after him. "How?"

He shrugs. "It's this feeling"—he touches a hand to his stomach—"in here, connecting me to the door. In the Halls, I'm always able to find my way even though they're infinite. I suppose it's an angel thing."

"Useful," I say. "Is that how you knew I was a warlock? A feeling in your stomach?"

He shrugs. "Sort of. Every soul has a kind of feeling about it. A vibration. The souls of witches feel a bit different. I take it that's not something that humans can feel?"

"Nope. Definitely another angel thing."

He leads me down one street, then another, past houses with withered plants on their porches, until we stop at a plain house in the middle of its terraced row. The curtains are drawn, and the door's paint is a dull, peeling brown.

"This is it," Orpheus says.

I do a quick check to ensure we're out of view, then step up to the door and pull my wand from my bag.

"What are you doing?" Orpheus asks.

"I'm going to unlock it, obviously. It's a pretty easy spell."

Orpheus reaches out, turns the handle, and the door swings open.

I blink. "Is that an angel thing?"

"It wasn't locked."

"Oh." I feel my cheeks redden and step into the house, ready to pretend that that didn't just happen.

The hallway is dark, with water-stained wallpaper and a faint musty smell. The door closes as Orpheus enters, dimming the external light further. I reach out to a door on my left and follow it through to the living room. Pale light filters in through the curtains, revealing a pair of worn sofas facing a small TV. A coffee table littered with newspapers sits in the centre, and there are cabinets against the walls decorated with ornaments and framed photos.

"Was it like this when you were here before?" I ask.

"Yes," says Orpheus, who is running his hand along the edge of one of the sofas.

"And the door was unlocked then, too?"

"Yes."

I step around the coffee table. "Why?"

"Well, don't people remove the body after someone dies?" he asks.

"They do. But I'm pretty sure that's done by a paramedic or a doctor or a mortician or someone official. They wouldn't just leave the door unlocked. I guess the family might have forgotten to lock it, but . . . I don't know, it seems odd."

Orpheus pauses in the corner of the room and reaches his hand out as though placing it against something in the air.

"Oh," he says, catching me staring. "Sorry, I guess you can't see it. It only becomes visible for the human it belongs to, and only when they're dead." He moves his hand downwards, almost stroking the air. "It's the door to the Halls of Styx."

"Really?" I join him, facing the empty space. "Just here?" I reach out, feeling nothing, but the more I focus, the more I notice a strange haze in the air. It's like the mirages that form over roads on a super-hot day – a sort of wobbliness. It's subtle, but it's there. "Can you open it?"

He shakes his head. "I could, but I shouldn't. It's bad enough that it's unlocked. If I open it, the impact on the Halls will be even worse."

I recall the flash of memory of his mother explaining what happened. "Entropy, right?"

"Indeed."

I leave Orpheus with the door and take a look at the cabinet against the back wall. There are all sorts here: a porcelain tortoise, a set of unused candles, a half-painted model aeroplane. But what catches my eye is one of the framed photos. The dead man – or at least who I assume to be the dead man; he looks closer to forty than the seventyish he must have been when he died – is stood beside a woman while a young girl stands in front of them. Wife and daughter, I suppose, but what strikes me is the wife. I know her face. She's younger, of course, but even without the tight grey bun of hair, I recognise the sour expression of Eloise Morgan.

"Orpheus?" I say, lifting the frame from the shelf.

He walks over to me.

"I know her." I point at Eloise. "She's the Witchfinder General."

"The what?"

"The woman in charge of the witchfinders. My dad's boss. The one who gives the orders. I think . . . well, this looks like they're a family, doesn't it?"

I look at the photo again, trying to recall all I know of Eloise's family.

"I've never heard of a husband," I say, "but I know she has a daughter. I'm pretty sure she works for her too."

Orpheus' eyebrows knit together. "But what does this mean?"

I shake my head. "I don't know, but if the man whose death let someone steal the keys to the afterlife is related to the Witchfinder General . . . that can't be a coincidence. I think . . . well, maybe the thief killed him. We're assuming the thief is a witch, right?"

Orpheus nods.

"And who do witches hate more than the woman who makes their lives hell?"

Orpheus looks at the picture, into the eyes of Eloise Morgan. I wonder how it must feel to see her without having had your life so heavily impacted by her bigotry.

"So," he says, "you think a witch killed the old man as a sort of revenge?"

"Maybe."

I set the frame down on the cabinet and look back over to the corner where the door to the afterlife apparently stands.

"And maybe . . . a spell big enough to let a witch break into the afterlife would leave a trace."

Orpheus follows my gaze, then looks back at me. "Meaning?"

"Meaning I might be able to see how it was done."

I close my eyes and take a deep breath, letting that old familiar feeling wash over me before opening them to the web of threads. And oh, it really did leave a trace.

There are tangled threads still glowing many colours other than the plain gold that they would be if they didn't have a spell running through them. They're bound to each other to form thick rows of stitches which make the outline of the invisible door clear, with a particular mass of stitches at the point where the keyhole would be. There are stitches in other positions too, all across the door, stitches that would have been formed as part of a spell, but which are so complex and tight that they haven't yet unravelled. They're still glowing, too, in striking lines of colour, not quite as brightly as if a witch were still feeding magic into them, but bright enough that the magic still remains.

"What can you see?" Orpheus asks.

"The spell was more complex than any I've ever seen." I reach out to a row of purple stitches and flinch as a shock of energy moves through my hand. The vestiges of the magic that was used to cast the spell.

"When a simple spell is cast," I explain, "the stitches that a witch has formed in the fabric of the universe unravel within minutes. But here . . . the stitches are still tightly bound almost an entire day later. I'm not sure any individual witch would be capable of a spell so complex by themselves."

I follow the glowing threads away from the door, crouching down to view a spot on the floor just below where they form a final set of stitches. Here the threads form a pentagon with the thickest rows of stitches at each corner. I realise there's only one thing that could leave a trace like that.

"They used an artefact," I say, letting my vision return to normal and facing Orpheus.

"An artefact?"

I get to my feet, running my hands through my hair as I piece things together. "There's a limit to the spells a witch can cast on their own. Sometimes, the stitches we need to form in the threads just aren't possible with a single wand. The more complex the spell, the more difficult it is to cast without additional help." I take a seat on the edge of the coffee table, not wanting to risk the sofa where a dead body might have been. "So either you can use multiple witches with their own wands, *or* you can use an artefact."

I run my fingers along my own wand. "Very minor magical effects can be done with fingers alone, but wands are necessary for anything worthwhile. They're made of a certain metal alloy capable of conducting magic and touching the threads. It's been around for a long time, but back in the Victorian times, some witches realised they could use this alloy to make clockwork devices called artefacts that, if held by a witch, could form stitches in the threads for them by effectively using multiple mini wands. At first, they were a useful aid for those less able to use their hands for whatever reason, but as the technology developed, they were able to create artefacts that could cast spells too complicated for an average witch to perform on their own."

Orpheus sits on the sofa, engrossed. "And that's how the thief did it? They had an artefact that could hold open the door?"

"I think so. It must have been designed by a necromancer. Whether the designer is the one who used it is another question. Artefacts have been illegal for years. The witchfinders do raids on dealers all the time."

There's a knock at the door.

I sit bolt upright and stare at Orpheus. Both of us are silent.

There's another knock.

Shit, shit, shit.

My blood runs cold as I hear the front door creak open. Driven by instinct alone, I grab Orpheus' hand and drag him across the room to a dark corner. He flinches at my contact, and if it were any other situation, I'd apologise. I shift my vision and start moving my fingers, gathering a net of blue, pink, orange and green threads around us and feeding them onto the hook of my wand to start working them into stitches, hoping I can remember how to do this properly. It's one of the earliest things my Gran taught me, but it isn't easy. The order needs to be perfect. Please let me remember. *Please.*

The door to the living room swings open at the exact moment I let a pulse of magic out into the web I've tied around us. I can feel Orpheus motionless, pressed against my side, while I stare at the two men entering the room. One is white, tall, with a shaved head, wearing a denim jacket and chewing gum while he surveys the room. The other is brown, his hair short and black, wearing a long dark coat while typing something into his phone. Both look to be in their mid-thirties.

The white man's eyes pass right over me and Orpheus, but he doesn't flinch. The spell is holding, thank God.

"What did she even want us to do?" he asks.

The other man looks up briefly from his phone. "Clear it out."

"All of it?"

"Obviously."

The first man groans. "Alright, I'll start upstairs. You do the kitchen?"

"Sure."

They both leave the room, the second's eyes still glued to his phone.

I turn to look at Orpheus, and in the softest whisper I've ever spoken, I say, "We need to leave, *very* slowly and *very* quietly. And as soon as we're out, we run."

He nods without question. I reach my hand down to his and hold it tightly. He flinches again, but not as strongly as before. I make a mental note to apologise once we're out of here.

With a deep breath, I begin to walk as calmly as I can, Orpheus in tow, towards the door. There's thudding upstairs and clanging in the kitchen, both men out of sight. I keep walking, praying that the spell is still holding, until we reach the front door.

"Ready?" I whisper, turning the handle.

Orpheus nods.

"Run."

Chapter Nine
Orpheus

"Who were they?" I ask between breaths, doubled over at the corner of a small playground.

"No idea," says Evan. He's out of breath too, but not quite as exhausted as me. In fact, he's laughing. "Did you see how good that cloaking spell was, though? I haven't done one of those in years!"

There's a woman staring at us from across the road while she pushes a pram.

"Evan," I say.

"What?"

I nod towards the woman.

"Oh, right. Come on, let's find somewhere private."

As I follow him to a narrow path at a nearby treeline, I find my eyes wandering to his hand. Specifically, the one which held mine when we ran out of the house. It was a strange sensation, having my hand in his. It's not something I've ever done before, and it surprised me when it happened. But it felt nice. Granted, I was mainly focused on the fear that Evan seemed to be consumed by.

When we heard those knocks at the door, I didn't know what to think. Evan made it pretty clear that it was something to be worried about and to stay completely silent. But when he grabbed my hand . . . and when I was right next to him in the corner of the room . . . there was something strangely comforting about the physical contact, as though whatever it was that made Evan so afraid wouldn't be able to hurt either of us if we were together.

"I don't know who those men were," Evan repeats, coming to a stop at the top of a set of stone stairs that lead further into the woods, "but maybe they know the witch who stole the keys. Or maybe they're the dead man's family. Whoever they are, something weird is going on."

"At least we know an artefact was involved."

Evan nods. "And I think I know where we need to go next."

"You do?"

"We're going to need some leads for who might have the artefact, and I've got a friend who knows way more about this stuff than me."

"Another witch? But Mother said I mustn't involve too many—"

"Not a witch," Evan says, cutting me off by placing a hand on my shoulder.

I'm suddenly very aware of the physical contact and forget what I meant to say. Instead, I look over at Evan's hand.

"Oh, sorry," he says, removing it.

"No, I—"

"And sorry for grabbing your hand earlier, I'd normally have asked, but—"

"We were in a stressful situation; it's fine. And I didn't mind."

Evan nods. "Well, sorry anyway."

I consider telling him I actually quite liked it, but the words never come and are instead replaced with, "So, this person you know?"

"Right, yes. They're my best friend, but they're not a witch. In fact, they don't even know that I'm a warlock. You'll need to make sure you don't mention that. And we won't tell them what we're really doing."

I blink, trying to keep up and oddly feeling like I wish he hadn't removed his hand from my shoulder.

"If they're not a witch, how can they help?"

Evan smiles. "They're a bit of a magic expert. It's their autistic special interest."

I raise an eyebrow. "Autistic?" I think I may have heard the word from a spirit once, but I don't know what it means.

"Oh, right." Evan scratches his head. "Basically, people's brains work in different ways, and there are some ways that are considered typical and others that aren't. Autistic people are in the atypical group because they have difficulties with socialising; or they can be under- or over-sensitive to sensory input; or they might have really intense interests called special interests; or they might struggle with changes to routine. There are all sorts of criteria."

"I see." I wonder what levels of the things Evan described count as atypical. At what point are you being over- or under-sensitive? How intense does an interest have to be to be considered special? And what is considered a difficulty when it comes to socialising? As far as I've seen, socialising with mortals is inherently difficult, what with all their unspoken rules.

"But yeah," Evan continues, "if anyone will be able to give us a lead, it's them. We'll just have to be subtle about it. And we'll need some sort of cover story for you." He looks me up and down. "You could be a visiting cousin making a trip to see my dad before he dies? No, a family friend; I would have mentioned a cousin before."

"Whatever you think makes sense."

"And maybe we'll get you a change of clothes. Something a bit less conspicuous."

I remember thinking that maybe the weird looks I've been getting from everyone have been due to my clothes. The white robes don't really match the clothes I've been seeing people wearing, and I doubt the stains from my tomato excursion have helped much.

"I think Wren is about your size," Evan says, "and I'm sure they won't mind you borrowing something." He pulls out his phone and checks the screen. "If we set off now, they should be home from school by the time we get there."

"Wren is their name, I take it?"

"Oh, yeah, and they're non-binary, by the way. They use they/them pronouns. Do you . . . know what that means?"

I smile. It's fascinating to see what Evan thinks, or rather doesn't think, I'll have picked up in my talks with spirits.

"Yes," I say. "I've met non-binary people before."

The bus is busier than earlier, with more children dressed similarly to Evan with a blazer and tie, though theirs has different colouring to his.

"What is this?" I ask, pointing at his clothes.

"My uniform?"

I nod.

He laughs. "Well, it's . . . you know what school is, I assume?"

"Yes."

"Right, well, some schools – pretty much all schools in this country – make their students wear the same thing. A uniform." He shrugs. "It's meant to give us a sense of equality or something."

"And you wear this all the time?"

"God, no. Just while at school. I'd normally have been there at the time you met me; I just left early because of my dad. Not that I think delivering him some clothes was a good enough excuse, but when the school knows your parent is dying, they'll let you out for anything."

It's odd, the way he talks about his dad. One thing about human death that has always been clear is that it is considered sad. That when a friend or a relative or a lover passes away, you mourn for them. Or that when you know someone is going to die, you feel sorrow. And yet when Evan talks about his dying dad, he sounds almost bored.

"You and your dad," I say, "you don't get along, do you?"

He snorts. "You could say that. I hate him."

There's that word again. That powerful, harmful word. "Why?"

He rolls his eyes, looking frustrated. "Because he would hate me if . . ." His tone quietens, since there are a lot of people around. ". . . if he knew what I am. He hated his own mother because of what she was. And even without knowing the truth, he's always been cruel to me. Believe me, if you had a dad as hateful as mine, you wouldn't love him either."

I frown. It must hurt to be the son of someone so hateful. I can't imagine how that must feel.

"I never knew my father," I say.

"No?"

I shake my head. "He died soon after I was born." A group of children at the back of the bus start arguing loudly about someone called Mr Jones, so I know I won't be overheard. "Mortals aren't supposed to live in the Halls of Styx. The way time works there doesn't fit with their biology. Mother tried to make him leave so that he could live a full life here on Earth, but instead, he stayed and died before I was old enough to remember him."

Evan puts a hand on my thigh. "I'm sorry."

"Sorry for what?"

He chuckles softly. "It's just an expression."

"Oh." I glance at his hand, feeling that comforting closeness again, then back to his dark eyes. "Thank you?"

He smiles. I guess that was the right thing to say.

The children at the back of the bus start playing loud sounds from their phones, snapping my attention away. They blast short snippets of people speaking and fragments of music.

Evan removes his hand from my thigh, folding his arms. "You should be glad you don't have to deal with being around schoolkids every day."

He's not wrong. The noise is intense, and at each stop, more people get on the bus. Soon, it's not just schoolkids blasting noise from their phones that I'm hearing; it's twenty different conversations all happening around us. I catch random sentences from each, never enough to understand what they're discussing but always enough to feel overwhelmed. The hospital was similar. I wonder how many places are like this. How often do mortals have to deal with this onslaught of noise every day?

"Are you okay?" asks Evan at one point. I'm not sure how long it's been since he last spoke. I've been too caught up in the conversations around me.

"Um . . ." I say, not sure how to put it into words. "It's just . . . loud."

He frowns and leans over me to glance out of the window. "We could walk from here. Do you want to get off?"

I look at him, his wide eyes searching mine for an answer, and nod.

He presses the stop button.

The relief I feel when we're off the bus is beautifully intense. It's like a wave of quiet has descended over me. The cool air is a welcome change from the warm breaths of fellow passengers.

"Thank you," I say to Evan, who looks at me with a tilted head.

"It's okay," he says. "It was way too loud, wasn't it?"

"You thought so too?"

He pauses, which confuses me. Surely the answer is obvious.

"Sure," he says before turning on his heel. "Wren's house is this way."

I follow him past a library where a couple of young kids are pulling on their mother's arms, eager to enter; a shop selling pieces of paper with words such as *Happy Birthday* or *Congratulations* spread across them; and a bizarre building where a man is sitting in a chair facing a mirror while another man cuts his hair with scissors.

"It's a barber's," Evan says, noticing my confused look. "It's where you go to get your hair cut. Do you not need to cut your hair in the Halls of Styx?"

"No," I say, still perplexed, "it just sort of . . . stays how it is."

Evan laughs. "Well, I imagine it's growing now that you're here."

I run a hand through my hair, wondering how quickly it grows in this world. I've already seen so many different styles in this one short day, let alone the many spirits I've come across.

"People care about what their hair looks like, don't they?" I ponder aloud.

"Yeah, I suppose so." Evan turns a corner.

"And their clothes, too?"

He nods. "You'll find humans are a pretty vain species. We're always thinking about what others think of us."

"Why?"

"Now, that's far too deep a question for me to have the answer."

We cross the road and come to a stop outside a small metal gate in front of a house. It's not part of a row of attached houses, like the dead man's. Instead, this one stands alone. All the houses on this road are like that. They're all the same shape and size but with little differences like the colours of their front doors or the designs of the windows.

Evan opens the gate and walks up to the door, passing a row of bright flowers. He knocks on the door, and within seconds, it swings open. A person around Evan's – and, I suppose, my – age stands there, wearing the same white shirt as Evan but without the blazer or tie. Their skin is a light brown, decorated with freckles, and their hair is jet black, short at the sides and much longer at the back than the front.

"Oh, hey!" they say, taken aback by Evan's presence. "What are . . ." Their eyes wander past Evan's shoulders to me.

"Did you not get my text?" Evan asks.

"Phone died. Only just got back. Who's this?" They point at me.

Evan turns and gestures for me to come forward, which I do while also forming an attempt at a smile. Wren looks utterly baffled, so I'm not sure it works.

"This is Orpheus. His mum is a family friend; they're just visiting to see my dad before he . . . you know?"

"Oh. Well, nice to meet you." They hold out a hand.

I stare at it.

"Not a handshaker? That's cool. Nice name, by the way!" They lower their hand. "Do you two want to come in?"

"If that's okay?" Evan asks.

Wren steps aside, and I follow Evan across the threshold into a hallway. There's a flight of stairs to the right and a door to the left. Wren closes the door behind us, and it suddenly feels a whole lot warmer.

"What can I do for you?" Wren asks, shoving their hands into their pockets.

"Bit of a weird one," Evan says. "Is there any chance Orpheus could borrow some clothes? Just for today? He, uh, didn't come prepared, and we're not exactly the same size."

Wren giggles and looks at me. "I was gonna say that's an interesting choice for October. Bit cold for ancient Greek cosplay, isn't it?" They get a sudden panicked look in their eyes. "That wasn't an insult, by the way! I actually used to do the same. It was one of my early special interests. Is that where you got your name from?"

Evan clears his throat.

"Oh, right, sorry, change of clothes! Follow me."

If Evan hadn't told me that Wren was deeply interested in magic, their bedroom would have given it away. The walls are covered in illustrations of witches casting spells or close-ups of the rows of stitches in the fabric of the universe being formed by fingers and wands. There are stacks of books on every surface with titles like *Magic: A Hidden History* and *Weaving the Threads*, and on the far wall is a whiteboard with the words *witch* and *warlock* written above a list of words I don't recognise: *witchlock, wiccle, magis*.

"He's not anti-witch, is he?" I hear Wren whisper to Evan.

"No, no, he's cool."

"Whiteboard caught your eye?" Wren says, moving over to my side.

I nod.

"It's just a little pet project of mine. So, you've got *witch* for the girls and *warlock* for the boys, but I think it's a bit stupid that there isn't a non-binary equivalent."

Evan opens his mouth to speak, but Wren raises a finger and continues. "And yes, I know that *witch* is also the generic name to encompass all magic users, but I think that's just the same as when we use *man* to refer to all humans."

"Touché," says Evan.

There's a smile on his face, but his eyes tell a different story. I wonder how it feels for him to have a friend who is clearly so supportive of witches but who he can't be honest about his identity with. It seems to me that Wren would be delighted to find out they have a best friend who is a warlock.

"Anyway . . ." Wren says, throwing open their wardrobe. They riffle through their clothes, grabbing a selection of shirts and trousers and throwing them backwards onto their bed. "Will those do?"

I stare at the clothes, unsure of what the difference is between any of them.

"I like the flannel," Evan says, stepping forward and grabbing a long-sleeved shirt with a green check pattern on it. "And maybe these?" He picks up a pair of black trousers and hands them and the shirt to me.

"Okay," I say, accepting the pile.

I reach up to the fabric around my neck and start pulling it away.

Evan suddenly steps forward, face turning red. "Um, the bathroom is that way!" He points at the door across the landing. "You can get changed in there."

I'm puzzled by the statement at first, but then realise that if humans are always clothed, they probably don't tend to take their clothes off in front of people. So many rules. How do they cope?

Chapter Ten
Evan

"He seems nice," Wren says once Orpheus is shut away in the bathroom, "if a bit aloof. Is he autistic?"

I snort. Trust Wren to pick up on that within minutes.

"I'm starting to think so, yeah," I say.

The redness in my cheeks starts to fade as I perch on the edge of Wren's bed. I shake my head at myself. I didn't need to get that panicked over the sight of Orpheus' bare shoulder. It's not like he pulled the whole robe off.

Once Wren has put away the other clothes they got out, they sit beside me on their bed.

"You've never mentioned him before," they say.

"I hadn't met him until today."

"Interesting." They stare at me as though studying me for clues.

"What?"

"Nothing."

I don't believe that for a second, but I let it slide. "How was school?"

Wren shrugs. "Boring. Quiet. More people went home after lunch, and all the teachers were distracted by the news. Mrs Choudhry didn't even notice when Marcus Smith graffitied her display."

"That's not like her."

"No." Wren sighs. "Oh, and I'm pretty sure Zara was looking for you all afternoon."

I roll my eyes.

"No, seriously. She grabbed me at the end of the day and asked where you'd gone."

I bite my tongue. Ignoring me in history but then asking about me when I'm gone? It's a classic Zara move, really. She hadn't even crossed my mind since I left school this morning. Until now.

"I didn't tell her where you'd gone, by the way," Wren continues. "I just said it's none of her business anymore."

"Thanks."

They nudge my side. "You know I'm Team Evan for life."

That gets a laugh out of me.

"That's more like it."

"Enough Zara talk. I'd rather hear your theories about the whole immortality thing."

Their eyebrows practically fly off their face. "Really? You didn't seem that interested this morning."

"Well, I've changed my mind. I actually have some theories of my own."

Wren scoffs. "Evan Weaver has theories about magic? Is it my birthday?"

I nudge them back. "Shut up. I was just thinking about what you said about the size of the spell. How it must have been huge. Maybe they used an artefact, like you said?"

They look over at a chaotic spread of books on the floor, one of which is a catalogue of artefacts. On the front cover is an image of a pentagonal metal box, brass coloured, with an open top showing layers of clockwork within and hooked metal arms sticking up at each corner of the pentagon.

"They could have," Wren says. "I've not heard of an artefact that could do something like this, but that doesn't mean it doesn't exist."

"Could it have been made by necromancers?"

Wren's eyes narrow. "What's gotten into you? You've never been this interested in magic. I don't think I've ever even heard you say the word *necromancer* before."

I feel my cheeks turning red once again and am grateful for the eternally dim lighting of Wren's bedroom. This would be so much easier if they knew the truth about me, but I've been risky enough today already, and the promise I made to Gran stands firm in the back of my mind, like always.

"Well, we've never been in the middle of a global magical crisis before," I say. "And it is kind of the only thing keeping my dad alive, so yeah, I'm interested."

Their eyes hold onto suspicion, but they relax a little. "Okay, well, yes, it could have been necromancers. Not that many of those exist anymore. There are rumours of a few lingering covens, though."

I try to hold back to avoid sounding too eager. "Oh, really? Whereabouts would they be?"

"There's potentially one nearby. I was reading about it recently. Up on the moors about an hour away. People say it's a weak point between this world and the afterlife, like the veil that separates us from that world is at its thinnest. And there's all those old abandoned houses up there – it's the perfect place to get up to some illegal magic. I've been meaning to take a look myself, actually."

Local necromancers? There's no way that's a coincidence.

"Cool," I say. "Can you show me where you mean? On your phone?"

"Seriously? Who are you and what have you done with Evan?"

I laugh, hoping Wren's eagerness to talk about their special interest will overpower their suspicion. Which it does. They pull out their phone and open up a map.

"Somewhere around here," they say, pointing at a wide area of moorland. I know it, vaguely. There's a reservoir nearby which we once visited on a school trip, and there's a small car park somewhere overlooking the valley where Gran once took me. I remember standing with her, shivering in the strong winds yet still eating an ice cream from the van that for some bizarre reason considered the remote spot to be a good place for business.

I can feel Wren staring at me and know they're about to probe deeper about my newfound magical curiosity, but whatever they were going to say remains unspoken when the door swings open. Orpheus stands there, looking like an entirely new person in Wren's clothes. I was right – they fit him perfectly. Better, even, than they fit Wren. In fact, there's something oddly handsome about him dressed in that flannel.

"Is this right?" he asks, scratching his messy hair, eyes catching mine.

I clear my throat. "You look . . . good."

"You look great," Wren adds. "I'll have those clothes back when you're done, though, mind!"

"Of course," says Orpheus, before adding, "Thank you."

I push myself up off the bed. "Right, we'd better be off. But thanks, Wren. For everything."

The suspicious squint returns. "Are you sure you don't want to stay a bit?"

"We really need to be off. But I'll message you later, yeah?"

They hesitate, but eventually say, "Alright," and open their arms for a hug.

I oblige, as always, then lead Orpheus downstairs to the door.

"See you both!" Wren calls. "And nice to meet you, Orpheus!"

"And you!" Orpheus says as we step outside. He looks to me when the door closes. "So, did you find anything out?"

I nod. "Looks like we're going to the moors." My stomach groans. "Though maybe we should grab some food first?"

The Elm Café is one of my favourite spots in town. Gran used to bring me as a kid, then later I showed it to Wren, and then it even became my first date spot with Zara. It's small and cosy, with cushions literally everywhere, and the bright flowers that decorate it make it feel like springtime even in the middle of autumn.

Orpheus and I take seats at a corner table, right beside a window which looks out at the nearby clocktower.

"What do you fancy?" I ask.

Orpheus responds with one of his classic confused looks, and I realise that the afterlife probably doesn't have a café.

"Here." I pass him the menu. "Choose something off the list. Just ideally something less than a tenner. I've not got much money on me."

Orpheus studies the menu like it's the most important document he's ever held. I hide a smile behind one hand and pull out my phone with the other. There's a news report about how soldiers in warzones aren't sure what they're supposed to do now that they can't kill their enemies. One account describes the horrific scenes in a village where a bomb was let off, leaving countless people injured beyond belief but unable to die.

There's another headline just below, claiming that Eloise Morgan has refused to give any update on the witchfinders' search for the cause of the immortality. In fact, she still hasn't made a public appearance.

"That's not like her," I mutter, setting down my phone and looking out of the window. Nobody outside has any idea that two boys sat in this café might be the only people with a lead as to how to bring death back to the world.

A waitress arrives at our table. She's not much older than me, face still dotted with the last remnants of teenage acne.

"What can I get for you?" she asks, cheery.

"Um, the vegan sourdough sandwich and an oat milk latte, please."

Orpheus looks from the waitress to me and back again. "I'll have the same."

"And can we get those to go, please?" I add.

The waitress nods and walks away.

"I just feel like we should keep moving," I say to Orpheus, the article about warzones flashing in my mind. "No time to waste, is there?"

Orpheus shakes his head. "Not really."

"Last time I was here, I was on a date." I scoff at how ridiculous it sounds. "Didn't think the next time would be the middle of a quest to save the world."

"A date?" asks Orpheus. "That's a romantic thing, isn't it? An activity with a partner?"

"Yeah."

"So, you have a . . . girlfriend? Boyfriend?"

"*Had* a girlfriend. We're not together anymore." I catch his eye. "I am bi, though, if . . . if you're wondering."

His expression gives nothing away, if that is indeed what he was asking. "Why did you break up?"

"She cheated on me. Got with someone else behind my back."

"Do you miss her?"

"You ask a lot of questions, don't you?" I smirk, but I know he's not doing it to be rude. I think Wren was onto something with their potential diagnosis. "But yes. And no. It's complicated. We only broke up recently. I don't want to get back with her, but that doesn't mean I'm over it, you know?"

He nods. "I heard about a lot of relationships from the spirits."

"Yeah?"

"It seems to be one of the things humans value the most."

"Relationships?"

"Love." He smiles when he says it. "It's what people usually think about, in the end. Whether it's romantic or platonic, love persists, beyond life."

There's a look in his eyes when he speaks, like he's lost in a wistful reverie. As though all those stories the spirits told him are swirling in their blue waters. I think maybe he understands humans far better than I gave him credit for.

"That's a total of fourteen fifty," comes the voice of the waitress, snapping me back to reality. She sets down our cups and wrapped sandwiches, and I pass her some cash.

"Keep the change."

We ride the bus mostly in silence, though I do find some amusement in watching Orpheus experience an Elm Café sandwich for the first time. I think perhaps the food he's used to doesn't have much flavour. From the wildness of his eyes, you'd think he'd just taken a bite of the greatest food on the planet.

"What's in this?" he asks with a mouth full of food. "It's amazing."

I stifle a laugh. "Facon – that's vegan bacon," I add after his puzzled look, "peppers, onions, lettuce and tomato."

"Tomato?" he says, shocked. "Interesting."

"Is it?"

He studies the half-eaten sandwich, staring into its apparently fascinating depths. "I ate tomatoes this morning, and they didn't taste like this."

I recall the pale red stains from his robes. "Please tell me you didn't eat whole tomatoes with nothing else."

Orpheus looks panicked. "Was I not supposed to?"

I smirk. "I mean, you can, but no wonder you didn't like them." I point at the sandwich. "Please continue to enjoy them the way they're supposed to be eaten."

He returns to his wonderment. It's hard not to enjoy being in the company of someone who finds such joy in the small things. I can't help but get swept up in it, forgetting for a moment that we're trying to save the world.

The scenery outside the bus shifts from rows of houses to rolling green hills, and by the time we've lost sight of the town, the sun is already starting to set.

When we make our way off the bus, the driver says, "Are you sure you two will be okay? There aren't many buses after this one tonight."

"We'll be fine," I say.

The instant we're off, I realise why he asked. It was cold in the town, but up here, in the vast open moors, the wind is biting. The bus drives away, up the single long road which doesn't even have a pavement at its edge. Orpheus and I are stood next to a dry stone wall with a step stile built into it. There's not a single other person or building in sight, just vast swathes of green and brown and the occasional purple patch of heather.

"One second," I say when I realise Orpheus is shivering.

I pull off my backpack and rummage inside, retrieving my grimoire. The spell I need is just three pages in. I study it briefly, reminding myself of the simple steps. It's been a while since I've cast this one.

"Okay. Hold these." I pass him my bag and grimoire. "And hold still."

I pull out my wand, and then, with a deep breath, I shift my vision to reveal the threads. They're somehow less chaotic out here, where nature takes hold. They're just as numerous, but it feels like they vibrate more gently. I hold my intention in mind and observe as dull gold transforms into lilac and orange. I reach out at a pair around Orpheus and loop them around my wand's hook, creating the stitches displayed in the grimoire: a row above Orpheus' head, another on each shoulder, one around each hand, knee and foot. Then I repeat the process on myself, loop a thread connected to each of us over my wand and bring out that blissful spark of magic from within.

Energy ripples out through the glowing wand, igniting the stitches and turning them into a vibrant pink. Orpheus sighs with relief at the exact instant I feel the warmth pass over me.

"That should keep us toasty for a while," I say.

I'm about to remove the threads from my vision when I notice a gentle white glow at Orpheus' chest. I look closer and see stitches I never tied. Many tiny, sprawling rows of stitches, all surrounding his necklace. The anchor. I suppose it makes sense that it would be connected to magic somehow.

"What's wrong?" Orpheus asks.

"Nothing; I just . . . I didn't realise your anchor uses magic."

I shift my vision back so that the anchor is no longer obscured by glowing threads and I can see it properly. A brass-coloured disc with an intricate set of clockwork within.

"I wonder if it's the same metal as wands and the artefacts," I say. "It's the right colour. And it uses clockwork."

Orpheus shrugs. "Probably. Though it was designed by the gods."

"Bit more complex than human artefacts, then?"

Orpheus laughs. "I suppose so. Thank you, by the way."

"For what?"

"The warmth."

"Oh." I smile, taking back the backpack and grimoire. "It's nothing. A pretty simple spell. I can cast it again in a few hours if we need it."

I clamber up the stile, looking out at the unmarked footpath beyond.

"If I remember correctly, there's a rocky outcrop in that direction. We should have a good view of the valley from there. We might be able to see where the necromancers operate from."

"I'm not sure we'll be able to see anything soon." Orpheus nods towards the orange haze of the setting sun.

"Good thing we don't need normal vision, then." I climb down the other side of the stile. "We've got the threads to guide us."

It's not long before we reach the rocks, which — thankfully — are where I expected them to be. They jut out from the moorland, forming a jagged platform from which you can see for miles. There's a reservoir down in the bottom of the valley, reflecting the last of the sunlight, and further out, I can see a couple of the old, abandoned houses that Wren mentioned. If we're lucky, the necromancer coven will be in one of those.

"Wow," says Orpheus when he arrives at my side. "This is . . ." He stares out at the moors, open-mouthed.

"Beautiful?"

"Yeah."

It's easy to forget, when you live near a view like this, how beautiful it really is. I remember once, one of my cousins from London came to visit and was shocked by the natural landscape. Being here now, I can't help but think of those old trips with Gran. Remote, natural places like this were perfect for practising magic. She used to say it was important to remember our connection to nature.

"Magic is the most natural thing in the world," she said. "Don't ever let anyone make you forget that."

Orpheus leans back and breathes in the cold air, taking it all in. "It's a shame we can't just stay here," he says.

I have a feeling Gran would have liked him.

"We can always come back," I say, watching his silhouette against the sunset. "Once we've ... you know ... saved the world."

"That would be nice."

I feel an odd pang of sadness at that, which feels wrong. As though part of me hopes we won't be finished any time soon. But I can't actually believe that, not when there's such a huge responsibility on our shoulders. I suppose it's just that there's been something freeing about being open with my magic in front of someone. To share a part of me that's normally so private. Something I've not even shared with my best friend or ex-girlfriend.

I shake my head. There's no time for dwelling on that. I look out at the valley below and reveal the threads. I survey them, hoping to see some sort of disturbance, and—yes!

"There!" I say, pointing out at a distant abandoned house. "You see that building?"

"Just about," says Orpheus.

"The threads over there are glowing bright. I think they've even formed a shape, like a sort of dome around the house."

"Meaning there are spells being cast?"

"Definitely."

I banish the threads and grab Orpheus' hand.

"Come on!"

Chapter Eleven
Orpheus

I hold Evan's hand for as long as I can, but the ground quickly becomes too uneven, and I need both hands free for balance. This place might be beautiful, but it's not easy to walk around, especially with the sun continuing to set. It's looking pretty certain now that by the time we reach the house, it's going to be fully dark.

When I trip for the fifth time, Evan pulls out his wand and conjures up some light, stitching a glowing orb into existence in seconds. It hovers by his hand as we walk, reminding me of the whispering orbs in Mother's cave.

"I'd put it above us," Evan says, "but if anyone happens to spot us, I'd rather it look like I'm holding a torch."

It's hard to see much beyond the light the orb casts, but the moon is full and adds a silvery glow to the moorland around us. The house we're heading for looks like nothing more than a black shape in the distance. I wonder if this is how the spirits feel when Mother guides them through the Halls of Styx, when they find themselves stepping into an unfamiliar world and being led down a path by a stranger, not knowing what's coming next.

Evan isn't a stranger, though. Not anymore. At least, that's how I like to think of him. Whether he feels the same about me is another question entirely, one which I feel strangely concerned about the answer to. But he probably doesn't feel the same, now that I think about it. He's lived all his life in the mortal world, surrounded by fellow humans. He's had years to build countless connections. What could someone he's known for mere hours possibly mean to him? And more importantly, why do I seem to think it matters?

I focus on the sky above us, snapping myself out of my spiralling thoughts. The stars have begun to decorate the sky. I've heard stories of them before, described as part of a romantic backdrop to two lovers' camping trip, or as the lifelong obsession of an old scientist. I've imagined them countless times in my mind's eye, and I've even caught a glimpse of them through an open door once or twice, but I've never truly seen them. Not to this degree.

But despite the beauty high above, there's something eerie about the dark. I know from my talks with the spirits that humans are often afraid of the dark, and I've never quite understood why. The dark is something I've experienced plenty of times myself in the Halls of Styx, through the night cycle of the central forest, and it's never scared me. But I think I understand the fear now.

The dark here is different to back home. In the Halls, I always know what's around me. There's Mother and the spirits she guides. Nothing else is concealed in the shadows. Even if an unwilling spirit runs from Mother and flees to the edges of the Halls, I know they'll never come near my cabin. There's a certainty to existence in that space. Here, however, in this world filled with so many lives, there could be all manner of things hiding in the dark, beyond the glow of Evan's orb. The fear isn't of the dark; it's of what might lurk within it. The unknown.

"When we get there, let me do the talking," says Evan. "We don't want to give away exactly what we're doing unless we need to. If there are witches in there, I should be safe saying I'm one of them."

Beyond our footsteps, I can hear occasional movement – small animals racing through the heather. Other than that, there is only silence. We're too far from the road now to hear cars if there are any. The closer we get to the house, though, the more unsettling the silence becomes.

If there are witches in there, surely we should be able to hear them by now.

Soon we're close enough that I can make out the house more clearly. The roof has multiple holes, and one of the stone walls has completely crumbled. As far as I can see, there's no glass in the windows. It's clear no one has lived here in a long time.

Evan slows down the closer we get until he pauses completely, and I think I know why. Something feels wrong. It's like the air itself is warning us of danger. The silence is deafening.

Until it's pierced by a distant howl.

I don't even think before slipping my hand right back into Evan's.

"What was that?" I whisper.

"It sounded like . . . a wolf," Evan whispers back, his body tense against mine. "But there are no wolves here."

The howl sounds again, closer this time. Evan and I both turn in its direction, somewhere back where we just came from.

"Evan?"

"Yeah?"

"Can you hear that?"

It's a new sound. Not howling. Running. The sound of an animal getting closer and closer, heading straight for us.

Evan raises his hand – the one with the glowing orb – and thrusts it forwards. The orb moves away, lighting up the path we just walked along, travelling farther and farther until it shows us exactly what's heading our way.

I've seen dogs before, and I know that wolves are similar, and this is what I've always imagined wolves to look like. Except it's more than that. It's like it's made of smoke. A mass of black smoke in the shape of a wolf, with luminous white eyes, running full speed in our direction, baring its teeth. It'll be on us in seconds—

"Get back!" shouts a voice I don't recognise.

Suddenly, Evan and I are both falling backwards, colliding with the rough stone wall of the house. Evan's light is extinguished, but a new one forms as the wolf collides with a glowing magenta wall in front of us.

It whimpers and runs away, and the magenta wall fades, leaving only the dim light of the moon to show the woman now standing above us. Wild-eyed, with her red hair loosely tied back, dressed in a long black coat, she stares from me to Evan and back.

"Both of you, inside. Now!"

The house is just as shabby inside as it is out, with crumbled walls and grass all across the floor – except for the centre, where a thick rug has been placed. With a quick movement of the woman's fingers around the tip of her wand, a set of candles light up across the room, each jammed between different stones. Now I can see a pile of grimoires atop a flimsy-looking wooden table and a sleeping bag at one end of the rug.

"Who the hell are you two?" the woman asks. "And don't bother lying." She looks at Evan. "I saw that light spell; I know you're a warlock."

"Right, yes, I am." His voice is shaky, not as clear as usual, and he's shivering.

As am I. The warmth from Evan's earlier spell is gone. Though I can't help but wonder if we're also shaking out of fear for whatever that shadowy beast was.

"I'm Evan," he says. "And this is Orpheus. And . . ." He shakes his head. "Sorry, what the hell was that thing out there?"

The woman scowls and picks at the nail on one of her fingers. Her lips stay sealed.

"Okay, you don't want to tell us," Evan says. "Fine." He glances my way, and I can see in his eyes that he isn't sure what to do. "Can you at least tell us your name?"

"Charlotte," she says.

I move to stand in front of her. "What if we tell you why we're here?"

She stops picking at her nail. "Go on."

I look at Evan and nod.

"We want to know what caused the immortality," he says, stepping forward, "and we heard there might be a coven of necromancers out here, so we thought we'd investigate."

Charlotte scoffs. "Well, you're a bit late for a coven."

Evan's brow furrows in uncertainty.

"And we definitely didn't cause the immortality," Charlotte continues. "But you can add that thing out there to the list of problems it's brought."

"I don't understand," says Evan.

Charlotte shakes her head. "Join the club." She stares off into space, thinking, then nods to herself and says, "At least if I tell you, you might be able to help." She sits down in the centre of the rug and gestures for us to join.

I look to Evan, who nods, and take a seat beside him.

"You know we're necromancers, so you know we research magic relating to death."

"We?" Evan asks.

"I'll get to that."

In the distance, the howl sounds again, and I find myself edging closer to Evan.

"It won't surprise you that one of our greatest pursuits is that of a resurrection spell – a way to bring someone back from the dead. Of course, it's no easy feat, and necromancers have been trying to find the solution for literal centuries. There are stories of necromancers communicating with the dead and even summoning ghosts to our world, but never quite managing true resurrection."

I doubt this necromancer has ever summoned a ghost, not while Mother's Halls of Styx have stood strong. The days of ghosts and poltergeists are long over. She's too good at her job to let them slip through the cracks.

"A year or so ago, a member of our coven was able to procure this." Charlotte reaches behind herself and pulls something out of a bag. It's a small pentagonal metal box the colour of brass.

"Is that—" I start.

"An artefact," says Evan, eyes lighting up.

"Rumours suggested that it is the closest thing any witch has to a true resurrection spell. We tried to use it many times, to no avail, but on the night of the immortality, we thought perhaps the usual rules that keep the dead separate from the living no longer applied. So we used it once more, hoping to resurrect a dead member of the coven. But instead, the artefact summoned that beast you saw outside."

"But what is it?" I ask. "The beast. The wolf. It's not just an animal, is it?"

She shakes her head. "It's a gytrash."

Evan's eyebrows rise in recognition.

"A what?"

"A gytrash?" repeats Evan.

Charlotte nods.

Evan looks at me. "It's an evil spirit that was said to haunt the roads of West Yorkshire many years ago. The Brontës – famous authors – wrote about them. They'd come in the shape of animals like dogs or horses and attack lonely travellers." He turns to Charlotte. "Right?"

"Indeed. And now there's one on the loose again, and I haven't been able to contain it. I've set up a protection spell around this house, but it doesn't hold for long. I have to keep recasting it."

"But what does the gytrash do?" Evan asks. "Can it hurt us?"

Charlotte sighs and looks over at a dark corner of the room. She raises her wand in the air again, manoeuvring her fingers around the hook until another pair of candles light up, revealing what was hidden in the darkness. There, on the floor, lie three bodies.

"Oh my God," says Evan, racing over to them.

I follow, getting closer. I've seen plenty of corpses through the doors, and these look eerily similar. The nearest body is that of a woman, similar in age to Charlotte but with darker skin and shorter hair. Her eyes are open but unseeing, like a haze has descended across her pupils. I reach out a hand and place it on her forehead. She's cold to the touch, but not as cold as I expected.

Beside her are two men, one with a youthful face that can't be older than twenty and the other much older than the rest, with wiry, receding grey hair. Both wear the same vacant expression as the woman, eyes as cold as the autumn air.

"Are they dead?" I ask.

"No," says Charlotte. "I don't know what they are. But the gytrash passed through them, and now . . . I'm the only one of the coven left standing."

I stand up, staring at the three bodies while Evan continues to check them, placing his fingers on their necks to confirm they have a pulse. There's something we're missing. Something obvious.

I face Charlotte. "You said you were trying to resurrect someone specific?"

She nods. "Amelia. She was one of us. One of the coven. In fact, she's the one who procured the artefact in the first place."

"Where from?" Evan asks.

Charlotte shrugs. "A dealer; she never said who."

The howl sounds again, conjuring up the image of the gytrash in my mind. The black swirling smoke. Where have I seen that before? Think, think, think.

A memory stirs. Mother, trying to calm an aggressive spirit. The spirit refusing to co-operate. An anger like I'd never seen. The edges of the spirit starting to darken, like wisps of jet-black smoke. It was a sight that stopped me ever hanging around when spirits got angry in future.

"The artefact worked," I say, drawing the attention of both Charlotte and Evan.

"Not properly," says Evan.

"Yes, properly." I point at Charlotte. "You wanted to bring back your friend Amelia, yes?"

She hesitates, thrown by my words. "Yes."

"And that's exactly what you did." I turn to face one of the glassless windows, listening out for the chilling howl. "Amelia is the gytrash."

Chapter Twelve
Evan

Orpheus looks at us both from the window, a delighted smile across his face, proud of his revelation. But Charlotte looks horrified.

"Sorry, what?" she says.

"When someone dies," Orpheus says, hands animated, "they travel through a liminal space before reaching the true afterlife. But they don't always go willingly. Some spirits outright refuse to pass on, consumed by rage, running away and getting lost on the edges of that liminal space."

I notice he's avoiding naming the Halls. It's a smart move – it could be dangerous to let Charlotte know the truth of his identity.

"Those lost spirits become corrupted," he continues. "They lose their sense of self, even their human form. I think maybe the gytrash is the result." He looks at the bodies of the other coven members. "And maybe the corruption rubbed off on their spirits too."

Charlotte shakes her head in disbelief.

Orpheus walks over to the artefact and picks it up. "I don't think this will ever be capable of truly bringing back the dead, but while a door to the afterlife is left open, it could help a corrupted spirit on the edge of existence slip through."

"How can you possibly know all of this?" Charlotte asks, voice thick with uncertainty and, below that, anger.

"It's a theory!" I say before Orpheus has a chance to reply. "But it makes sense, doesn't it? You're a necromancer; surely you know something of how the afterlife works?"

She narrows her eyes in suspicion. "The stories do say there's a liminal space to pass through before reaching the true afterlife, though what exactly that space is seems to differ throughout history. I've heard stories of forests, frozen landscapes, and mazes."

I spot a glint of recognition in Orpheus' eyes. Charlotte must be referring to the realms designed by previous psychopomps.

"There's always a guide, though," Charlotte continues. "Someone to walk you to the next life."

"How old was Amelia when she died?" I ask.

Charlotte breaks eye contact. There's a painful memory there.

"Twenty-seven," she says.

"So she probably wasn't ready to go."

"Of course she wasn't!" Charlotte retorts, venom on her tongue. "It was an accident, a car crash. She was gone in an instant. She should have had decades left!"

I hold up my hands. "Of course, of course. I'm not denying that. But . . . it would make sense that she'd refuse to pass on, wouldn't it?"

Charlotte's scornful face softens slightly. There's another howl in the distance, but this time, instead of fear, I find myself feeling sad.

I turn to Orpheus. "Can we help her? Can we, I don't know, uncorrupt her spirit?" I glance at the bodies, wondering if they're still conscious behind their frozen expressions. "Can we save them?"

"I don't know," he says. I can see in his face that he wishes that weren't true.

I take in the room – the bodies in the corner, the sleeping bag, the piles of grimoires.

"Have you been here since last night?" I ask Charlotte.

She shakes her head. "The gytrash disappears in the daylight. It attacked the others last night, but I made it to morning. I came back with all of this"—she gestures at the grimoires—"to try and banish it. I don't want it – *her* – to hurt anyone else."

There's another problem at play too. If Orpheus is right, and the gytrash is Amelia, then we're going to need a way to speak to her. A necromantic artefact is a rare thing, and apparently, Amelia knew a dealer with access to one. That dealer could also be the closest thing we have to a lead in finding the person who stole Orpheus' mother's keys. We need to know who they are.

"Okay," I say, bending down to grab a grimoire, "let's figure this out."

All three of us scour through the grimoires, searching for a spell that could help. There are diagrams of ghostly apparitions and countless ways of allegedly communicating with the dead, but not a lot about gytrashes, just an entry describing one warlock's encounter with one in 1853. He tells of how he put up a shield to protect himself – the very one that Charlotte has cast around this house – and waited until dawn to run away.

"Why can't the gytrash manifest in daylight?" I ask.

Charlotte shrugs. "It's always been the way of spirits."

"Spirits don't belong in this world outside a body," Orpheus says. "Maybe the sun is one of nature's ways of preventing them from lingering."

I'm not sure there's much of a logical basis for that answer, but it reminds me of what Orpheus said about religion: that outside the mortal realm, contradictory things can be simultaneously true. Maybe I shouldn't search for logic when it comes to spirits.

I grab the artefact and look at it closely. Unopened, it's just a dull metal box, save for a carving on its base that shows a blooming flower, the word *resurrection* written beneath it. With one twist, however, it opens up to reveal layers of clockwork and five thin metal rods that rise up at each corner, each with a hook on its end. Without magic flowing through it, the clockwork remains stationary, but I know that if it were activated, the rods would work just like wands but doing the jobs of fingers as well. They'd catch the threads and loop them over each other, forming rows of stitches with far more ease and precision than a human. It's almost like a miniature sewing machine.

"Does it work in reverse?" I ask. "Could it be used to send her back?"

"No," Charlotte says. "You'd need an entirely different artefact for that. It was built for one spell and one spell only."

I've only seen an artefact in person once before (not counting Orpheus' god-made pendant), when Gran took me to visit one of her friends. The friend was in her late eighties and didn't have much mobility left. For her, artefacts were her only way of casting spells. She didn't use them for anything particularly fancy, just simple spells like summoning objects to her or warming herself up in the winter. It wasn't long after the witchfinders confiscated her artefacts that she died.

Possession of a necromantic artefact like Charlotte's, on the other hand, would incur a far worse punishment from the witchfinders than simply having it confiscated. If she were caught, there's no doubt in my mind that she'd face a forced conversion. Her magic would be stripped away, leaving her missing a huge part of who she is. A shell of her former self. I wonder if that's how Amelia feels, if there's anything of her left inside the beast.

"Hey," Orpheus mutters from my side. His hand hovers hesitantly over my shoulder, like he's reaching out to comfort me but doesn't know if he's allowed. "Are you okay?"

"Hmm? Yeah, I'm fine." I rub my eyes, only now realising that tears have begun to form in them. "I was just . . . thinking."

Charlotte slams down her grimoire. "There's nothing! Nothing to help any of them!" She buries her face in her hands, breathing heavily.

I exchange a look with Orpheus, frowning.

"What do we do?" I ask him quietly. "You know we need to speak to Amelia, don't you? We need to know where she got the artefact."

Orpheus nods.

I bite my tongue. If we can't uncorrupt the gytrash, maybe we need a different strategy. "What would happen if I entered her mind?"

"I don't know," says Orpheus. "I don't know how much of her mind there is left."

"But it might work?"

"I . . . maybe?"

Charlotte drops her hands. "You want to enter the mind of a gytrash? Are you insane? How would you even get close enough?"

"You've proven you can cast a shield that it can't get past." I point at the walls of the house. "What if we made a new shield? But this time, around the gytrash, trapping it – *her*."

Charlotte walks me through the spell again. The patterns are simple enough; the problem is speed. We're going to have to be fast if this is going to work. The plan is to form a smaller partial shield inside the house. Charlotte will drop the one outside; we'll lure the gytrash in and seal the smaller shield around it. It won't be banished, and the other coven members will still be corrupted, but at least it won't be able to harm anybody else. And, if we're lucky, I'll be able to enter Amelia's mind.

"Okay," Charlotte says after I form a row of stitches again, "I think you've got it. I'll start on the new shield." She drags the rug, with the grimoires on top, to the edge of the room, making a clear space to begin the spell.

Orpheus stands at the doorway, looking out into the night. He hasn't said much since Charlotte and I started preparing.

"Hey," I say, walking up to his side. I shiver against the cold night air.

"Hey."

I keep my voice low to ensure Charlotte can't overhear. "You know, for someone who's only half-human, you're pretty easy to read." I nudge him playfully. "You're worried, aren't you?"

"I don't want you to get hurt." He faces me, eyes glowing in the moonlight. "I don't want you to end up like those people. If that happens to you, I won't know how to help you."

I put my hands on his shoulders, steadying him. I can feel him tremble.

"It's going to be fine," I say. "I won't end up like them; I promise."

He shakes his head. "You can't promise something that's out of your control."

"I can promise to try." I move my hands down his arms, stopping at his wrists. "Trust me. We don't have another option."

He sighs and looks into the room, towards the bodies in the corner. "I know. I just wish we could fix all of this."

"And we will. Once we find the keys, things will go back to normal. Your mum can retrieve the gytrash, can't she?"

"I think so. But I don't think she can help them." He nods at the bodies.

I raise a hand up to his face and tilt it to face me. His skin is cold but soft, and I find myself running my fingers gently down his cheek. He lets out a steady breath as his eyes study mine, looking down at me.

"One problem at a time," I say. "We've got the whole world to save."

Charlotte clears her throat. "If you two are done flirting, we have work to do."

"We weren't . . ." I feel my face flush as I return both my hands to my pockets. "We were just . . ."

"I don't need to hear it. Just come and help."

I shift my vision to reveal the threads once we're all in position. Orpheus is outside, stood at the edge of the shield. Charlotte is out there too, ready to tear down the shield when the gytrash approaches. I'm inside, stood to the side of the doorway, studying the almost-completed shield dome in the centre of the room, flexing my fingers and steadying my wand, ready to finish the job.

My heart is pounding hard and fast, but I try to calm myself with slow breaths. Part of me – quite a large part, actually – wishes I'd given in to Orpheus' wish to stay on the rocky outcrop. We could be there right now, gazing up at the stars, pretending the fate of humanity isn't resting on our shoulders.

But here we are. And now is the time.

"Go!" I shout.

I can't see him from my position, but I know Orpheus will now be stepping beyond the boundary of the outer shield.

"Amelia!" he shouts. "Over here!"

There's a howl and then silence as we wait.

Wait.

Wait.

Then the sound of the gytrash approaching.

Orpheus hurtles into the room, through the centre, passing straight through the inner shield. Charlotte will be bringing down the outer shield so that—yes!

The gytrash leaps into the room, still pursuing Orpheus but colliding with the shield before it can reach him. The magenta light shines brighter as the beast struggles against it. I step forwards and move my wand and hand faster than ever before, forming new red-and-blue stitches to complete the dome.

But I fumble. I lose grip of one of the threads.

The gytrash turns to face me.

It bares its teeth.

It pounces right at me.

And the room fills with white light.

Chapter Thirteen
Orpheus

I don't think. Or rather, I have only one thought clear in my mind: I must protect Evan. But that thought is enough to drive my hand to reach for the chain around my neck and tear off the anchor, throwing it to the ground.

Bright white light fills the room, radiating out of me in all directions as I feel myself rise from the floor. My wings, not of this world, pass straight through my shirt, spreading wide and allowing me to levitate. Everything seems to slow down. The gytrash moves towards Evan, ready to turn him into the same husk of a person that Charlotte's fellow coven members have become.

But I won't allow it.

I reach out and place my hands on the sides of the gytrash's wolven face. The moment I make contact, I feel its anguish. All the rage and fear and desperation that corrupted Amelia's spirit is there in the black smoke. But it softens at my touch. The tension in its spiritual body dims as I focus on a single word.

Calm.

The gytrash slows further. No longer is it ready to attack. Instead, it sits. The black smoke remains, but it will not harm anyone – at least, not for now.

I feel something else, too. Below the emotion that defines the gytrash's form, there's something more familiar. I know it well from my time in the Halls of Styx: the aura of a human spirit, the gentle vibration. There's a spark in amongst it that reminds me of Evan's – the soul of a witch.

But this one is lost. Corrupted. It's like she's been physically torn apart. Yet I can sense fragments.

I move my hands further into the smoke, reaching out. Reaching *in*. Searching for something, anything. Any part of who Amelia was.

My vision blurs, and suddenly, a new image comes into focus. I'm watching a young girl on a swing at a playground being pushed by a man. Purple blossom flutters through the air as the girl giggles.

"Higher!" she cries, pigtails swaying to and fro on the sides of her head.

The man obeys, laughing as he pushes her higher and higher. As I watch him, I feel an emotion that isn't my own, as though I can trust this man with my life. I hear a woman's voice in my mind calling, "Dad!"

With another push on the swing, my surroundings blur once again, swirling out of focus as though they were merely a reflection on a pond which has now been disturbed. A new scene comes into focus.

A woman throws a graduation cap in the air with her university friends against the backdrop of a grand old building. The sounds of cheers fill the air.

"Here's to the future!" one of her friends says.

"Here's to years of debt," the woman replies.

I'm not sure how, but I know her to be the same person as the girl on the swing. I know her to be Amelia.

And there's that voice in my mind again, this time as I look at each of Amelia's friends. "Samantha," it calls. "Charlie, Diane, Gareth!" And there are those emotions that aren't my own, a deep love for each of these people I've never met.

The scene changes again, graduation caps turning into black smears against the sky before the dappled canopy of a forest comes into being.

As a teenager, Amelia wanders through woodland, checking behind her to see if she's being followed. When she finds a clearing, she sits down, runs her fingers through the grass, and takes a deep breath. From the pocket of her hoodie, she draws a wand. Its metal surface glistens in the sunlight. She raises it along with her spare hand and begins reaching out to threads that I can't see and looping them over the hook, casting a spell.

I feel her fear of being caught. This must be what Evan experiences every day.

"Can't let them see," the voice says. "Mustn't let them see."

The sunlight gets brighter, then fades as a new scene appears.

Amelia enters the old abandoned house on the moors to find Charlotte and the other members of the coven stood drinking steaming liquid from flasks. Charlotte smiles when she sees her and shakes her hand.

"Home," the voice says. With it comes an overwhelming sense of belonging, like a weight has been lifted. "A new family."

The house transforms into one filled with shelves of ornaments. Amelia sits across from a dark-haired woman, who holds an artefact in her hands. Music plays in the background.

"You understand this is a particularly rare find?" the dark-haired woman says.

"I understand."

"And you know if the witchfinders catch you using it, you'll face a severe punishment?"

Amelia nods. "The coven has been looking for something like this for years."

"I don't doubt it." She passes the artefact to Amelia, and as she does, I hear the voice in my mind again.

"Tamara O'Sullivan," it says.

"And you'll keep the promise?" the woman – Tamara, it would seem – asks.

Amelia nods. "I won't tell Charlotte I got it from you."

The house vanishes into ripples.

As a toddler, Amelia cries after bumping her head, and I can't help but want to cry too. Her father holds her close and kisses her cheek, cooing in the hopes he'll calm her down.

"It hurts," says the voice. "Make it better!"

A screeching sound fills the air, and I'm suddenly in the back of a car. Amelia screams as it swerves off the road.

"Too soon."

I recoil back, hands stinging, and let go as the room comes back into focus. The gytrash continues to sit calmly on the floor.

Time catches up, and Evan falls to the ground, shielding his eyes from the light and gasping with panic. Charlotte runs in, shielding her eyes too.

"What happened?" she cries.

Evan sits up, blinking until his eyes have adjusted to the light, and taking in what he can see.

"Orpheus?" he says, open-mouthed.

"It's okay," I say, and though all of this is new to me, I know it to be true. "She won't harm you."

Charlotte stumbles over to Evan's side, staring at me in disbelief.

"You're . . ." she mutters. "You're an angel?"

"Half-angel," I correct her.

I check the ground and find the anchor in the grass at the edge of the rug. I let myself lower to the floor, folding in my wings, and pick up the pendant.

"But what did you . . . ?" Evan asks, looking from me to the gytrash.

I put the anchor back on and feel a shift in my body as my angelic form is locked back within its human shell. I can almost hear the bones knocking together as I become more solid. The light I was emitting fades away, and I feel my wings retract, like wisps of white smoke being drawn into my flesh. Charlotte and Evan continue to stare in awe.

"I calmed her, I think. It's something my mother does; it seems I can do it too."

The gytrash remains seated, its black smoke seeming to move a little more gently than when it was attacking. It is no longer a hungry beast seeking to destroy whatever it can set its jaws on.

"I don't know if it'll last forever, though. You might want to seal that shield."

Charlotte doesn't question me. She gets to work, stitching the final rows and forming the full dome.

Evan stands up, facing me. "You saved me."

I shrug. "I had to."

He throws his arms around me and pulls me tightly against him.

"What—"

"It's a hug. I'm hugging you." His voice is muffled against my shoulder.

I copy him, wrapping my arms around his back.

There's a muffled laugh. "You've not done this before, have you?" He lets go, and we separate.

"No," I reply. I'd like to say I'd love to do it again, but I choose to keep that quiet. "I think I found the artefact dealer, by the way."

"Wait, what?"

I nod towards the gytrash, which, if Charlotte's exasperated sigh is anything to go by, is now properly trapped inside a shield.

"I saw her memories. The dealer is called Tamara O'Sullivan."

"Great! And where is she?"

Ah. "I don't know."

Evan rolls his eyes. "Right, well, I'd better go into her mind myself."

He starts to walk over to the gytrash, but I grab his blazer and stop him.

"I don't think you should," I say, recalling how I was thrown out of the last memory, hands stinging. "I think she showed me all she'll ever show."

He sighs. "A name is better than nothing, I suppose."

"It's a lot more than we had before."

Charlotte does a final flourish with her wand and, seeming satisfied with the shield, faces me.

"Who are you, really?" she says, moving strands of wild hair out of her face.

I feel there's no point in lying to her now, not after everything she's seen. "I'm Orpheus, son of the current psychopomp of the afterlife."

"Psychopomp?"

"Death," Evan says. "He's the son of Death. And he's here to try and fix what's gone wrong. To stop the immortality."

Her face is drained of all colour. "How?" she asks, voice quieter than ever before.

"Well," I say, "apparently, we need to find a witch named Tamara O'Sullivan."

Charlotte laughs, slowly at first, but it soon turns into a hysterical giggle that has her doubled over. I look at Evan, hoping he'll tell me this is a normal human reaction, but instead, he looks as baffled as I feel.

"Charlotte?" I say.

She composes herself slowly and stands up straight again. "Tamara O'Sullivan? As if this day couldn't get any stranger."

"What's so strange about Tamara?" asks Evan.

Charlotte lets out a final weak laugh. "Tamara O'Sullivan is my ex-wife."

Evan casts his warming spell on all three of us and the bodies of the other coven members as we sit on the rug once again. Amelia, still in her gytrash form, sits patiently where we trapped her, a dog in a cage. Tame, at least for now.

"She did always have an interest in artefacts," Charlotte tells us while lighting a new set of candles. "But I never thought she'd become a dealer."

I shared what I saw in Amelia's memories, including Tamara's line about not telling Charlotte. It seems a far-from-amicable breakup is the real reason Amelia never revealed who her artefact dealer was.

"She was never much of a risk taker," Charlotte continues, "at least, not while we were together. I mean, you should have seen how worried she used to get when I'd practise necromancy at home. Always afraid that the witchfinders would come calling. Simple magic in the privacy of your own home is perfectly legal. But necromancy?" She fakes a laugh. "Guaranteed ticket to conversion."

"But so is artefact dealing, isn't it?" Evan asks.

"Indeed, it is. Which begs the question, what led her down that path?" She pauses. "Unless . . ." Her eyes widen, and suddenly, the wolf's face isn't the scariest thing in the room. "Of course. That lying b—"

Evan clears his throat. "Care to explain?"

"She was doing it behind my back," Charlotte says, shaking her head in anger. "I *knew* she was up to something. She claimed she was helping run her family's business, but it 'involved highly delicate goods', so I wasn't allowed to see it. But no, this is what she was doing all along! Of course she didn't want me practising necromancy – she didn't want any witchfinders investigating me because if they did, they might realise what she was doing!"

Evan looks at me and raises his eyebrows as if to say, *I wasn't expecting that*. I do the same back. I think it's safe to say a lot of things have happened today that we didn't expect.

"Um," Evan says, "I'm sorry that happened to you, Charlotte, but is there any chance you could tell us where we might find Tamara?"

Charlotte doesn't look either of us in the eye; instead, she's staring up at the ceiling, seemingly reliving her entire marriage in her mind. I've heard many failed marriage stories from spirits. Often, they'll look back in their final moments and have an epiphany or two. I hadn't considered that humans might have such huge revelations while still alive.

"Last I heard, she'd moved into her parents' old place," Charlotte says, making threatening faces at the crumbled ceiling.

"Which would be where, exactly?"

"Eighty-seven Crestfield Road, Manchester. I bet you she wouldn't have *my* parents' address memorised."

"Right . . . thanks." Evan waves at me and mouths, *We should go*.

I get up off the rug, feeling a sense of guilt. We'll be leaving her with the bodies of her coven and a gytrash, but there's nothing more we can do for them. The best thing we can do is continue the search for the keys.

"Charlotte," I say, "we're going to go now, if that's okay."

"Sure," she says, apathetic, but then she pauses, looks at us both, and realises what I actually said. "Oh. Are you sure?"

"The longer we wait, the worse things are going to get," I say.

"Will it work? Whatever your plan is?" She looks specifically at me now, and I get the feeling she's still picturing the wings behind my back.

"We hope so."

"Sorry," Evan adds, "for what happened to your friends."

She smiles sadly. "Thank you."

I hesitate, unable to turn away as Charlotte gazes over at the bodies. "What will you do now?" I ask.

She shrugs. "Maybe I'll take them to a hospital, and I'll keep researching a way to fix the damage. There are other necromancers out there; I can try to contact them. But I'm not sure much will change until the immortality stops."

"It will stop," Evan says, his words resolute in their conviction. "We promise."

And with that, we both step out into the dark, this time knowing there's no gytrash on the loose.

It's a long walk back up to the road, but Evan makes it easier with his warming spell and an orb of light. It feels strange to see the road again, as though we've travelled in time. That remote house, surrounded by natural land, must be how many people used to live, before cars and buses and cafés and hospitals. I wonder how much change an average human sees in their lifetime. Do they mourn for the eras they'll never witness?

"There's one bus left, thank God," Evan says, shining the orb's light on the bus stop sign before extinguishing it. "We're really getting our money's worth out of these day riders."

"Will they get us to Manchester?"

Evan laughs. "No. And we're too late for the last train. We'll have to go there tomorrow morning."

"What do we do until then?"

"Ideally?" He yawns. "We sleep. You do know what sleep is, right?"

I grin. "Yes, I know what sleep is. I even do it sometimes."

"Wow, check you out!" His voice takes on a higher pitch than usual, and I'm not sure why, nor am I sure what he means. But he's smiling, so I think it's something positive, and I smile back.

He laughs, shaking his head. "You're cute, you know that?"

"Cute?"

"It means . . . attractive, in a . . . soft, nice way. Or something. Just ignore me." He stuffs his hands in his pockets and looks down, cheeks turning a little red.

I'm not sure how to react. "I'm . . . attractive?"

His face gets redder, and he throws his hands in the air. "It means hot. And not hot like the temperature, hot like . . . like . . ." He closes his fingers as though hoping to catch whatever word he's looking for. "I just mean you look nice."

"Um, thank you?"

He looks as though he might laugh again, but instead, he opts for, "You're welcome," and I can't help feeling I'm meant to say something else.

After an incredibly long moment of silence, I offer, "You look nice, too."

"Honestly, Orpheus," he says, smirking as he sticks his arm out for an approaching bus, "never change."

His meaning is lost on me again, but I follow him onto the bus – which is mercifully free of other passengers – and sit beside him near the back.

"Where are we going to sleep?" I ask.

"Good question." He pulls out his phone. "I think I'm gonna owe Wren about a thousand favours by the time we find the keys."

Chapter Fourteen
Evan

It never feels good to lie to Wren, and I hate how easy it feels after lying to them almost every day. I feel even worse about how quick they are to offer help when I claim I've had a huge argument with my parents. Though, to be fair, if I did go home, I almost certainly *would* end up in an argument with them.

When they open their front door, they're wearing a sympathetic smile.

"Do I ever tell you how much I love you?" I ask.

"Not nearly enough," they say, stepping aside to let me and Orpheus in. "And it's them you should be thanking." They gesture through the door to the living room, where both their parents are sat on the sofa.

"Thank you!" I call through.

"Any time, Evan!" says Wren's mum, Halima.

"Always a pleasure!" adds Wren's dad, Nadir.

Wren heads down the hall, and I follow, with Orpheus lagging behind. He mutters a "Thank you" too, and I just about make out an, "It's really no bother" from Halima, but I'm already through the kitchen and into the conservatory.

"It might get a bit cold," Wren says. "But Dad brought through the electric heater, and there's a tonne of blankets. Also, the sun will probably wake you up, but there's not much we can do about that." They gesture at the glass roof.

It's a spacious room with an easel at one end beside a stack of canvases and a tall lamp. The glass-topped coffee table that normally sits in the centre has been pushed against the wall, and the many houseplants have been moved around to make room for the sofa, which has been opened up to become a double bed. A whole host of patterned blankets have been thrown across it.

"You don't mind sharing, do you?" Wren asks.

"No," Orpheus and I both say simultaneously, and a little too quickly. I feel my face redden yet again.

Wren attempts to hide a grin. "Cool. There are some extra clothes for Orpheus on the table over there, plus some pyjamas for you both. Don't say I never treat you."

"Thanks, Wren." I say.

They wink as they leave the room, leaving only an awkward silence to fill it.

Orpheus looks up at the glass ceiling, which is currently reflecting the light of the lamp. "Will we be able to see the stars?" he asks.

I turn off the lamp, and sure enough, the stars become visible in the cloudless sky above. I watch Orpheus in the moonlight, joy spreading across his face as he stares out at the cosmos. There's something beautiful about the way he appreciates the little things, the things so common to the normal human experience that most people take them for granted. The landscape of the moors. The magic of the stars. Even a mundane ride on a bus or the taste of a sandwich.

"I'm gonna go get changed in the bathroom," I say, scooping up the clothes. "I'll give you a few minutes to change before I come back. The pyjamas are the ones on top of the pile."

His eyes turn from the stars to the clothes, which he starts running through his fingers, feeling the different fabrics.

"Thank you," he says.

Wren is waiting for me at the top of the stairs, arms folded, leaning against the frame of their bedroom door with one leg crossed over the other. "Just a family friend, is he?"

I roll my eyes, heading for the bathroom.

"Oh, come on, Evan! I haven't seen you like this since you first started dating Zara. You like him, don't you?"

"I barely know him."

"I've never met Alan Turing, but I still think he's hot."

I pause. "The mathematician who died in the 1950s? *That's* your go-to example of hotness?"

"I didn't come here to be shamed! My point is, you don't need to know someone that well to fancy them. I'm not claiming you're in love."

"I . . ."

Wren pulls their "you know I'm right" face.

"He's . . . Alright, I think he's cute. In fact, I actually told him that earlier."

Their jaw drops. "Wait, what? What did he say?"

"Nothing. He . . ." I look behind them, into their room, at the space on the floor beside their bed. "Hang on; last time I stayed, you had a blow-up mattress in your room. Have you forced us both on the sofa-bed on purpose?"

They start to shake their head but give up when they realise I'll see right through it. "I just figured maybe you'd appreciate a helping hand to move this crush along."

I laugh in sheer disbelief. "You are unbelievable; you know that?"

"Hey." They jab their finger into my chest. "Who is it that got their parents to let you *and* a boy they've never met spend the night at very short notice?"

I jab them back. "The best friend ever."

"Exactly. So you go enjoy being close to your new Romeo, and I'll go theorise about what you've really been getting up to all evening."

"What do you—"

"If you'd really just come from an argument with your parents, you would have brought pyjamas with you."

Damn. I should have thought about that. "No, I just had to leave quickly because—"

Wren holds their hands up and steps backwards into their room. "Tell me the truth when you're ready. I'm gonna go to bed."

They close the door, and I feel a whole new wave of guilt. Maybe it really would be easier if I told Wren everything. The fact that they've let me and Orpheus stay the night when they don't even believe my lie is the strongest proof I think I've ever had of their friendship. I could knock on their door right now and tell them everything. I could show them a spell, let them read my grimoire, chat about all the things I've never been able to share with them. All it would take is one knock on their door.

But I don't. I can't. Not yet.

I think of Gran in her final days, how miserable she looked. How empty. She wasn't herself, not fully, not after the conversion. That would be my fate too if Dad had his way. If the immortality continues, and the witchfinders manage to pin the blame on all witches, then things will only get worse for us. If Eloise Morgan has her way, magic won't just be illegal in public; it'll be illegal completely. All it would take is one decision from the government, and conversion would be the fate of every witch in the country.

I'd trust Wren with my life, but until something changes, I can't risk anyone else finding out I'm a warlock. I won't let what happened to Gran happen to me.

Orpheus is already lying on the sofa-bed when I return to the conservatory. He's covered by the blankets, and his eyes flicker open when I close the door.

"Hi," I say.

"Hi."

I shuffle my way onto the space beside him and grab one of the many blankets, pulling it up around myself and leaning back onto the cushions. I stare up through the glass to the starry sky beyond and relax into the quiet, hearing only Orpheus' steady breathing.

"Wren's a good friend," Orpheus says, voice quiet, gentle.

"Yeah, they're the best friend I've ever had."

"When did you meet them?"

I turn my head slightly to see Orpheus' profile. The blue of his eyes is just about visible in the moonlight.

"Way back," I say. "We would have been about seven. Long enough ago that I can't remember our first meeting. We were in the same class at junior school, though. I don't think we were super close, but we both ended up at the same high school, and that's when we properly became friends."

Orpheus turns to face me too, and we both end up awkwardly shuffling about until we're on our sides so we can see each other properly. Well, as properly as we can without the lamp.

"It must be nice to be so close to someone for so long," he says. There's a sadness in his voice.

"Does it get lonely?" I ask. "In the Halls of Styx?"

Orpheus takes a moment to think before answering. "I've never known any different – until today, I suppose. It's always just been me and Mother."

"You must be close with her, then?"

He pauses again. "I used to think so, but I've heard many spirits talk about their children or their parents, and I can't say my experience is similar. My mother is . . . distant?" He sighs. "I'm not sure there are words for it. She talks to me, and she creates the things I need, and I'm sure she cares about me, but . . ."

I want to reach out, offer a hand of comfort, but I'm not sure it would help.

"I wish I had known who she was when my father was around," he says. "He fell in love with her, after all. There must have been an emotional connection. I think his death made her afraid of that. Like she doesn't want to open up again."

"Have you ever told her all of this?"

"Not really."

"It might help."

"Do you talk about this sort of thing with your parents?"

I almost laugh. "No. We have a different sort of difficult relationship, what with my dad being what he is."

"Of course. I'm sorry. That can't be easy."

I sigh. "It's not. Things were better when Gran was around. I could always talk to her."

There's a silence again, but it isn't awkward; it's comfortable.

"What was her name?" Orpheus asks.

Her kind face fills my memory. "Sylvia."

"What happened to her?"

I hesitate, unsure if I want to share everything that happened. Like my magic, this is one of many things I've never spoken to anyone about. But Orpheus has already seen that side of me. Perhaps he should see this side, too.

"She was always open about being a witch," I say. "But my dad was just as open about his hatred of witches. Gran told me he wasn't always like that, especially as a child. But when he got older, he got radicalised, like a lot of people do. When the government is anti-magic, it's easy to fall into that frame of thinking. Eventually, my dad became a witchfinder, and he started asking Gran to undergo conversion."

"Conversion? Charlotte mentioned that."

I nod. "It's this process invented by the witchfinders. They use a machine made out of the same alloy as the wands and artefacts – the one that conducts magic – to remove a witch's magic completely. It helps to think of it like blood. If you lose a little bit of blood, you're fine; your body will make more. It's the same with magic: every time you cast a spell, your body replenishes the magic inside you. If you lost too much blood at once, you'd die. That doesn't happen with magic, but if you lose too much at once, it's gone forever. It can't be replenished. The conversion machine drains all your magic from you."

Orpheus listens intently, his moonlit face the picture of horrified fascination. It's reassuring, in a way, to see such a reaction from him. So many people around the world don't care that this is happening to witches. They don't feel sorry for them. Yet here's a boy who is completely new to this information, and he's already disgusted.

"The witchfinders want magic gone from the world completely," I continue. "In some countries, magic is completely illegal, and conversion is forced on all witches. Here, most forms of magic are legal if done in private."

"But not artefacts or necromancy?"

"Exactly. As long as you don't break the law, you don't have to go through conversion, but it's always there as an option. Some witches, whether it's because they've been forced or because they've been made to feel so ashamed about what they are, volunteer to be converted."

"That's horrible."

A lump forms in my throat, and I cough it away. "Gran kept refusing, obviously. Until one day, my dad gave her an ultimatum." The lump returns, making my voice thick, but I can't get rid of it. "He told her that if she didn't get converted, he'd never allow her to see me again." Tears begin to pool in my eyes, and I wipe them away quickly, not wanting Orpheus to see.

"Evan . . ."

"I tried to get her to say no, but she wouldn't listen." The tears come back. "She said she'd rather face a hundred conversions than never see me again. So she . . ." I can't stop them now, and the lump in my throat is too big to be able to speak over it. Instead, all I do is sob.

And Orpheus holds me. He wraps his arms around me and lets me cry into his shoulder. He rubs a hand gently on my back and whispers the words "It's okay," over and over again until my sobs quieten. Until I manage to breathe clearly.

"She was never the same after that," I say softly into the blankets. "And she died a few months later."

"I'm sorry," Orpheus says, voice as delicate as the feathers of his wings.

We stay like that, the two of us pressed together, breaths getting slower and steadier until they're completely synchronous. And beneath the moonlit sky, in the arms of a half-angel, I drift into a dreamless sleep.

Chapter Fifteen
Orpheus

When I wake, Evan is gone. I reach out my arms to find nothing but flat blankets and a cold void. I sit up, bleary-eyed, and look around, stopping when I see Wren stood in the open door. They're holding up two cartons.

"Orange or apple?" they ask.

I rub my eyes. "What?"

"Juice." They shake the cartons, filling what was a peaceful room with the sound of sloshing liquids. "For breakfast."

"Um . . . apple?"

"I knew you'd say apple! It's because of the bits, isn't it? I can't stand them either."

I start to wonder if I somehow fell through another door while I slept into a different world entirely.

"Where's Evan?" I ask.

"Oh, right." They sit down on the ledge below the doorframe, placing the cartons on the floor by their feet. "Sorry, got distracted. I'll add this to the list of examples for my ADHD assessment." They pull their phone out of their pocket and start typing.

I clear my throat.

"Oh! Evan's gone home. He said he wanted to grab some clothes, but he'll be back in a bit. You were fast asleep, and he didn't want to wake you, which I think is insanely cute. Good morning, by the way."

I take a moment to let myself fully remember where I am and wait for my mind to catch up with what Wren's just told me.

"Good . . . morning?" I say.

They pocket their phone and retrieve the two cartons, shaking them again as they stand and walk out of the room.

"Breakfast is this way!" they call.

I stumble off the bed and follow Wren through to a room where there is barely an inch of wall not taken up by a framed photo of them and their family. I see Wren at many different ages (and many changing hairstyles), smiling with their parents. In the centre of the room is a long wooden table with six chairs around it, and on the table is a plate stacked high with thick golden discs beside a bowl of fruit.

"So, we went on holiday to America last summer," Wren says, using a fork to move a couple of the discs onto their own plate, "and ever since then, my parents have been obsessed with making pancakes for breakfast, especially when we have guests over."

I watch as they spoon pieces of fruit onto the golden discs and then drizzle them with some sort of viscous liquid. They notice me watching and point a fork at the stack.

"That was your cue. Pancakes. Please eat."

I grab my own plate and copy exactly what Wren has done, right down to the way they cut the pancakes into smaller pieces. Wren observes me with what can only be described as fascination, but I try to ignore them and take a bite of what is clearly a form of food. And wow, it tastes like nothing I've ever tasted before. The fruit and syrup and whatever on Earth a pancake is combine to form a bizarre yet amazing mixture of flavours and textures.

I immediately devour another piece, which Wren seems to find funny, though they hide their laughter behind their glass of apple juice.

"My parents are out, by the way," they say. "Mum's got this big art show in Leeds, and they wanted to beat the traffic. People are saying there'll be some protests about the immortality in all the big cities today, what with it being the weekend."

I take a sip of juice.

"You're not very talkative, are you? That's okay; I'm like that sometimes, if you can believe it. I would love to hear what you think of Evan, though."

"What I think of him?"

"Yeah. You know . . . ?" They wiggle their eyebrows, which I assume is supposed to convey some sort of meaning.

"I'm not sure I under—"

There's a high-pitched ping, and Wren grabs their phone.

"Sorry," they say, "I've got news alerts turned on." They swipe on the screen, and their eyes widen. Then, without saying a word, they run into the next room.

I've seen televisions through many doors before, whenever people die at home, but it's rare that I see one switched on. Wren's is far larger than the one in the dead man's house. It's playing a news report focused on the ongoing immortality. There is footage of hospitals at maximum capacity and an interview with a doctor with bloodshot eyes. She says the staff at her hospital are exhausted and terrified about how long this will go on for.

"For many, the scenes at this hospital and others will bring back memories of the height of the COVID pandemic," says the reporter.

Even I have memories of that. I have multiple diaries filled with COVID stories back home. For Mother, it was just an expected part of the job. All psychopomps are bound to work through a pandemic or two, apparently. I can only imagine how scary a time it must have been for the mortals.

"Similar, too, are the scenes at our supermarkets," the reporter continues, "where people are panic-buying supplies despite the Prime Minister's advice not to."

"People never learn," Wren says bitterly.

Next, a graph appears showing average birth rates and death rates along with population growth. Then the population graph is adjusted for the death rate being set to zero, and what was a steady gradient becomes a far steeper incline.

"Knowing our government, we'll be getting forcibly sterilised soon," Wren says. I'm not sure whether they're being serious.

The reporter returns. "And now we go live to the Witchfinder Headquarters, where Lily Morgan, daughter of Eloise Morgan, Witchfinder General, is about to answer questions."

Wren leans closer to the screen. Maybe this is what their phone informed them about. I watch too, intrigued as to what these witchfinders I've heard so much about are really like.

The woman who appears on screen is in her mid-thirties, with straight shoulder-length blonde hair and a surprisingly nervous look in her eyes. She's dressed in a lime-green suit, and below her microphone, she is picking at her fingernails. There are camera flashes and raised hands from the crowd of reporters, all of them seemingly desperate to ask a question.

She clears her throat and says, "Good morning. My mother is currently very busy with the ongoing investigation into the cause of the immortality, so she has asked that I answer your questions for her today." There's a quiver in her bottom lip, but she continues. "She wishes to reassure you all that the witchfinders are working tirelessly and have no intention of stopping."

There's an immediate wave of noise from the crowd, and Lily picks her fingernails more aggressively. A man in dark clothes enters the crowd with a microphone, passing it to one of the many people with their hands raised.

"Hello," says the chosen person. "Do the witchfinders have any leads on the culprit or culprits?"

Lily hesitates, then says, "We are following multiple leads at the moment, but for obvious reasons, I can't give further details."

Another person receives the microphone. "We know you're searching for the cause, but are you also searching for a solution? I think I speak for us all when I say we're worried that the immortality might last forever."

"We're certainly looking into that, as are many teams of scientists across the world."

"To counter that point," says the next person, "what do you have to say to those who think the immortality is a positive thing? That we should celebrate a potential gift from God?"

Lily glances down at her feet before answering. "I say that the witchfinders know a perverted use of magic when we see one, and this is certainly not a gift from God. You only have to look at the state of the hospitals to see that."

The microphone is passed again. "Good morning. I was wondering if you have any comment on the rumours that your mother is deeply unwell, hence her absence today."

Lily looks taken aback by this question. The lip quiver returns, and she hesitates for far longer than before. When she speaks, her voice is noticeably quieter. "Um, I stated at the beginning that my mother is busy with work. I'm not sure what rumours you're referring to, but I can assure you they are unfounded."

"Holy shit," says Wren. "That was the most obvious lie in the world." They look at me. "Wasn't it?"

I nod. I may not be the best reader of humans, but even I could tell Lily was lying. It was the change in volume. Her surprise at the question. Her face, shifting ever so slightly with every word as she tried to form her sentence. It's like the inner workings of her brain were on display. Every little quiver of the faces of humans really does tell a story.

The questions for Lily continue, but they're mostly asking for the same updates in different ways, of which Lily has none. Meanwhile, Wren's eyes are fixed to their phone, where they're reading a myriad of reactions on the internet. According to them, the internet is "blowing up" with theories about Eloise's mystery illness.

"Chantelle Adeyemi is having a field day. I hope Evan's seeing all this," they say.

Chapter Sixteen
Evan

I run straight to the bathroom when I get home, ignoring Mum's calls from the living room. I don't have time for her inevitable questions. I take a shower, welcoming the relief of the warm water. My thoughts turn to Orpheus as I worry how he'll manage being alone with Wren. I wouldn't have left him if I didn't trust that he'd be okay, but maybe I should have woken him up. There was just something about his face as he slept that I didn't want to disturb. He looked so peaceful.

There's a banging on the bathroom door.

"Evan? Is that you?" comes the voice of my dad, laced with anger as it often is. "Where the hell have you been?"

"Darling, you should be in bed," says Mum. I picture her holding his shoulders, rubbing them in the hopes she might calm him down. It's something she always tries but which never works.

"I told you!" I shout over the noise of the shower. "I stayed at Wren's!"

"That good-for-nothing—"

"Arthur, *please*," says Mum, desperate now. "You need rest. Come on; let's get you back in bed."

I hear them both shuffle away.

There's a thought that's been lingering at the back of my mind ever since I agreed to help Orpheus search for the keys. It's the fact that if we succeed, and he returns them to his mother, bringing death back to the world, my dad will die. And the reason I hide that thought away is because it *doesn't* upset me. If I never see him again, I'll be happy. I don't want to reconnect; I don't want to hug it out; I want him gone. And I've wanted him gone for years. But I know that makes me a bad person.

I can't help but wonder what Orpheus would say if I told him that. He never even got the chance to meet his own dad, yet here I am wishing my own dad dead. Maybe he'd understand – he knows the truth of what Dad did to Gran, after all.

The warmth of the shower is nothing compared to being hugged by him last night. I felt so safe, so understood. It's hard to believe I feel so close to him after, what, not even an entire day? And yet that's the way it is. It's been so freeing to be so open around him.

I relish the feeling of changing into something that isn't my school uniform. I don a thick jumper and cram a full change of clothes into my bag in case I'm out for over a day again. When I head back downstairs, Mum is waiting for me. Her eyes are dark and tired, her hair is unkempt, and she looks like she's been crying.

"Where are you going?" she asks weakly.

"Out." I move past her to the front door, slinging my bag onto my back.

"Evan?"

I pause, hand on the doorknob, and turn back to face her.

"I know you hate him. But he's your dad."

I shake my head. "He hasn't been that for a long time."

I leave without another word, almost jogging up the driveway, keeping my eyes fixed straight ahead. There's guilt clawing at me, whispering into my ear that I should at least be nice to my mum. And it's true: I don't hate her. My dad's bigotry isn't her fault, and though she often goes along with it, there've been many times that I've seen that she doesn't completely agree with him. She tried to talk him out of what he did to Gran, and it was always her who took me for visits to Gran's house.

When Dad's gone, maybe I'll find a new closeness with Mum. I'm truly not sure how I'll handle her grief, though. I won't be able to sit around and say nice things about Dad. I won't reminisce on happy times. But I'll be there for her, at the very least. We'll get through it, somehow.

My phone buzzes, and I pull it out to see a message from Wren about Eloise Morgan. It's a link to an updates page about a speech her daughter's just given on TV. I press it and feel my mouth fall slowly open as I see what Lily has said. Immediately, I start searching for discussion forums, specifically about the rumours that Eloise is ill. There are countless posts, many citing the fact that beyond alleged written statements, Eloise hasn't been seen or heard from in weeks. Chantelle Adeyemi has posted a video stating that this is proof people shouldn't listen to the witchfinders.

"They rule with misinformation. Don't be fooled!"

Of course, the lack of a day without a public appearance wouldn't normally be a sign of anything unusual. But during a global crisis which the witchfinders are claiming is the fault of witches, it does seem very suspicious that Eloise hasn't been seen. And you'd think, if she were ill, that the witchfinders would just admit it. Instead, they've got Lily Morgan telling blatant lies.

I continue to watch Chantelle's video. It's gaining a lot of traction, probably because she's proposing the wildest theory yet:

"What if the witchfinders are doing a bad job on purpose?" she says, staring into the camera with the confidence that comes with being an outspoken activist. "If they're trying to cover up Eloise's mystery illness, surely that implies it's something serious. What if it's terminal? What if Eloise is dying?" She pauses, then holds up her hands to frame what she knows is a bombshell of a theory. "What if the immortality is the only thing keeping her alive, and the whole reason the witchfinders have no updates about the witch behind the immortality is because they don't actually want to fix it?"

I rewatch it over and over again and read the many replies arguing for or against. It's an out-there theory, but I can't help but think it makes a certain sense. Why would Lily be so cagey about the illness if it wasn't something serious? Maybe the witchfinders really are just lying about the investigation and hoping the immortality continues, all while distracting people with their usual spiel about magic being a "perversion".

If it's true, then Eloise is an even worse person than I already know her to be. But hey, maybe this is exactly the sort of conspiracy that could turn the public against the witchfinders. Also, if it means Orpheus and I are closer to solving the problem than them, then that can only be good for us.

When I reach Wren's house, they answer the door with Orpheus eagerly bounding behind them. He's in a new outfit – a plain black T-shirt with one of Wren's many hoodies on top – and yet again, he looks great. I'd love to know what his own style would be if he were let loose in a clothes shop. Maybe after all this is done, I'll take him to one.

"Did you see?" Wren asks, and I instantly know they're talking about the Eloise stuff.

"Yeah. It's crazy."

"Isn't it? I've never seen so many people doubting the witchfinders before; it's great! I'm looking into whether people are setting up protests against them. Do you want to join?"

"Um . . . I'd love to, but Orpheus and I had really better go."

Wren's eyes bounce between me and Orpheus. "Where are you off to this time?"

There's that guilt again. They knew I lied last night; how am I supposed to lie again now?

"We're going to Manchester," Orpheus says before I have chance to reply.

Wren hesitates, and I get the sense they're giving me a chance to tell them the truth. And I want to. I really do. But I just keep hearing myself making a promise to Gran. A promise I've already broken with Orpheus and Charlotte. Maybe it would be easier just to break it again.

"Well, you two have fun." Wren says, giving up on probing me for now. They send me an overly enthusiastic wink which I pretend not to notice.

"Thank you for breakfast," Orpheus says before stepping out to join me, beaming as he does.

"I'll pass it on to my parents." Wren holds up a hand to say goodbye and closes the door.

Orpheus and I walk side by side up the road. We're close enough that our arms occasionally brush, sending my mind back to the warm embrace he held me in last night. I open my mouth to thank him for that, but he gets his words out first.

"How was it seeing your parents?"

"Oh. Not great, I won't lie. I didn't even actually see my dad, just heard him. He wasn't exactly happy I hadn't spent the night at home."

"And your mum?"

I shrug. "She's just sad about Dad."

Orpheus puts a comforting hand on my shoulder, which surprises me, but I'm not complaining. It does make me slow to a stop, though, at the corner of the road. A tree arches over us, with its brown leaves hanging perilously from the branches.

"Families are confusing, aren't they?" he says.

I laugh. "I'm not sure mine is comparable to yours, but yeah. You're right."

He moves his hand down my arm, letting go just before the wrist, and I realise I did the same thing to him last night when we were preparing to catch the gytrash. I'm reminded of a conversation I once had with Wren, back when they were preparing for their autism assessment. They told me how one way in which autistic people mask is by copying the behaviours they see neurotypical people do.

"You know that thing you just did?" I ask Orpheus now. "With your hand, on my arm?"

He nods.

"Why did you do it?"

He gets a panicked look. "Was it not right? Did I do it wrong?"

"No, no. It was nice. I just wondered what made you do it."

He pauses. Thinks. "You laughed, but your eyes were sad. When you held my arms last night, it made me feel better. I wanted to do the same for you."

I look up, into his eyes, as an orange leaf falls behind him. I was worried that he was forcing himself to fit in with this world that he isn't used to, but that's not what he's doing at all. He isn't masking; he's being kind.

"I never said thank you," I say. "For last night, I mean. When I told you all that stuff about my gran. It felt nice when you held me."

He blinks, and I can't tell what he's thinking behind those ocean eyes.

"Thank you."

"You're welcome," he says, and more leaves fall behind him.

My eyes drift to his lips. If I asked, would he let me kiss him, I wonder? Unless he's been kissing spirits in the Halls of Styx, which I highly doubt, it would be his first. Would he grant me that honour? Or am I reading too much into these kind acts he's doing for me? In any case, now probably isn't the time.

"Bus stop's this way," I say.

The train station is probably the busiest place I've taken Orpheus yet, and I can see the stress in his face. Once I buy our tickets, I lead him to the point on the platform where I know the doors to the quiet coach always end up being. I've caught enough trains with Wren to have noise reduction strategies memorised by now. It doesn't help that it's a Saturday and that we're heading to a city, and I can't imagine things will be quieter once we're in Manchester, but at least Tamara's address isn't in the centre.

"Watch out!" comes the voice of a woman nearby.

I turn to see a boy who can't be much older than me bursting through the doors of the station and out onto the platform. People move out of his way, then collectively gasp in horror as he leaps down onto the train tracks.

There are cries of alarm, and a few people run back into the station to try and grab the attention of someone official. The boy, meanwhile, is howling with laughter as he runs along the tracks, hopping from one set to the other.

"What the hell are you doing?" shouts a man in a fluorescent orange vest showcasing the logo of one of the train companies.

"No risk anymore, is there?" the boy shouts back, laughing maniacally.

An electronic voice sounds over the speakers, announcing that a train is approaching, which only adds to the commotion as more and more people shout at the boy, begging him to get off the tracks.

I remain frozen to the spot, heart pounding when I hear the sound of the approaching train. The boy keeps bouncing between the tracks, hooting and laughing. More people in fluorescent vests charge in, some shouting into walkie-talkies. And then the boy stops running.

The train hurtles into view, slowing as it normally would but still moving fast enough to kill anyone who gets in its way. The boy stands with a foot on each rail, facing the oncoming train with his arms held wide. He waits till the very last moment, then jumps to the left. But he isn't fast enough.

The train collides with one of his legs, and I turn away, pulling Orpheus with me to face the wall before we're able to see exactly what happens. Then the station fills with screams.

Chapter Seventeen
Orpheus

"I don't understand why he did it," I say. I'm sat across from Evan in the train station café, hands around a cup of coffee.

"Looks like a whole new epidemic," Evan says, scrolling on his phone. "People are engaging in high-risk behaviour because without death, they think there's no danger." He turns his phone to show me the article he's found about it. "Apparently, in America, people have started filming themselves shooting each other."

"No death doesn't mean no injury."

"Try telling them that. It says here one man got taken to hospital with a bullet hole straight through his brain. They've got no idea whether he's even still thinking, but he's still alive."

I grit my teeth, pushing away the image that comes to mind. What would Mother say if she were here? What must she be doing now, trapped in the Halls of Styx, unable to carry out her job? What must the gods be thinking as they look upon this new world where the basic laws of existence have been torn apart?

"The rail replacement bus service is now arriving," says a voice over the speakers.

"That's us," Evan says. "Come on."

I follow him, along with the few other people who were on the platform earlier. After what we witnessed, most went home. Part of me wishes I could do the same. Though Evan turned my head at the moment of impact, it was impossible not to see the blood when we turned back around. I've seen blood before – not every scene that Mother opens the doors to is peaceful. But it's different being on this side. It's more tangible. A reminder of how fragile humans are.

There's an intense quiet on the bus when we take our seats. I'm grateful, but I know it's because no one quite knows what to say after what happened. Evan continues to read about similar incidents on his phone while I stare out of the window. I watch as we pass families and couples and solitary shoppers. Countless lives which, if the world were working as it's supposed to, could end at any moment.

The reporter on the news this morning said that, on average, over one hundred and fifty thousand people die every day. That means that since the moment the keys were stolen, there have likely been at least two hundred thousand people saved by the immortality. Two hundred thousand people who will gradually drop dead once I return the keys to Mother. Two hundred thousand stories cut short.

It's easy to see why there are people out there who think the immortality is a blessing. For humans, life brings so much potential. They are driven by the hopes and dreams of what they might do before they die. But if death were gone forever, what would happen to those dreams? What would push them to live life to the fullest? Death has been woven into the fabric of the universe from its very beginning, and the world of mortals is not built to cope with the reality of immortality.

I look at Evan, his strawberry blond curls and gentle face. What dreams drive him? What future awaits him in his mortal life? Perhaps, when this is all done, I'll stick around and find out. I have the anchor now, after all. I'd like the chance to experience a human life when the world isn't in chaos. It would be nice to experience it with him.

"What's up?" Evan asks, noticing me looking.

I smile. "Nothing."

Manchester is very different to Elmwood Vale. The buildings are taller, the streets are busier; there are roadworks and building sites and a whole lot of noise. I also see people wrapped in dirty blankets, sat at the foot of buildings or sheltering under bridges. This sight isn't new to me. Too many times, I've seen Mother open a door to a dead homeless person. Too many times, I've heard stories of how people have lost everything and have had to live and die on the streets.

I've heard also of the way in which most people will walk straight past the homeless without even looking at them. Even Evan keeps up his pace as we wander past a man holding out a cup containing nothing more than a couple of coins. I tug on Evan's sleeve, slowing him down, and ask him if he has any change.

Evan looks puzzled, but his eyes drift over my shoulder to the man on the ground, and he digs into his pockets, handing me a collection of coins. I take them over to the man, dropping them into his cup.

"Thank you," the man says. The surprise in his face hurts to see.

"You're welcome." If I had time, I'd stay and talk to him more. I'd ask for his story, just like all the spirits in the Halls. Instead, I simply ask, "What's your name?"

He blinks, surprised again, I think. But he answers, "George."

"I wish you well, George," I say, before turning back to Evan.

Evan doesn't say anything, but he looks at me with an expression I can't decipher. It's as though he's admiring a brand-new face entirely.

"That'll happen to more people if we don't fix things, won't it?" I say.

"What will?"

"Homelessness." I think back to the statistics on the news this morning. "If the number of people rises, the food supply gets smaller, and the price of everything goes up."

Evan nods. "That's capitalism for you. The poor suffer the worst in times of crisis. Our world really does suck sometimes."

"All the more reason for us to fix it."

I'm not sure why, but Evan slides his hand into mine, interlocking our fingers. He smiles up at me, and I tighten my grip, enjoying the feeling of closeness.

"You're a good person," he says. "I hope you know that." He gently swings my arm. "Piccadilly Gardens is this way."

We walk through an area surrounded on all sides by roads but clearly set apart for pedestrians. There are large patches of grass, a water fountain, and a statue of a long-dead monarch. A crowd has begun to form around the statue. People are holding placards with various captions written on them. I manage to make out *WE WANT ANSWERS* and *WHAT ARE THE WITCHFINDERS HIDING?* A person stands on the uppermost step at the statue's base, raising a megaphone to her mouth.

"People of Manchester," she shouts, "are you ready to make your voices heard?"

The crowd cheer in agreement, and more people filter from the streets towards them. I have a feeling this place will get very loud very soon.

"Just imagine if all of them turned their doubts about the witchfinders into support of witches," says Evan.

"Maybe one day they will."

Evan smiles, but I see the doubt in his eyes. "Maybe."

We head away from the crowd to a raised platform beside what look almost like train tracks built into the paved ground. Moments later, a long set of yellow carriages weave along the tracks towards us.

"It's a tram," Evan says, smirking. "Kind of like a mix between a train and a bus."

The tram doors slide open, and Evan leads me on, hand still in mine. We take a pair of seats, and the rest around us fill up with other passengers.

"You have an awful lot of different things that all do the same job," I mutter, flinching at the sound of the doors shutting.

"Just wait till you here about the London Underground."

I don't even ask.

With a shudder, the tram starts moving. There's space for far more people than the buses, so there are a lot more conversations around me. I catch snippets of concern about immortality, complaints about the protest, and even what one man is considering having for lunch. The accents here are different to Elmwood Vale. I've always found it quite beautiful how varied accents can be in the spirits I've met, not to mention the languages.

It does make me wonder, though, how in a world so diverse do people manage to harbour hatred towards others. Isn't everybody different in their own way? Is that not what makes humans so interesting? My piles of diaries wouldn't exist if every story were the same. It seems to me that if differences were embraced by society, everyone's experience would be richer. The witches could bring magic to mundane lives.

Tamara's neighbourhood is much quieter than the city centre. It's an area of red brick houses as far as the eye can see. I walk hand in hand with Evan to Crestfield Road. Number 87 has an iron gate built into the wall and a small front garden filled with gnomes. A bird bath stands in the corner, and, though there is no water in it, a small bird with red feathers on its breast is perched on the edge. It flies away when Evan opens the gate.

The front door is a dark brown, with a golden knocker beneath a set of three small windows. Evan knocks, and the two of us wait. There's a large window to our right, but the curtains are drawn. Dark clouds are beginning to gather up above.

There's no answer, so Evan knocks again.

"What if she's not in?" I ask.

The curtains twitch.

"Looks like she is."

There's movement behind the door, and a voice that somehow carries no emotion at all says, "Who's there?"

"Tamara?" Evan says. He quietens his voice, putting his face close to the door. "I was wondering if I could talk to you about artefacts?"

"I don't talk about those."

Evan looks back at me. "Is anyone watching?"

"I don't think so," I say, checking around. There's no one else on the road, and as far as I can see, no one is peeking out of their windows, either.

"Tamara?" he whispers. "I'm like you. I'm a warlock. Please can you let me and my friend in? We just want to talk."

She doesn't reply, but I hear her move. Her footsteps get distant.

Evan sighs. He turns his head, quickly checking for onlookers. After a deep breath, he discreetly pulls his wand from a pocket and casts a spell. The door's lock clicks.

"I hope I don't regret this," he says, pushing the door open.

Chapter Eighteen
Evan

Tamara's house is as dark as the dead old man's, but I keep the threads in my vision. I walk down the hall, hands raised and ready to cast another spell if necessary. Breaking into a witch's house might be the stupidest thing I've done yet, but we need answers from her whether she likes it or not.

I step through the first open door on the right, into the living room. The wallpaper is a dull red, while the furniture is brown leather. A fireplace stands unlit against one wall, and shelves and cabinets fill the others. What's odd, however, is that they're all empty, aside from a record player on a table below the window.

Tamara sits in an armchair, dark hair falling in chaotic curls just below her shoulders. She's wearing a rough-looking white dressing gown and is staring at the fireplace, a vacant expression on her face. She barely even reacts to us entering the room, just the slightest glance in our direction.

I dispel the threads as I realise we're not in any danger. I've seen this before. The vacant expression. The empty voice. It's exactly what Gran was like in her final days.

"Tamara?" I move across the room, kneeling down on the hard wood floor in front of her.

Her eyes fall slowly to meet mine, but she says nothing.

"What's wrong with her?" asks Orpheus.

"I think—" I pause, correcting myself. "No, I *know* she's been converted."

Orpheus stumbles over. He kneels down beside me. Tamara looks into the middle distance between us both.

"Who are you?" she asks.

I reach out, placing my hands on top of hers. They're cold to the touch.

"I'm sorry, Tamara. I'm sorry for what they did to you."

I shift my vision back to the threads and cast my usual warming spell over her. Then I turn to the fireplace and stitch a fire into existence. It takes a little while, but I know it'll be worth it. Tamara probably hasn't felt comfortable in a long time. As I loop threads over the hook of my wand, I can hear her muttering absently to herself.

"There," I say once the fire is lit. I return to Tamara's side, where Orpheus is biting his lip in uncertainty. "That's better, isn't it?"

Tamara nods weakly, and I swallow away a new lump in my throat. Gran was exactly like this. Barely coherent. No longer herself. The conversion process doesn't just remove magic; it traumatises the witch it's done to. Damages them beyond repair.

"Orpheus, can you see if she has any music anywhere?" I place my hands back on Tamara's. "There's a record player, so there must be some vinyl somewhere. You know what those look like, right?"

"I think so." He gets up and starts searching the room.

I wipe away a tear. Some of Gran's only lucid moments near the end were when we listened to her favourite music. Maybe the same thing will work on Tamara.

"There's something here," Orpheus says from a cupboard at the other end of the room. He brings over a seven-inch record and passes it to me.

"Fleetwood Mac? Nice." I smile at Tamara, but her face remains blank. "Trust a witch to like Stevie Nicks."

The record player is covered in dust, but it's plugged in. I give it a quick wipedown, then set the record going. The room fills with the opening notes of "Silver Springs". Immediately, Tamara's head perks up. She closes her eyes and begins to sway gently as Stevie sings. Orpheus watches in wonder, a sad smile spreading across his face.

I return to my kneeling position. What does Tamara think of when she hears this song, I wonder? Is it a reminder of what went wrong with Charlotte? Whatever it is, it brings some of her back to the world.

"Tamara?" I say.

She opens her eyes, still swaying.

"Can I ask you about the artefacts? You were a dealer, weren't you?"

She nods.

"Did the witchfinders catch you?"

She screws her eyes up tight but nods again. It's a painful memory, undoubtedly.

"I'm sorry." I reach for her hands again.

The music continues, building in complexity as it progresses and soothing Tamara at the same time. It's almost like a spell in its own way.

"Tamara?"

"Yes?"

I share a look with Orpheus before I continue. "Did you have an artefact that could hold open the door to the afterlife?"

Her eyes snap open, and I feel her hands tense beneath mine. "How do you know about that?" Her voice is weak but panicked.

"It's okay. It's fine." I keep my voice gentle, hoping to counter the anxiety that's radiating from her. "We just . . . We think maybe someone used it, and we think maybe you could help us work out who."

She shakes her head violently and starts rocking back and forth. "Can't say. Mustn't say. Can't say."

I try to soothe her, rubbing her hands and saying, "It's okay," over and over again. But it doesn't work. Orpheus watches, eyes frantic. I wonder if he's ever seen a human in this state before. Do spirits ever get in this state?

The song continues, approaching the bridge, and I do the only other thing I can think of: I sing along. It does nothing at first, but as I keep going, Tamara's movements slow. She returns to the gentle sway of before and hums along.

"Tamara?" I say again, voice as soothing as I can possibly make it. "If you can't tell me, can you show me? Can I look at your memories?"

Her swaying stops, but she remains calm. She pauses, then nods.

"Thank you."

I bring the threads back into view and reach for the ones that flow into her head. I create the same simple stitches that I made when doing this to Orpheus just yesterday. Then, with one last deep breath, I fill the threads with magic, and the world around me dissolves.

What was a dark and dusty room becomes bright, with the curtains wide open and the shelves filled with books and ornaments. There's a record playing, but it's not a song I recognise. Tamara is sat in the same armchair, grimoire in hand, wand on her lap, with a smile on her face as she studies a spell.

There's a knock at the door, and she immediately stands, stowing her wand and grimoire beneath a cushion. She glances out of the window, checking who is outside. Whoever it is must shock her because her body immediately tenses, and she takes a moment to steady herself before heading out of the room. I would run to the window and check for myself, but I need to stay close to Tamara, or the memory will fade away.

I follow her to the front door, arriving by her side just as she opens it.

"Tamara O'Sullivan?" asks the man on the other side. He's dressed in a police uniform.

"Yes?"

The policeman clears his throat. "According to the Witchfinder Act of 1981, you are to be detained on suspicion of illegal magical activity and the dealing of prohibited magical items." He steps forward, brandishing handcuffs.

Tamara backs away. "No, you can't; I never—"

"You do not have to say anything. But it may harm your defence if you do not mention when questioned something which you later rely on in court. Anything you do say may be given in evidence."

"Please, you can't."

He grabs her by the shoulders and slams her against the wall before grappling her hands and fitting the handcuffs around them.

Two other men enter the house, and I freeze on the spot when I see their faces. It's the same two men that almost caught me and Orpheus in the old man's house. They're not in police uniforms, but they are both wearing blazers with a crest embroidered onto the breast pocket. A crest I know all too well. The crest of the witchfinders.

The policeman turns to face them and shoves Tamara in their direction while she writhes and cries out for help.

"She's all yours," he says.

The men grip her on either side, dragging her out of her house and into the back of an unmarked black car. All I can do is watch on in horror as Tamara screams. I've never seen the Witchfinder Act in action, but its meaning has been burned into my brain ever since Gran told me. It states that if a person is accused of illegal witchcraft, the witchfinders have the right to detain them in their headquarters rather than a standard prison. It also states that if enough evidence is gathered, the witch does not have the right to a trial, and the witchfinders may carry out the conversion process.

As the doors of the car slam shut, the world around me swirls and warps into an entirely new scene.

Tamara sits alone in a small box of a room, dressed in plain black overalls. Her eyes are red, and her hair looks like it hasn't been washed in days. The walls and floor of the room are all made of the same white tiles. There's a small metal table in the centre. Tamara is in a chair at one side of it, facing an empty chair on the other. I don't need to delve any deeper into her mind to know that we're at Witchfinder HQ.

There's a click, and a door opens. Lily Morgan walks in, flanked by the same two men from before. She's wearing high heels, a sleek dress, and has a large black handbag draped over one shoulder. Her hair is tied up, just like her mother's always is, and it's clear she's trying to exude the same intimidating aura that Eloise always does. But it doesn't work. Her eyes still bear the same naivety as they did in her TV interview. It's a painfully obvious false confidence for someone who is clearly out of her depth.

"Leave us," she says.

The two men walk out, closing the door behind them. She takes the seat opposite Tamara.

Tamara looks her up and down, sour-faced, fuming, before letting out a forced chuckle. "When they told me I was going to be questioned, I didn't think it would be by the daughter of the great Eloise Morgan."

"My name is Lily."

"I know." Her stare could cut a hole in the toughest material in the world.

"I have some questions for you about the artefacts we recovered from your home."

"Why? You've already found me guilty. I'm being converted tomorrow. What more could you possibly want?"

Lily places her handbag on the floor, delves into it, and places an artefact on the centre of the table. Unlike the one I saw with Charlotte, this artefact is triangular rather than pentagonal, though it is still the same style of small metal box. As Lily rotates it in her hands, I spot the image of a knife carved onto the bottom and runes on each side of the triangle.

"Our team have been able to identify the purpose of most of the items," she says. "Levitation, pyrokinesis, teleportation. But they weren't certain about this one."

Tamara grits her teeth. I can't even begin to imagine the misery she's experiencing, but I admire the way she still makes her hatred of the witchfinders abundantly clear. I wish I could have known her before she was converted.

"Those symbols on the side, they represent necromancy, don't they?"

"How do you know that?"

Lily looks strangely proud. "I've done my research."

Tamara stares at the artefact. "It's one I had no intention of selling. Or using."

"What does it do?"

Tamara chews on her lip, bravado fading. "It kills people."

Lily's eyes light up.

"How?" *she asks.*

"It severs the connection between spirit and body."

"Fascinating."

I wish I could kick her off her chair. How dare she take such an interest in magic when she works for an organisation that wants our kind eliminated?

She returns the artefact to her bag and pulls out another one. This one is pentagonal, and the same runes are carved into the edge, but on the bottom, rather than a knife, is the image of a door. She places it on the table with a metallic clunk.

"And this? Necromancy again, isn't it?"

Tamara scowls. "Why should I answer any more of your questions? It's not like you're going to let me go."

Lily smirks. "Quite."

"Then I'm telling you nothing."

There's a moment of silence as both women study each other intently through gritted teeth. But then Lily chuckles to herself.

"It's my understanding," *Lily says, summoning that fake bravado again,* "that you used to be married. Is that correct?"

Tamara's gaze falters. "Why do you care?"

"I don't particularly, but as far as I'm aware, this ex-wife of yours is a witch like you, isn't she?"

There's no response from Tamara.

Lily runs a fingernail along one of the artefact's edges. "Now, I can't be sure how your marriage ended, but I think given your disgust *for the conversion process that even if your divorce wasn't amicable, you probably don't want Charlotte to have to go through it as well, do you?"*

I can almost feel a shift in the air around Tamara. She sits up straighter, and the concern in her eyes instantly betrays the fact that she does still feel something for Charlotte, whatever that may be.

"Charlotte hasn't broken any laws," she says, though it's clear she doesn't entirely believe her own words. She knows, after all, that her ex-wife is in a coven of necromancers.

"Not that the witchfinders are aware of, but that could change."

"You leave Charlotte out of this!"

Lily grins, and I feel sick at the sight. She's relishing her position of power.

"Gladly," she says, "provided you tell me about this artefact."

Tamara's eyes sink to the ground. She can't face Lily, and I can't blame her.

"So," Lily continues, "this artefact also uses necromancy, doesn't it?"

"Yes." Tamara sounds deflated, no longer the spite-filled woman who was arguing before. She's much closer to the Tamara I met in the present.

"But it does something different?" Lily asks.

"Yes."

"How so?" There's a disturbing sense of hunger to her words that makes me hate her more and more. From her TV interview, I thought she was a bumbling idiot, but it's clear now that she's her mother's daughter. She might not have the commanding presence, but she harbours the same hatred in her heart and even adds to it with this hypocritical interest in how magic works.

"It's a particularly rare find," says Tamara. "Allegedly, it can hold open the door to the afterlife when a person dies."

My heart races, and it seems Lily's does too because she leans forward at Tamara's words. This is it. This is the artefact behind the immortality. This is what allowed someone to enter the Halls and steal the psychopomp's keys. But I don't understand. If the witchfinders have it, how could a witch have used it?

"Allegedly?" Lily repeats.

"Well, I've never seen it used. The warlock who invented it went missing, years ago."

Lily picks up the artefact and turns it in her hands.

"Could a living person step through the door?" she asks.

Tamara leans back, taking in the sight of Lily, confused.

"If they used this," Lily adds, "could they?"

"That's what they say happened to the inventor. That he walked through the door and was never seen again."

A warlock in the Halls of Styx? Never seen again? Surely Orpheus would have mentioned if that had happened. It could just be a story, I suppose, but—

No.

He didn't mention a warlock, but he did mention a man. A mortal. His father.

Lily returns the artefact to her bag and stands.

"Thank you for your information," she says. "It has been most enlightening."

Tamara shakes her head. No "you're welcome" will leave her lips.

The world swirls around me once again. Now that I have my answers – even if they've only given me more questions – I can leave. I will myself to escape, to let go of the connection I've formed with Tamara. But something holds me back, and a new scene begins to form. It's like Tamara wants me here, like she has something more to show me, and I find myself curious to see what it is.

Tamara is weeping uncontrollably. She's in another white-tiled room, but this one is larger, and there's a whole team of people watching her from behind a glass screen. She's strapped down on her back, unable to move, while a large metal arm descends from above. It's the same brass colour as wands and artefacts, with similar hooked prongs poking out just above Tamara's chest.

There's a whirring sound, and the prongs begin to move, spinning around each other and bending in much the same way as they do in artefacts. As they move, a golden light begins to emanate from Tamara's chest.

"Please!" she cries. "Please don't!"

The movements get faster, and the golden energy rises up, being caught by the prongs and travelling into the arm of the machine. Small glass windows reveal the clockwork within, and I watch as the energy flows through cogs, up to where the arm is attached to the ceiling. I turn around to watch the team of people behind the glass wall.

One man and one woman stand at what looks like a control panel covered in levers and buttons. Behind them, others observe another metal arm descending from the ceiling. I see the golden glow move through it, too, and realise it is the same arm as the one above Tamara. It must extend through the ceiling between this room and the one beyond the glass screen. At the base of the arm on their side, the golden light pools into a glass jar encased within a mesh of the brass-like metal.

Tamara screams, and I face her again. The golden light is pouring rapidly out of her now, captured by the metal prongs and sent through the device. It's her magic. Her power. That mystical energy that has been part of her since birth. It's all being ripped away from her and stored in a jar. Her screams get louder, and I cover my ears. I can't listen to this, not anymore. There's such pain in her voice. Such misery.

I close my eyes, but then all I can picture is the same scene but with Gran in Tamara's place. This is what happened to her too. This has been the fate of so many people for just being themselves.

"No!" I shout.

And the world goes black.

Chapter Nineteen
Orpheus

Evan falls back from Tamara, and I catch him.

"No!" he shouts, eyes closed, hands flying to his ears. "No! Make it stop! Make it stop!"

I hold him tightly, just like I did last night, one hand moving up to the back of his head, gently running my fingers through his hair.

"It's okay," I say. "It's okay; you're safe; you're here."

His breaths come thick and fast, but they begin to slow.

"You're okay."

His hands fall away from his ears, moving instead around me, reciprocating the hug.

"Orpheus?" he mutters.

"I'm here."

The dull crackle of the record player fills the silence. The song reached its end just after Evan went into Tamara's mind. It was strange, watching them while they were connected. Their bodies remained still, but their eyes were moving rapidly beneath closed eyelids.

Now Tamara has returned to rocking back and forth, murmuring something unintelligible.

Evan leans back but keeps his hands on my body. His eyes are filled with tears.

"What happened?" I ask. "What did you see?"

"She showed me her conversion," he says, voice catching on a sob. "It was horrible."

I look over at Tamara. Is her conversion what she thinks of while she's rocking? Is it replaying in her mind, too?

Evan sniffs and removes one of his hands from me so that he can wipe his eyes.

"I'm sorry you had to see that," I say.

He shakes his head. "I think I needed to. I never knew what it was like before. Not properly. But now I do. The thing they use . . . it's like a giant artefact. Like they're using our own technology against us." He frowns as his eyes drift towards Tamara. "She was strong, right up to the end. I think she wanted me to see what happens in that horrible place."

I rub his shoulder. "Did you see anything else?"

"Yes. But I'm not sure I understand."

He tells me everything, from the arrest and the presence of the same men we saw in the dead man's house to the revelation that the artefact is in the hands of the witchfinders. But he leaves one thing until last.

"And Tamara mentioned that the artefact was made by a warlock," he says. "A warlock who used it and went missing."

"Strange."

He takes my hand. "Orpheus, I think she was talking about your dad."

I stare back in disbelief. "My . . . What?"

"He must have got into the Halls somehow. And other than dying, it seems like this artefact is the only way to do that."

"But Mother never said he was a warlock."

"Did she tell you much about him at all?"

That stops me. Because no, she didn't. And Evan is right – how would he have accessed the Halls of Styx without magic? But it feels so strange to think that I could be learning more about him now, here, on Earth. That he might have invented the very thing that caused Mother to send me here. That he, like Evan, was a warlock in a world that hates magic. I've always wanted to know more about him, but I never considered that this would be how I found out.

"You might be right," I say quietly, still wading through the disbelief.

"You can ask your mum about it when you go home."

"Right. Yes." I hold Evan's hand tighter. "Home."

Tamara's murmuring fades away, and she returns to the absent stare that we saw when we first entered her house.

"What I don't understand," Evan says, "is how a witch could have taken an artefact from the witchfinders. I've heard Wren talk about their headquarters before – they're impenetrable. They keep artefacts locked away in a vault."

"Could a witch have gotten in with a spell? Teleporting or something?"

Evan shakes his head. "Not easily. It'd take a whole coven to cast a spell like that, or an artefact. I think we're missing something."

I think back to what he said. To Lily's words. Her fascination with the artefact.

"What about Lily?" I ask.

"What do you mean?"

"She wanted to know if someone could walk through the door held open by the artefact, right?"

"Yes."

"So, what if she used it?"

Evan looks at me as though I've said something completely ridiculous. "She's not a witch."

"Do we know that for certain?"

"She's the daughter of the Witchfinder General!"

"So?"

"She's a witchfinder herself!"

"I've spoken to enough spirits to know that internalised oppression exists in plenty of people in your world."

Evan hesitates at that.

"We can't rule it out as a possibility," I say. "And if she isn't a witch, then couldn't she persuade a witch to do it for her? She could offer them an escape from conversion or something, couldn't she?"

Evan scrunches up his face, thinking my words over. I understand why he wouldn't want to believe them. It can't be easy to think a witchfinder might have used the very thing they claim to hate above all else. But he's already said the conversion device reminded him of the artefacts. The hypocrisy is already present.

"Let's say you're right," he says. "Let's say somehow Lily used the artefact. What would she gain from it? Why would she want to—" He stops, eyes widening. He looks up at me, right into my eyes, and says a single word. "Eloise."

"Eloise?"

"She's ill. Allegedly. Right?"

"That's what people seem to think."

He gets up off the floor and starts pacing, hands gripping the hair on either side of his head.

"Evan? What's—"

"I was looking at theories online this morning, speculation about Eloise. Some people suggested that her illness, whatever it is, is terminal. Guaranteed to kill her."

"Okay . . ."

He faces me with a look I've never seen on him before. It's more than disbelief; it's like everything he understands about the world has been turned on its head. It's way beyond his reaction to when I revealed my identity to him yesterday morning.

"If you were a human," he says, "and your mum was dying, and you had access to a device that could get you close to the angel of death . . ."

My skin runs cold as I realise what he's saying.

"You'd try to stop death ever reaching your mum."

We run flat out to the tram stop. A light drizzle has begun to fall; it feels like tiny ice-cold pins as it hits the skin, but Evan doesn't slow for anything. There's a focus in his eyes and a tenseness in his jaw that I know come from the same place: anger. I feel it radiating from him.

All his life, the witchfinders have preached a hatred of magic, and now here Evan is with the knowledge that one of them used magic to save the life of the Witchfinder General. They're the reason his grandmother died in misery, the reason he has such a distant relationship with his parents. Not only that, they're also the reason witches like Evan all across the country have suffered countless years of trauma. And they're hypocrites.

Evan stays silent as we ride the tram, and I choose not to pry into how he's feeling. I'm here if he needs to talk; I have to hope that's enough. The rain is getting heavier now, beating on the windows and blurring the view. If only it could wash away all our problems; Evan and I could run out into the rain, carefree, him showing me the joys of mortal life.

When the tram stops, the protest is in full swing. The crowd is huge now, all those people chanting and waving their placards despite the rain. But it's chaotic. They're all chanting different things, and now there are multiple people with megaphones, all with smaller groups around them.

"They should know the truth," Evan says as we walk past them, heading for the shelter of a line of shop fronts. "They've got no common cause right now. If they knew what Lily had done, they'd rally together."

"Maybe you can spread the word once this is all over."

"Maybe."

We continue to the train station. I keep my hood up, but the rain is starting to soak through. Evan's hair turns darker the wetter it gets, the slight curls turning into flat waves against his head.

"Where are we going now?" I ask.

"London. Witchfinder HQ." He turns into the station, practically marching with determination.

"How will we get in?"

"We'll figure that out later." His voice is deeper than usual, laced with rage.

It's the first time since meeting him that he's made me feel uncomfortable.

He steps up to a ticket machine. "Cover me."

"What?"

He doesn't answer, but he's already pulled out his wand and is moving his spare hand in the way I know can only mean he's casting a spell – here, in the open.

"Evan!" I look around, checking if anyone can see us. There are so many people, not to mention security cameras. Anyone might see him.

The machine's screen blurs and fizzles out before displaying the words *Ticket Purchase Successful*. Evan stuffs his wand into his backpack and pulls tickets out from a hatch at the bottom of the machine.

"Did you just—" I start to say.

"It's expensive to get to London." He walks towards the barriers as if there's nothing wrong at all.

I follow, still checking whether we've been seen. "Evan, you can't–"

"Can't what?" He spits the words at me, stopping and turning on the spot.

My instinct is to move away from him, but I hold my ground, even when heads start to turn our way.

"Can't break the rules?" he says, even louder. "Why not? Why does it matter what I do if the people who make the rules are breaking them themselves?"

"I understand." I can feel more eyes aiming at us from every angle. "But you can't get caught."

"I don't care!" His throws his hands up in fury, but in mere seconds, what was a wrathful face melts into misery as his tears begin falling.

A uniformed man starts to approach, but I hold up my hand, and he hesitates.

"It's okay," I say, stepping towards Evan and putting an arm around his shoulders. I start to move, and through his uncontrollable sobbing, Evan follows. The uniformed man backs off. I'm sure if he'd seen Evan's magic, he'd pounce, but instead of a dangerous warlock, Evan is just an upset teenager. Other onlookers move on too.

When I manage to get Evan all the way to the wall, out of the way of commuters, I wrap my other arm around him as well.

"It's okay," I say again. "I know you're angry. I understand. But do you know how we solve all of this?"

He sniffs. "How?"

"By succeeding at what we set out to do. By getting those keys back. And if we're right about Lily, then once we fix everything, you can tell the whole world about what she's done, can't you? You can spread the word and give people a solid reason to hate the witchfinders."

Another sniff, but Evan is nodding.

I stand back, keeping my hands on his sides, and give him the biggest smile I can muster. A toothless, half-hearted smile breaks through his red face in return, and he wipes away the tears.

"I'm sorry," he says.

"There's nothing to forgive. Just . . . maybe don't do any more risky spells in public."

He laughs weakly, takes my hand, and sets off walking towards the barriers once again.

The train to London looks different to the one we almost caught to Manchester. Where that one's logo and chairs were blue, this one's are red. I'm reminded of all the businesses I've seen as we've travelled through this city. So many brands and companies, all driven by the desperation to earn and spend money. It's odd, I think, the way humans seem desperate to tie everything back to money. Like it's become their reason to exist. I wonder, if I'd been around for a previous psychopomp's tenure, how different would mortal society have been? Would they have had similar quirks like this? Will they still have this when it becomes time for the next psychopomp?

Evan lets me take the window seat again. I lean my forehead against the glass, enjoying the slight vibration of the train's engine as it prepares to set off. There's a sign just above my head indicating that this is the quiet coach; I make a mental note to thank Evan later for choosing this one. After a series of rapid beeps, I hear the doors slide closed, and a very welcome silence descends across the carriage.

The train starts moving, and I lean my head back off the window, ready to properly take in whatever new views this journey brings me. But it's only a moment later when Evan's hand grips my leg. I turn to see panic in his face as he stares down the carriage. I follow his gaze and immediately see what has him so shaken.

There, in the open space between the carriage doors, stands a tall man with a shaved head wearing a denim jacket. The same man we saw in the dead old man's house on Friday night and who Evan saw in Tamara's memories. He has an unsettling smirk across his face.

And he's staring right at us.

Without a word, Evan's hand moves from my leg, interlocking with my fingers, and he stands up, slinging his bag loosely onto his back with his spare hand. I rise with him as he drags me in the opposite direction to the man. But then we both freeze. Because at the other end of the carriage is the other man. The one in the long dark coat. He, too, is smirking with horrifying glee, eyes fixed on Evan and me.

There's no time to question how or why – it's clear they're here for us.

"What do we do?" asks Evan, voice trembling.

And all my words about avoiding risky magic fade away. It's impossible to be discreet now. But what exactly can we do?

The man in the dark coat starts pacing towards us, and I don't need to turn to know the other is doing the same. I look up at the ceiling, a plan forming. A wild, stupid plan, but a plan nonetheless. I reach for the anchor with one hand while wrapping the other around Evan's waist.

"Do you trust me?" I ask him.

His eyes, still red from his earlier tears, meet mine. It's like I can see the last two days replay in super speed across his pupils.

"Yes," he says.

"Then hold on tight and don't let go."

I tear the anchor from my neck, stuffing it into a pocket, and the carriage fills with white light. I feel my body shift from mortal flesh to something beyond the laws of this world. As my wings spread into existence, I rise from the floor, bringing Evan with me. The weight of his body means nothing when I'm in this form; he's as light as my feathers.

I don't pause to see the reaction of the witchfinders. Instead, I rise up with impossible speed, manoeuvring myself so that Evan is sheltered as my body collides with the roof of the train. Where a human body would bruise and break, mine remains strong, tearing a hole in the metal as easily as passing through water.

With Evan holding on tight, I take to the sky.

Chapter Twenty
Evan

We're flying. Really, actually flying. I'm clinging on to Orpheus with every bit of strength I have, but I know in my soul that the arm he has around me is enough to stop me falling. The train becomes little more than a speck as we ascend above the city. The air grows colder, and the rain becomes painful, but I'm too dumbstruck to care. We soar past the tops of the tallest buildings and head outwards beyond the city, where the buildings change from skyscrapers to tiny houses, becoming more and more scattered.

Every so often, I turn my head to see Orpheus' wings. Their span is vast, far greater than any bird, and they're feathered but not quite solid. There's an ethereal quality to them, much like the glow that pours from Orpheus' skin. It's like he's shrouded in wisps of pale smoke. It's similar to the gytrash, though where that seemed to carry anger and sorrow, Orpheus carries hope.

"Where are we going?" I call out to him when the city is almost out of sight.

He either doesn't hear me or chooses not to answer. The wind is strong up here, so there's every chance he's deafened.

The journey becomes less painful as we leave the rain behind. And with the weather, the landscape below changes too. The industrial streets give way to swathes of moorland, those dark green rolling hills I know all too well. I wonder if Charlotte is down there somewhere, still trying to save her unconscious coven. Is she looking up at us, I wonder? Is anyone?

When I first saw Orpheus' angel form down there, moments from being attacked by the gytrash, I barely had chance to process it. There was just so much going on, and really, the same can be said of now. So many questions. How did Lily manage to use an artefact? How did those two men find us? How are we going to reach Witchfinder HQ if we're apparently being hunted? Even if we do get there, how will we get the keys?

My head should be on the verge of exploding. And yet up here, holding on to an angel, I feel the most peaceful I've felt since this whole ordeal began. My fingers may be going numb, and my ears might feel like they're about to freeze solid, but I know I'm safe. Here, I can watch the world pass by without it ever touching me. Here, I can pretend I'm not in the world at all. The sky is a liminal space, just like the Halls of Styx. Neither here nor there. Separate from reality.

We glide over reservoirs and rocky outcrops. We pass collections of villages and winding country roads. Eventually, we find ourselves over a forest. The trees are densely packed, and with their autumn leaves turned red and orange, it looks like a blanket of fire below us. That's when Orpheus falters.

It's subtle at first, just a slight wobble in what has so far been an incredibly smooth flight. But then we drop five feet without warning.

"Orpheus?" I yell, looking up at his face.

His eyes are rolling back like he's about to faint. Behind him, his wings begin flailing wildly.

"Orpheus!"

I feel his hand slip, and I cling on to him, every ounce of safety I felt before gone in an instant. We drop again, and now my dangling feet are almost brushing the tops of the trees.

Blearily, Orpheus manages to mutter, "Evan... the anchor..." before his eyes fall closed and his head rolls forward.

The two of us fall from the sky.

"Beautiful, isn't it?" says Gran, hands on her hips as she surveys the green fields down below.

I step up to her side, still catching my breath from the steep walk, and nod.

"This is history, this place," she says, planting a hand on my shoulder. "This hill, the land around it. It's our history."

"I thought we were from Yorkshire."

She chuckles. "We are, my love. But I'm not talking about our family." She bends down to get closer to my level. I've not yet had the growth spurt Mum claims is on the way.

"Then who do you mean?"

Gran moves her hands onto mine, palms to palms, fingers splayed. She wiggles each digit the way she did when first teaching me how to loop the threads around the hook of a wand, and I realise what she's talking about.

"Witches?"

"Exactly."

She grins, and I copy her. Our chats about magic are my favourite. It's a secret topic, just between us. Not even Mum and Dad know that I'm a warlock. I didn't either, until a few weeks ago.

"This is Pendle Hill," she says. "Have you ever heard about that in history at school?"

I shake my head.

Gran rolls her eyes. "Of course not." She sits down on the grass, baked dry by the summer sun, and pats the space beside her.

I take a seat.

"Hundreds of years ago, there was a coven of witches who lived around here."

"A coven?"

She gets a sad look in her eyes at that question, but she hides it with a smile. "It's what a group of witches is called. In the past, they were quite common. These days, witches mostly stay apart."

"Why?"

She sighs. "Because together, we are strong, and that makes mundane people scared."

I scrunch up my face. "Why?"

"That's a very good question, Evan. In a coven, witches are able to share knowledge and cast more complex spells. For people who hate magic, that seems like a dangerous thing."

I think back to the moment Gran told me I'm a warlock. How much she stressed that I must never tell anyone, and that although it was a beautiful thing, it put me in terrible danger. I can't help but wonder what it would be like to be in a coven. How much freer both Gran and I could be.

"What happened to the coven that lived here?" I ask.

Gran gazes out at the vibrant green fields. "They were falsely accused of using their magic to commit murder, and most of them were executed."

I stare at her, horrified. "That's terrible."

She nods solemnly. "Our history is not a happy one, I'm afraid. And it's because of trials like that of the Pendle witches that there are barely any covens left. Together, witches are powerful, but they are also a more visible target. Sometimes – well, most of the time – it is safer to be alone."

"Are we a coven?" I ask. "Me and you?"

Gran's eyes soften as she looks at me. I think she might be about to cry. She takes a moment, returns both her hands to mine, and smiles.

"Yes," she says. "And I'll always be there to help you, no matter what."

"Gran!" I yell, eyes snapping open. I'm looking up at the rusted canopy of the forest. There's a broken set of branches directly above me, allowing the grey sky to peek through. That must be where I fell from.

"Orpheus?" I say, though it turns into a wince as I sit up. Pain shoots through my body, sharp, coming from everywhere at once. I grit my teeth and scrunch my eyes closed, short bursts of breath escaping from my nose. I remain still, letting the worst of the pain ebb away, before opening my eyes again.

"Orpheus?" I turn, slowly, and see him sprawled on the ground a few feet from me. His glow is faltering, like a lightbulb that's about to die, and his wings look to be losing their shape. The feathers blur into each other, becoming vague wing-shaped planes of mist.

I crawl towards him, over damp earth and fallen leaves, trying my best to ignore the pain that accompanies every movement. When I'm close enough to see his face, I feel my heart drop. He's unconscious, and his skin is cracked like a porcelain doll. Dark rivulets cover his face, and they're spreading. They've already covered his neck, and now they're running along his arms, right to the tips of his fingers. His right hand is outstretched, and just inches from it, I spot the familiar brass disc that is the anchor.

Instantly, I recall one of the memories he showed me when we first met. His mother, telling him what the anchor was and how his body would fall apart without it. Her words echo in my head: *You could last an hour at most.* I lunge for the anchor, sending shockwaves of agony through my body.

In the back of my mind, I hear my swimming instructor's first aid speech.

"Don't move his head," she'd say. "You might break his neck." But she never had to deal with an injured angel.

I lift Orpheus' head and return the chain to his neck, resting the anchor on his chest. The moment I let go, he returns to human form. The glow and the wings fade away.

The cracks fade, too, but they take longer. I was hoping for a movie moment where Orpheus would sit bolt upright with a huge intake of breath, but that doesn't happen. He stays where he is, eyes closed. He is breathing, but not strongly.

"Orpheus?" I say again, voice shaking. "Please, wake up."

I lean forward and cry out as another wave of pain spreads through me. My mind races. What am I supposed to do? I reach for my phone, only to find an empty pocket. I must have lost it in the fall. It could be anywhere. I look around, biting my lip so strongly against the pain that I draw blood, and see my backpack at the base of a tree just next to where I woke up.

I crawl to my bag, keeping an eye out for my phone but failing to see it anywhere. The bag is looking worse for wear, with scuff marks and tears in the fabric, but nothing has fallen out. I'd say luck is on my side if it weren't for Orpheus being unconscious. Inside my bag is a change of clothes, my wand and my grimoire. I pull the grimoire out, racing through the pages for an entry on healing. Near the centre, I find one on pain relief. Without hesitation, I grab my wand, shift my view to see the threads and start to loop them over the hook, forming the rows of stitches that the page describes, pulling on the coloured threads around my legs that correspond to blood flow and pain reception. I can't hope to help Orpheus if I can't even move without screaming.

It takes longer than a spell usually would, but I've only used this one once before, and until the pain is gone, I can barely think straight. Once I've formed the stitches, I summon a pulse of magic, and a wave of relief passes over me. The pain is still there, but hugely dulled. I'm not sure I'll be able to get rid of it completely on my own. There's nothing in the grimoire about spells to fix major injuries.

I push that worry away and return to Orpheus' side. His pulse is normal, I think, but his breathing is still shallow. I cast the same pain relief spell on him, hoping it might bring him some comfort if he's even a little aware of what's going on around him.

"Orpheus?" I repeat for what feels like the hundredth time. "Can you hear me? Orpheus?"

No response.

Maybe it takes time. Maybe his body is recovering from what happened. He must have been in his angel form for too long and come close to falling apart, like his mother warned him. But he'll be okay. I just have to wait. Right?

Without my phone, I can't be sure how much time passes. I can't even make out where the sun is in the sky thanks to the dense trees. But I have to recast the pain relief spell, and my stomach begins growling, so I assume it's been at least a couple of hours. As far as I can tell, I haven't broken any bones, but I know I'm going to be completely covered in bruises by tomorrow. There's still no response from Orpheus.

I've used magic to dry the ground around him and to keep us both warm. I've searched through the grimoire from cover to cover for anything that might help and found nothing. Well, almost nothing. There's a spell on the very last page that I remember Gran telling me about soon after our trip to Pendle Hill.

"Imagine the threads are like the strings of a violin," she told me. "The violinist can use her bow to send vibrations through the strings."

"And that's what we do with magic?" I asked.

"Precisely. And this spell lets us send those vibrations to other witches. It was often used by members of a coven to call on each other in times of need."

"So I could use it to call you? Like a phone?"

She ruffled my hair. "Just like a phone."

I stare at the page now. Gran taught me how to use the threads to send a message in the form of a thought directly to her, but the same could be done to any other witch. To be able to contact a specific witch, I'd need to know them well. Ideally, I'd need to have made mental contact with them in the past. But even without that, I could send a message out into the threads for any witch to pick up on.

It's not something I've ever witnessed, and I doubt many witches ever do it. Like Gran said, ever since the witch trials, most witches have chosen to practice magic alone. There'd be no way of predicting who would receive my message or what trouble it could cause, but maybe the time for being solitary is over. If Orpheus and I are right about Lily being behind the immortality, then for the first time in history, there might be a genuine reason for the world to turn against the witchfinders. Now, more than ever, perhaps it's time for witches to come together.

I look at Orpheus, his tall frame somehow looking so tiny and frail. Waiting and praying isn't going to save him. With a deep breath, I gather multiple threads in my hand. This isn't a normal spell; there'll be no rows of stitches or even a wand this time. I focus my thoughts on one word: *help*. And with a pulse of magic, I send that thought out into the world, vibrating along every nearby thread.

I curl up beside Orpheus, one arm across his body and the other gently stroking his hair. I slow my breathing to match his, close my eyes and hope.

Chapter Twenty-One
Orpheus

I'm falling. Falling so far and so fast. Falling from the sky without control. And the world is dark, and black, and cold.

Until it's not.

I stretch out my fingers, feeling soft blades of grass beneath them. I push myself up, blinking against the sudden light, and find myself in a field. It stretches out unobstructed for what must be miles. No trees, no buildings, no hills or valleys. It's an infinite plane of verdant green, though in the distance, I can see patches of dark, billowing smoke, as though the grass is on fire. The sky above is bright blue and cloudless, but the sun is absent.

"I often wondered if I'd ever meet you," comes a low voice from behind me.

I turn to see an old man with a fiercely wrinkled face and wisps of white hair, wearing a billowing grey cloak. He sits cross-legged on the grass beside a large wooden pole and regards me with large pale blue eyes. A pair of feathered black wings stretch out behind him.

"Who are you?" I ask.

The corners of his previously neutral mouth curve upwards. "Interesting."

"What is?"

"That you should choose that as your first question." He folds his arms. "Some would argue that 'Where am I?' would be more pertinent. But then, you have always had a fascination with people, haven't you?"

I take a moment and check my surroundings again. The sunless sky reminds me of the forest in the Halls of Styx.

That and the fact that there's an angel here is enough to tell me I'm not in the mortal world. But I'm not in the Halls, either. I'm somewhere else. Another plane of existence entirely.

"Who are you?" I repeat.

"I'm curious," he says, avoiding the question yet again. "What do you remember from before you arrived here?"

I bite my tongue. He's toying with me, and I want to know why, but I'm not exactly in a position to argue. I don't know where I am or how I got here, which means he has the upper hand.

"I was falling," I say.

"And before that?"

"I was . . ." I pause as the memory comes back. "I was flying. Evan . . . he was with me, and I . . . No!" I stand, hands flying to my head as I realise what happened. I'd been holding Evan, keeping him safe as we flew, but I went too far. I stayed in my angel form too long. I needed to land, to put the anchor back on. But I was too late.

The angel remains seated, clasping his hands together and resting them on his stomach.

"We were falling." I stare into the angel's eyes, fear rising in my chest. "Is he okay? Is Evan okay?"

The angel says nothing. No emotion crosses his face.

"I need to get back to him. Where am I?"

He smiles. "Now you ask." He gestures at the ground. "Please, sit."

I scoff. "I'm not here to play games!"

"Neither am I." He gestures again. "Sit."

With a deep reluctance, I do as he says, returning to the grass.

"What are the Halls of Styx?" he asks.

I frown, confused not by the question but by his tone. It's as though he isn't really questioning me. He knows the answer already.

"Go on," he says.

"They're a liminal space," I say hesitantly. "A transition between the mortal world and the afterlife. Between life and death."

He nods, then holds up his hands and looks to the sky. "This is a liminal space, too. Not between life and death, but between existence and oblivion. An infinite plane on the very edge of reality through which things pass when they cease to exist."

My heart drops as I recall Mother's warning to me about what would happen if I didn't wear the anchor.

"Is that what's happening to me?" I ask. "Am I . . . ceasing to exist?"

The angel considers me, tilting his head as his eyes pass over every inch of my body.

"No," he says after what feels like forever. "You're not entirely here."

"What do you mean?"

He reaches out and taps my upper arm. A white glow ripples across me from that point, and for a moment, my form becomes translucent.

"It seems someone got to you just in time," the angel says. "That anchor of yours is doing its job."

I touch my hand to my chest, at the point where the anchor would be, and smile. Evan must have put it back on my body before it was too late, which means he must be okay, or alive at the very least.

"I should be grateful, I suppose," the angel says. "Transition through here usually only lasts a few seconds. Most people simply float across the sky, never landing. It's been a long time since I've had the chance to speak to someone."

It's strange. From someone else, those words might be sad, but from him, they're apathetic. He's just stating a fact, not seeking sympathy.

"Who are you?" I try again.

He sighs. "Like your mother, I've gone by many names. But you likely know me as Charon."

If I were still standing, I think I'd fall in shock.

"Charon?" I repeat. "The *ferryman*?"

"The *original* psychopomp," he adds, "from long before your mother turned my river into a set of corridors."

I stare at the wooden pole by his side. Is that what he used to punt his boat across the water?

I shake my head. "But why are you here?"

"This is where I came after the gods retired me. While the new psychopomps ensure stability in whatever Styx they build, be it River or Halls, I ensure stability here. I hear whispers of their exploits, catch glimpses of the mortal realm. That's all that reaches this place – echoes." An unsettling smile creeps across his face. "More echoes than usual recently, in fact, thanks to your mother's mistake."

"What mistake?"

A chuckle escapes him. "The immortality. The missing keys. All that entropy flooding through the unlocked door into the Halls of Styx is causing quite a lot of damage."

He grabs the pole and waves it across the air between us, causing it to ripple like the water of his river. A chaotic amalgamation of voices emanates from the disturbance, too garbled to make anything out, but it fades almost as quickly as it came.

"Cracks are forming in the fabric of reality," he continues. "If those keys aren't found soon, the Halls may crumble completely. Gods only know what state humanity would be left in if that happened." He holds out his pole, directing it at the billowing smoke on the horizon. "Even this realm is feeling the impact."

I swallow nervously. My mind is flooded with concern for Mother. I can't help but picture her alone in the Halls as they fall apart around her. And yet here's Charon, an angel who was once in Mother's position, seemingly smiling at the idea of her downfall.

"You don't seem overly concerned," I say through gritted teeth.

He shrugs. "It makes little difference to me. I've rather enjoyed the change of scenery and the extra information I've been able to glean from the echoes. Normally, the most exciting thing around here is the occasional appearance of a corrupted spirit that has wandered too far."

"Gytrashes," I mutter.

"And ghosts. And poltergeists. If they don't slip into the mortal world, this is where they end up." He looks up at the sky. "They float peacefully overhead until they evaporate. Gone forever. Forgotten."

"And that's what would happen to me if I didn't wear the anchor?"

He nods. "I was rather intrigued when I realised you'd travelled to the mortal world. I've heard many echoes of you over the years. The half-human son of the psychopomp . . . it's a wonder your mother wasn't retired the moment she conceived you." His voice isn't so apathetic anymore; it's laced with bitterness. "It seems the gods of today are more forgiving than when I was the psychopomp. Though I can't imagine they'll forgive this immortality mess she's created."

My hands curl into fists. "She didn't create it."

"That's not how the gods will see things."

"I'm fixing it."

"So I hear, though I fear your ending may be as tragic as your namesake's."

I stand again. "You're wrong."

"Perhaps."

A shudder passes over me as my form glows and becomes translucent once again. Suddenly, the horizon looks to be moving upwards.

"What's happening?"

Charon stands, using the pole to steady himself, but he looks taller than I expected. I look down and realise that it's not the ground that's rising – it's me that's sinking. My feet have already vanished below the earth, and the rest of my body is following.

"You're returning to the mortal world," Charon says. "I do hope we'll meet again."

Chapter Twenty-Two
Evan

The crunch of nearby leaves makes me jump.

"Who's there?" I call, turning with a wince of pain while still sat on the leaves beside Orpheus.

A woman stands between two nearby trees, hands held aloft in surrender. She's dressed in a long patchwork coat, with her grey hair framing a face decorated with wrinkles.

"I'm here to help," she says with a kindly smile that's hard not to trust. "My name is Mary." She points at Orpheus. "May I?"

I'm not sure how long we've been here – hours, certainly – but he still hasn't stirred.

I nod, letting the tension in my body go as the woman approaches with a slight hobble to her walk.

"I sensed your call in the threads," she says, kneeling down to examine Orpheus. "What happened?"

I hesitate, looking up at the broken branches in the canopy. "It's complicated. We . . . fell."

Her eyes flit between me and Orpheus, puzzled, but then she begins manoeuvring her fingers above him, no doubt studying the threads. "He doesn't seem to be injured. A couple of bruises perhaps, but . . ." Her hands come to a stop above the anchor. She reaches out to touch it.

"Don't!" I push her arm away, then buckle over in pain. "Please," I say, eyes closed against the stabbing sensation. "He needs to keep wearing it."

Her hands find my sides, and she eases me slowly backwards.

"It seems you're in far more pain than he is," she says. "What's your name?"

I blink my eyes open, trying to breathe. "Evan."

Mary leans me on my back, leaves crunching beneath my head. "Let me help you, Evan," she says, pulling out her wand and beginning to cast a spell.

The relief comes almost instantly, passing through each part of my body as though flowing through my blood. I almost cry with joy.

"Tell me," Mary says while she continues to work, wand now over my legs, "what is that pendant your friend is wearing? The thread patterns around it are incredibly complex."

I try to think of a believable lie, but nothing comes.

"You don't trust me," Mary says. "I understand that. I take it from your lack of healing ability that you've not been around many fellow witches before?"

I prop myself up slightly on my elbows so that I can look her in the eyes.

"There's been no one to teach you?" she asks.

"There used to be."

She raises an eyebrow.

"My gran. But she was converted, and then . . ."

Mary frowns and stops moving her fingers. "She died?"

I nod. The pain is completely gone now. I pull my feet towards me and sit cross-legged. "Thank you."

"I confess I'm not entirely sure how to help your friend. That pendant seems to be doing far more complex magic than I'm capable of."

I look over at Orpheus' face. Can he hear us, I wonder, from wherever he is? Is he merely sleeping?

"Perhaps whatever spell it is casting takes time?" Mary suggests.

"Perhaps."

Mary stumbles to her feet and surveys the surroundings. "Whatever the case, I think we'd better move him. Do you know how to cast levitation?"

"I think so. It's been a while."

"Then cast with me." She stands beside Orpheus' feet. "You take his head. Sorry, what's his name?"

"Orpheus."

I move to stand opposite her, Orpheus lying between us. Mary holds her wand aloft, ready to begin casting, and I shift my vision to reveal the threads.

"Ready?" she says.

"Yes."

I copy her movements, creating rows of stitches around Orpheus as though forming a net with which to carry him. When we send our magic into the threads, his body rises slowly from the ground until he's hovering just below our heads.

"Now what?" I ask.

Mary gestures in the direction she originally came from. "You follow."

There's no well-worn path through the forest: it's all endless carpets of fallen leaves. Mary seems confident in her direction, though, and I'm hardly in a position to question that. Orpheus' hovering body follows us as we walk, and every so often, Mary will do a quick twiddle with her wand and fingers to rotate him so he can fit between the trees.

"Whereabouts are we?" I ask after one such twiddle.

"You don't know?"

"Like I said, it's complicated."

"You're asking an awful lot of trust from me given that you won't explain anything," she says. Her tone isn't aggressive, but I can hear her frustration.

"I know. I'm sorry. It's just—"

"Complicated?" She grins.

"Exactly."

She ponders for a moment. "We're around the southern end of the Peak District. Once we're out of the forest, it's a fifteen minute drive to my village. Thornbrook, if you've heard of it. Though your accent sounds a little more West Yorkshire, am I right?"

I chuckle lightly. "Yeah. I'm from Elmwood Vale."

"Can't say I've visited." She turns towards a gentle incline. "The road's just up here."

The slope is more tiring than it looks, but Mary trudges on as though she does this every day. It's very witch-like, I suppose, to be at home in the forest. Despite what the witchfinders might claim, magic is a natural thing. The threads are everywhere, all the time, even if they can't be seen by everyone.

"Are you open about being a witch?" I ask. "Like, do your family and friends know?"

"Yes," Mary says. "Those closest to me know, and so do some other witches from the local area."

"Other witches? Do you have a coven?"

She stops walking and looks at me with a deep sadness in her eyes. "Yes, my dear. And I think perhaps you're in need of a coven yourself."

"I've been fine on my own."

She shakes her head. "Witches aren't meant to be alone."

I think of Gran and Tamara. I think of Charlotte's unconscious coven members. I think of the Pendle witches and all the witches who were killed throughout history.

"It's safer that way," I say.

Mary sets off up the hill again. "You're not the first witch who has called for my help these last few days, you know."

"I'm not?"

"You won't have heard it on the news because they always try to hide the harm that's done to our kind, but violent attacks against witches have been increasing since the immortality started."

I wish I were shocked, but it makes sense. It's the natural result of the witchfinders claiming that witches are responsible for the immortality.

Mary continues. "I've taken in a few witches who were in danger."

As we reach the top of the slope, the treeline becomes visible. Just beyond it is a road, where a small, dirt-covered car that looks one short trip away from falling apart is parked.

"There's not much space left," Mary says, "but I'd be happy to bring you and Orpheus to my home too."

I slow down as we approach the car, instinctively reaching for my missing phone. If I still had it, I'd be calling Wren and asking if there's any chance they could help me again, although I'm not so sure it would be that easy. The witchfinders on the train were looking for me and Orpheus, and for all I know, they could have access to the police's phone tracking software. In fact, if they really wanted, they could spread my name to the public as a wanted criminal. Anxiety rises in my throat as I realise that they might already have done that. And here we are, about to get into the car of a stranger.

"Evan?" Mary says, the back door of her car already open. She's guiding Orpheus' body into the back seat. "I could use a bit of help."

I remain stood still. Mary has been kind so far, and I want to trust her, but how can I possibly trust anybody right now? The witchfinders could have offered anything for someone to hand us over to them. What if she's been lying this whole time?

"You can leave us here," I say.

Mary stares at me, Orpheus hovering at her side. "What?"

"You can leave us here. We'll be fine. We'll find our way."

Mary looks baffled. "I don't think your unconscious friend will be finding anything." Her eyebrows knit together. "Is something wrong?"

I bury my face in my hands. This is an impossible situation. Without Orpheus, I feel completely lost. If Mary leaves us, we're stranded. If we go with her, we could be walking into a trap. Either way, we're screwed. Without warning, I feel my eyes fill with tears, and I begin to sob.

"Oh, Evan," says Mary in the gentlest voice I think I've ever heard.

She places a hand on my arm, and I find myself crumpling to the ground, sobs becoming utterly uncontrollable.

"I don't know what to do," I say, though I'm not sure the words are particularly clear.

I wish there were a spell to send me back in time, to before any of this happened. To the day before the immortality, when the only thing I had to think about was how much longer the dad I hate had left to live or whether my ex-girlfriend would speak to me.

Except then I wouldn't know Orpheus.

"Evan?" comes a familiar voice.

I wipe away my tears to look behind Mary.

And there he is.

Chapter Twenty-Three
Orpheus

Evan collides with me so hard that I momentarily forget how to breathe.

"Orpheus!" he cries, squeezing me tightly before backing up so I can see his face. There are tears in his eyes, which I instinctively reach out to, wanting to wipe them away.

When my hand touches his face, his flies up to meet it. His palm is soft against my knuckles. It's a welcome sensation, especially after being in my angel form and then barely any form at all in Charon's realm. Evan's touch grounds me. It makes me feel human. It makes me feel alive.

"I thought I'd lost you," Evan says, voice thick with emotion.

I wipe away the last of his tears. "I'm not going anywhere."

My eyes drift to the old woman stood a few feet away. There's a twinkle in her eyes as she watches us.

"And there was me thinking you two were just friends," she says, approaching us.

I exchange a look with Evan, confused by the woman's words, but he blushes and barely meets my gaze.

"Er, Orpheus," he says, "this is Mary. She's a witch. She healed me and helped get you out of the woods."

Mary folds her arms. "And ideally, I'd like to take you both back to my home so that you can get properly rested and I can check you again for injuries."

"I'm still not sure that's—" Evan starts.

"Please," Mary says. "I'm not about to leave two teenagers out here alone. You can trust me, and the other witches. The coven is a place of sanctuary, not danger."

Evan looks to me, and it's like I see a thousand concerns swirl in his eyes. Is it any wonder? After those men found us on the train, who can say where safety lies, if anywhere? And yet I fear we have no choice but to seek help.

"We can't do this alone," I say, taking Evan's hands. "I think we should go with her."

I watch as the doubt fades from his face. He trusts me, and I hope to the gods that I've made the right choice.

"Okay," he says, turning to face Mary. "Let's go."

The car creaks and wobbles as it travels down the road, and I get the feeling from Evan's tight grip on his seatbelt that cars aren't really supposed to do that. Mary is fiddling with a dial on the dashboard, which seems to be filling the car with a mix of static and occasional snippets of music. The road outside is long and winding, with the forest stretching out on both sides. The sun is setting, so it looks like the autumn leaves are reflected in the sky. It's a beautiful reminder of how connected all of nature is.

Charon's words replay in my mind, especially what he said about the fabric of the universe. The disruption of the natural order has already caused chaos in the mortal world. I dread to think how much worse things could be if the universe itself started falling apart. Death might often fill this world with sadness, but it is a necessary part of life. The universe can't go on without it. The green leaves must turn red and fall to the ground if new ones are ever to grow.

A sharp screech of static pulls my attention away from the view, but it's quickly replaced with a man's voice.

"It's the news," Evan mutters. I must look confused. He nods to the car's console. "On the radio."

"Reports of widespread violence have begun to increase," the man's voice says. "It is believed that this is a result of the ongoing immortality, with people feeling that their violent actions carry less risk."

"Ha!" Mary says, scornfully. "Of course they only start reporting it when it happens to mundanes."

The man continues, "The witchfinders have continued to issue reassurances that they are pursuing the witch or witches behind the crisis. Any further information is still being withheld, much to the distaste of the public. Protests broke out in many major cities today as citizens made their concerns known."

Mary switches the radio off. "Where have these protests been every time a witch has been converted?" she says. "Trust the mundanes to fight back only when things impact them."

"Maybe this is the moment they start to see the truth," Evan says. "It could be a turning point."

Mary shakes her head. "Not when they catch the witch who caused the immortality. People are suffering. As soon as they're able to pin the blame for their suffering on a witch, it'll set progress back hundreds of years."

Evan and I glance at each other, no doubt both thinking about our suspicions around Lily Morgan. How, if we're right, the exact opposite of Mary's fears could be true. If the blame for the immortality falls on a witchfinder, this truly could be a turning point.

Evan mouths the words, *Do we tell her?*

"What are you whispering about back there?" Mary asks, eyes reflected in the rear-view mirror.

I nod at Evan. I meant what I said about not being able to do this alone. The help of another witch is exactly what we need.

"Mary," Evan says, "there's something we need to tell you."

By the time the story is finished, the car is turning into the driveway of a cobblestone cottage. There's a crunch of gravel below the tyres as the car slows. The branches of a large willow tree bend over the car's roof, sheltering it slightly from the light rain that has started to fall.

Mary takes a deep breath, one hand resting on the handbrake, the other on the steering wheel. She hasn't said a word since Evan began the story. She questioned nothing, just listened. I feel a ball of anxiety in the pit of my stomach as she turns to face us.

"If what you say is true, then the witchfinders are a house of cards. The lightest touch could topple them." There's a fire in her eyes as she speaks. A spark of hope. "If we take our time . . . gather evidence, build a case . . . we could bring them down."

"We can't take our time," I say before she has the chance to continue forming her grand plans. "The immortality needs to end as soon as possible. It's not just causing problems for humans; it's damaging the universe itself."

Evan raises an eyebrow. "What do you mean?"

"I went somewhere while I was unconscious in the forest – my mind or my soul, I mean. I went to the edge of existence, and I saw the damage that's happening." I don't mention Charon; it would only lead to more questions.

Mary shakes her head. "Then what are you going to do? How are you going to retrieve the keys?"

"I don't know yet," I say.

Evan shrugs.

"Well then," says Mary, "let's go inside and figure this out."

We exit the car and head for the cottage, almost jogging to avoid the rain as it grows heavier. The door is painted green, dulled and peeling with age. It reminds me of the last door I stepped through in the Halls of Styx. Mary twists her key and leads us in. Immediately, I feel a wave of warmth, as though Evan has cast his spell again. The light is low but homely, and I can just about make out the forest landscape paintings hanging on the wall. There's a clinking of crockery from another room, and Mary heads towards the sound.

I walk side by side with Evan into the kitchen, where a middle-aged man is filling cups of tea while a younger woman butters toast. They both look up when they realise we're in the room, but rather than wide eyes of surprise, they greet us with friendly smiles. It must be a common occurrence for Mary to bring guests.

"Orpheus, Evan," Mary says, "this is Jacob and Amara. They've been here since yesterday."

"Nice to meet you," says Amara. She sets down her toast and brushes the crumbs off her fingers before holding her hand out to Evan. She shakes his hand, then mine.

"And you," Evan says, with me echoing him.

"You're lucky I made more than enough tea," Jacob says, grabbing an extra pair of mugs.

"It's most appreciated," Mary says. She steps towards another door and waves Evan and I over.

It leads to the living room, where there are another four people. An elderly man sits on a rocking chair in the corner, reading a newspaper. A woman whose hair hangs in beaded braids is stoking the fireplace. And, given the way they're cosied up against each other beneath a blanket on the sofa, a man and woman who I assume are a couple are discussing something on the screen of one of their phones.

"Elijah, Chantelle, Christie and Ibrahim," Mary says, which prompts a quick glance from each person in turn, "this is Evan and Orpheus."

They all mumble greetings and give a quick wave before returning to what they were doing, but then I notice Evan staring at the woman with braids.

"Chantelle Adeyemi?" he says, open-mouthed.

Chantelle looks up from the fireplace, an awkward smile spreading across her face. "That's me."

"But . . ." Evan says, looking around as though baffled that no one else is reacting the same way. "Chantelle Adeyemi?!"

"Seems you have a fan," mutters the elderly man, Elijah.

"I'm not a fan," Evan says quickly. "Not that I'm *not* a fan; actually, my best friend is more of a fan. But you're. . . how. . . why. . ."

I reach out and take Evan's hand, which has become incredibly sweaty.

Mary chuckles. "Don't worry, Amara had the same reaction when Chantelle arrived this morning. Even celebrities need to hide from the angry mob of mundanes occasionally."

Chantelle chuckles. "Mary, I am not a celebrity."

"Compared to the rest of us, you are."

"Well, I for one think you are far more deserving of celebrity status than me."

"You're too kind." Mary wanders over to the staircase, which creaks as soon as she sets foot on it. "Now boys, if you have stopped gawping, I'll show you upstairs."

"Right, yes." Evan says, face bright red. "Sorry."

There's something strangely endearing about seeing Evan like this. I can't help but smile at his flusterment.

"Come on," I say, leading him towards the stairs.

We follow Mary to the top, where she shows us the bathroom and a bedroom which I imagine usually only sleeps one but now, with the hoard of blankets scattered about the floor, seems to be hosting multiple.

"As you can see, there's not much room," Mary says, "but I'm sure we can find some space in the living room if you two wish to spend the night."

Evan opens his mouth to respond, but Mary cuts him off.

"Which I highly recommend you do." Her voice is stern. "Whatever you decide to do next, you're going to need your strength." She waves in the direction of the staircase. "You're in a house full of witches; there's truly no better place to ensure you're fully healed. And I suspect if you told them what you told me, they'd jump at the chance to help. I know Chantelle certainly would."

There's an unexpected look on Evan's face. His eyes are glistening ever so slightly, but the corners of his mouth are turned upwards. He sniffs and wipes his eyes before saying, "Thank you, Mary. Could you give us a couple of minutes alone?"

"Of course, my dear." She hobbles away, back down the stairs. I hear her laugh at something one of the warlocks says.

Evan grips my hand tightly and leads me back into the bedroom.

"My gran always said I should keep my magic a secret," he says as soon as the door clicks shut. "In fact, she made me promise. And now I'm here, considering telling a house full of people, including a famous witch activist, that not only am I a warlock, but also that I'm on a quest with the half-angel son of Death and, oh yeah, that quest is leading us straight to the witchfinders, who happen to already be searching for us." He stares at me, pressing his hands into his hair so that the strawberry blond mop is messier than ever. "Am I completely mad?"

"Well, firstly, I think it's safe to assume the people in this house already know you're a warlock."

His stare remains unbroken, punctuating the silence that starts to form between us, until he completely loses his composure and starts laughing.

"Yeah," he says, breathless between giggles. "Yeah, I guess you're right."

I step towards him, placing my hands on his upper arms and letting his forehead collapse onto my chest. His laughs die down, and he takes a few deep breaths.

"And secondly," I continue, "I think if your gran were here, then she'd want you to find safety amongst other witches."

"A coven?" he mutters.

"Exactly."

I run a hand up into his hair. It's not as silky as the last time I felt it, and it's slightly damp from the rain, but as it slips between my fingers, I feel the same comforting closeness that I've felt so often these past few days. It's a feeling that distracts me from the rest of the world, as though right now, we are all that matters.

Evan leans back so that our eyes can meet. I gaze into them. The dark brown colour reminds me of the forest floor, like they're his connection back to nature. To the source of his magic. Evan's hand rises up to the back of my head, applying a very light pressure. He's not forcing anything, merely making a suggestion that I bring my head down lower, closer to his.

I give in to it, following a longing that seems almost instinctual. A longing that's been present for a while, but which I didn't understand until now. How could I when I've never felt this for anybody before?

I close my eyes.

We kiss.

And, just for this moment, we really are all that matters.

Chapter Twenty-Four
Evan

It should be wrong to feel this happy when there's so much at stake, but as I walk downstairs hand in hand with Orpheus, I feel like I'm flying all over again.

The others have gathered in the living room, some sitting on cushions on the floor, as the sofas and chairs are completely full. Fourteen eyes track us as we stumble over to a pair of cushions propped against an old wooden cabinet.

I find myself feeling a twinge of pride when some of the eyes drift briefly to our interlocked hands. What I've felt for Orpheus has been entirely private, hidden just beneath the surface, until now. It feels nice to be so close to him and have it be noticed by others. I hadn't realised quite how much I'd missed the feeling since ending things with Zara.

Once the both of us have planted ourselves on the cushions, I lean against Orpheus, and I feel him reciprocate. For the first time in God knows how long, I feel like I can relax, though I know it can't last.

"So," says Chantelle, looking from me and Orpheus to Mary, "is there something we should know?"

I feel Orpheus tense slightly, but he takes a deep breath and begins to tell the story of who he is and how we got here. I interject occasionally, but everyone else remains silent. They listen with wide eyes and open ears, taking in every detail of our story just as Mary did, and when we finish, the silence feels heavy.

Chantelle looks to Mary, "But this means—"

"I know."

"The witchfinders . . ." starts Jacob, staring at the floor, but he seems to lose whatever words were supposed to follow.

"But what's next?" asks Amara, hands clasped together as if in prayer. "How are you going to get the keys?"

I gulp. "That's why we're here. We need your help. All of you. If you'll give it."

"A scandal like this could bring down the witchfinders," says Jacob, finding his words. "Of course we'll help."

There are nods of agreement from everyone else, and my heart swells with gratitude.

"We should spread the word," says Ibrahim, adjusting his large round glasses. "If we got all the witches in the country together—"

"That may need to come later," says Mary. "The retrieval of the keys is the first priority." She sends me and Orpheus a brief nod, which I return.

"Before we came here," I say, "we were on our way to London. We were going to go to Witchfinder HQ, but then it turned out the witchfinders were already on our case."

"But see, that's what I don't understand," says Amara. "They were looking for you, which means they know you're onto them, and yet your names haven't been publicised anywhere."

"Maybe they don't know their names," suggests Jacob.

"But there have been no descriptions either. I've been checking the news all day, and there hasn't been one mention of two teenagers wanted by the witchfinders. If they wanted to catch you, why wouldn't they release that statement? Hell, they could claim you're suspected of causing the immortality if they wanted."

It's a good point. A great point, actually. Those witchfinders are very clearly targeting us, and if they want to know where we are, then the most logical thing to do would be to plaster our descriptions everywhere like we're wanted criminals. And yet they haven't.

"There's mention of the train roof damage online," says Chantelle, staring down at her phone screen, "but it all just says it was a freak accident. No comments from witnesses who saw you flying away or anything."

The heavy silence returns, with glances being exchanged in every direction.

"So, the witchfinders are keeping it a secret," says Amara. "But why?"

"Because we know the truth," says Orpheus.

Every head turns in his direction, mine included, which causes him to look a little taken aback. He squeezes my hand, and I squeeze back.

"Sorry," he says. "I can't claim to completely understand humans, but if we're right about Lily being responsible for the immortality, then she probably wants to keep that quiet. If she sent the whole country looking for us, what would stop us from revealing the truth to the first person we saw?"

I think he's getting quite good at reading human behaviour.

"Or," says Mary, voice gently serious, "maybe she knows she doesn't need to capture you, because if she waits long enough, you'll find her yourselves. She's likely sitting in Witchfinder HQ right now, awaiting your arrival."

"So walking up to the front door probably isn't a great idea," adds Amara.

I smirk. "That wouldn't have been my suggestion anyway."

I think back to my journey through Tamara's memories, especially those which took place in Witchfinder HQ. That awful moment where her magic was torn away from her. The interrogation between her and Lily. The artefacts on the table . . .

"Teleportation," I say, a half-formed thought slipping out of my mouth.

Puzzled faces are all I receive in reply.

"I've seen inside two rooms in Witchfinder HQ. If I hold the image of one of them in my mind, we could do a teleportation spell. It'd send Orpheus and me straight into the room."

There are scoffs of disapproval, judgemental laughs, and rolling eyes.

Mary is the first to speak. "Evan, my dear, teleportation is an incredibly advanced spell. It's the sort of thing usually reserved for artefacts."

"I know. They have a teleportation artefact in the vault – I heard Lily mention it in Tamara's memory – which means we'd have an easy way out."

"But not an easy way in."

I raise my hands, gesturing to the room. "You've got a whole coven here. Enough to cast the spell without an artefact."

"Evan." Mary offers a sympathetic smile, which I know means well but I can't help but find ever so slightly patronising. "None of us have attempted a spell as complex as that before."

Orpheus runs a hand up my back, relieving the tension I hadn't noticed had built up.

"Are you saying it's impossible?" I ask.

Mary pauses, exchanging uncertain looks with the others.

"Please, Mary," I say. "You must have the details of the spell in a grimoire somewhere. It's worth trying, surely."

Mary doesn't answer, but Jacob does. "Evan, I'm not sure you've thought this through. You'd be teleporting into a building crawling with witchfinders. A building which you, presumably, don't know the layout of, to find a set of keys that may or may not even be in there."

"They'll be in the vault, with all the artefacts," I say.

"You know that for a fact?"

I shake my head. "No, but it makes sense, doesn't it? The keys are a magical object; so are the artefacts."

"And if they're not in there?"

"Then we'll search the rest of the building."

"And if you can't even get in the vault?"

"I know how to unlock doors."

"And if you're surrounded by witchfinders?"

"I know a cloaking spell."

Jacob shakes his head. "This isn't a good plan."

"No," says Chantelle, "but it's not entirely terrible."

All eyes now fall on her.

"There are a million risks, it's true, but it's also the only way they're getting into the building. So what if we send them in the middle of the night, when there won't be as many witchfinders working? A cloaking spell could be enough to find the keys before being caught. Plus"—a grin spreads across her face—"we can cause a distraction from the outside."

She holds all our attention.

"If we start spreading the truth, not just telling other witches but also posting online, using my followers, telling the whole world, then the witchfinders will be scrambling to contain the fallout. We could kill two birds with one stone."

Mary looks baffled by Chantelle's positivity, but it can't be denied that there's a fire in her eyes now too – in everyone's eyes, in fact. A chance to cause the downfall of the witchfinders is too good an opportunity to miss. Mary's gaze drifts to a stack of grimoires in the corner of the room.

"Then I suppose we'd better get studying," she says.

It feels so strange to have access to so much magical knowledge. The grimoires here detail more spells than I've ever come across in my lifetime. The tome Gran left me is all I've ever known, its pages worn thin from years of my reading. Now here I am with a whole coven around me, all of us perusing Mary's books, studying the intricate diagrams of threads stitched together on the hooks of wands.

There are various accounts of teleportation spells, each claiming varying degrees of success. Witchcraft is inherently experimental – there is no one way of doing things. The threads that run through the world are infinite, all with different properties, and thus there are many ways of stitching them together to create similar results. But we need certainty.

Across the room, Jacob and Amara are practising part of a spell. They're working together, creating rows of stitches between them while Mary observes, grimoire in hand, making suggested improvements. I smile as I watch them, wishing the sight of witches working together wasn't so rare.

Elijah is muttering to himself as he switches between re-reading a page and practising the stitch pattern to match the description. Christie and Ibrahim are moving furniture to create a space for the spell to be cast when everyone is ready. Chantelle, meanwhile, is on her phone, pacing. She's making plans for spreading the truth online. As soon as Orpheus and I have been teleported away, she'll leak the news. By tomorrow, everybody will know that the blame for the immortality has never belonged to witches.

Orpheus walks across the room from the kitchen, having taken our empty plates in there after a much-needed meal that Mary provided. Now he's carrying a mug of steaming tea.

"Hey," he says when he reaches me, taking a seat on the cushion to my left and handing me the mug.

"Thanks." I take a sip, enjoying the warmth it brings and pretending not to notice how terrible it tastes. In hindsight, it might not have been best to leave the tea-brewing to someone who has never attempted it before.

"How are you feeling?" he asks.

I shake my head. "Honestly? I don't know. This has all been completely mad."

"It's certainly not been how I imagine an average human weekend."

I snort and choke on my tea. "You can say that again."

He looks at me, eyes vibrant even in the dim light. "Are you sure about the plan?"

I lower the mug, tapping my nail against the ceramic edge. "No. But I'm not sure we've got any better option. Best case scenario, we get into the vault quickly, find the keys and the teleportation artefact and get out. Worst case, we get caught, but the truth spreads regardless. Lily Morgan can't hide forever. Your mum will get her keys back, one way or another. I'm sure of it." I leave out the real worst-case scenario: that we get caught and no one believes the truth that Chantelle leaks. That all of this has been for nothing. I can't put that idea into Orpheus' head. We've come too far.

With my spare hand, I rub his arm. There's concern in his face. Worry. Fear. But it softens at my touch, even if I'm feeling the same things.

"You two should get some rest," says Mary, who has wandered over to us, leaving Jacob and Amara to continue stitching rows in the air.

"I'm fine," I say.

She shakes her head. "We'll be ready to cast the spell in a few hours. You've had a long day, and you're going to need some energy to pull this off." She waves a hand toward the stairs. "Please, use my bed; get some sleep. We'll wake you when we're ready."

I glance at Orpheus, who shrugs in response.

"It might be wise," he says.

I think of him mere hours ago, almost dead on the forest floor. A few hours in bed would be a blessing.

"Okay," I turn back to Mary. "Thank you."

"We're making a habit of this," I say, facing Orpheus in bed.

The room is dark, but my eyes have adjusted, and I can see the faint outline of his face against the black background.

"Though this is a bit more comfortable than Wren's sofa-bed," I add.

Orpheus chuckles lightly. "I like Wren."

"Yeah, I thought you would. You're quite similar in some ways."

"How so?"

"Just . . . the way you think. The way you take an interest in stuff. Remember you told me how you'd write down the life stories of the humans you'd meet in the Halls of Styx? I think it's cool how interested you are in humans. In our world."

"Like how Wren is interested in magic?"

"Exactly."

"You called it a 'special interest', didn't you?"

I nod, not that Orpheus can likely tell in the darkness. "Because they're autistic, yes. It's more intense than an interest or hobby that a neurotypical person would have."

There's a moment of quiet. The distant voices of Mary's coven echo through the floorboards, but they're muffled.

"Am I autistic?" Orpheus asks.

The question catches me off guard, but of the many things that have happened this weekend, this seems almost ordinary.

"I don't know," I say, thinking back on every social faux pas, sensory experience and burst of excitement at the sight of the human world that Orpheus has shown while I've been with him. "But I think you could be."

"Interesting."

His reply is surprisingly heartwarming in its simplicity. I've heard from Wren all about the ableist prejudices that most people have. A label can be a scary thing – it changes how the world perceives you and how you perceive yourself.

But Orpheus isn't from our world. He hasn't come here with prejudice. To him, the idea that he might be autistic is just one of many interesting things he's learned in his time here.

I shuffle closer to him and find his hand in amongst the bedsheets, entwining my fingers with his. All this talk of Wren has me thinking about home. About the normal life I was living before the moment the immortality struck. A life I'm not sure will ever be the same.

"Orpheus?" I say, close enough now that I can feel his breath.

"Yes?"

"What will you do after you return the keys to your mother?"

"What do you mean?"

"Will you stay with her, in the Halls?"

The quiet returns, and I feel my face get uncomfortably warm. I shouldn't have asked. It's none of my business, after all—

"Do you want me to?" His voice sounds strange. Scared, almost.

"What? No, I . . ." I pause, unsure how much to say. Of course I don't want him to stay in the Halls. After everything that's happened, I don't want him to leave. But we've only known each other for, what, barely two days? It's not fair of me to expect him to leave behind his life for me.

"What do *you* want?" I ask, squeezing his hand.

"I want to stay here."

He says it so simply, so matter-of-factly, and yet his words make my heart leap.

"There's a lot more of this world to see," he continues, "and, well, I don't want to say goodbye to you."

I bite my lip. "I don't want to say goodbye to you either."

I feel him move forward ever so slightly, and I do the same, meeting with a kiss. I feel like I'm swimming in

Orpheus' warm embrace. For the second night in a row, that embrace is where I fall asleep.

Chapter Twenty-Five
Orpheus

The coven are gathered in a circle in the living room when Evan and I descend the stairs. The light is dim, but there is still a glint against the metal wands that each witch and warlock holds tightly at their side. The room no longer has the homely warmth to it that welcomed us a few hours ago now that the fireplace holds only a few meagre embers. Mary and Jacob separate to allow us through, and we stand side by side, hand in hand, in the centre of the circle. Fourteen exhausted eyes gaze inwards at us, and I feel my palm become damp with sweat.

"It's 3:00 AM," Mary says, "so security should be minimal, but you should use your cloaking spell regardless."

Evan nods. He tucks his wand into his pocket. His bag remains in the bedroom upstairs. A wand is replaceable, but his grimoire belonged to his grandmother – it's better to leave it here than risk losing it.

"I've got posts and messages ready to go," Chantelle says. "As soon as you're gone, I'll start sending them out."

"Are you ready?" Mary asks, concern in her eyes as she looks at the pair of us.

"Yes," says Evan.

"Yes," I echo.

"Well then, let's begin."

Every witch save Evan takes in a deep breath and momentarily closes their eyes. I've seen this often enough now to know that they're all shifting their vision to reveal the threads that bind the world together. They raise their wands and hands, each pinching different sets of fingers in different positions, no doubt gathering the threads they need, ready to feed them onto the hooks and stitch them into rows.

"Evan," says Amara, "we're going to need you to picture the room you want us to send you to."

Evan nods and screws his eyes closed.

"Keep that image fixed in your mind and allow us to see it."

The witches start moving their hands, bringing the threads onto the hooks and looping them around each other, sometimes passing a thread to the person beside them or combining their stitches with another. It's far more complex than any spell I've seen Evan perform. I wish I could see what they're seeing; instead, I can only imagine it.

I keep my hand in Evan's but turn my head to watch each witch in turn. It's clear why this spell is usually only done with an artefact: each witch works frantically, clutching at threads from every angle, sometimes needing to stand on their tiptoes or kneel on the floor, bringing their wand along with them.

Eventually, they stop and return to their original standing positions. They glance around at each other.

"Ready?" Mary asks, not to me and Evan this time but to everyone else.

They all nod.

Mary looks directly into my eyes. "Good luck."

Every witch in the circle raises their wand and tenses their grip. There's a blinding flash of white light and a sickening lurch in my stomach as the ground below me feels like it gives way. A howling wind fills my ears. I call out to Evan but can't hear my own voice. I hear nothing but the wind. And I'm falling, falling so fast. But I still feel Evan's hand in mine.

As quickly as it began, the disorientation stops. The ground returns, the wind stops, and I'm stood exactly as I was before. But as I blink and the world around me comes back into view, it's clear I'm not where I was before at all.

Evan and I are stood in a large white-tiled room, half of which is set behind a large glass screen. Beside us is a chair of some sort, with open straps across it to bind whoever the unlucky occupant is. Above us, jutting out of the ceiling, is a strange metal contraption, brass coloured, made of intricate sets of gears with a set of hooked, wand-like prongs poking down towards the chair. It descends on the other side of the glass wall too.

"It worked," Evan mutters, dropping my hand and taking in the room around us. "It actually worked."

I think back to what Evan told me about Tamara's memories.

"Is this . . . ?" I start.

"The room where they force witches to lose their magic?" Evan finishes with a bitterness coating every word. "Yes."

I stare up at the machine, horrified. I can't even begin to imagine what it must be like to be strapped to that chair, having such a huge part of you torn away before your eyes, completely unable to stop it from happening. All for the simple crime of being yourself. How many witches have had to suffer through this?

"Hey," Evan says, placing a gentle hand on my shoulder. "Are you okay?"

I grit my teeth and turn away from the machine. "Sorry, it's just . . ." I can't even finish my sentence, but Evan's sad smile tells me I don't need to.

"We need to move," he says. "But I'll cast the cloaking spell first."

I nod and watch as he performs the same movements he did in the living room of the dead man's house, though this time with more care. That feels like a lifetime ago now.

"Okay," he says when he's finished. "That should do it. Let's go."

The corridor outside continues the white tile theme, stretching out beyond us and curving to a point I can't see beyond. There's something haunting about the gleam of the tiles in the electric light that fills this place. Perhaps it's the purity of it all, the sheer notion of coating a place where diabolical acts are regularly carried out in pristine white surfaces. To the witchfinders, I'm sure it hides the sadistic nature of this place, but to me, it only makes it more visible.

Evan and I move slowly, and I can't help but be reminded of home. I'm used to living in a space like this, where there seems to be nothing but endless corridors, but the comforts of home are completely absent here. Where the Halls of Styx felt tranquil, this place is clinical. There was always a sense of safety in the dim, ethereal lighting of the Halls, like you could blend into the surfaces, becoming one with the space. Here, I am exposed.

There's an eerie silence surrounding us, which could serve as comfort were it not for the fact that the slightest noise from us would easily echo far and wide. There are cameras poking out from the tops of the walls, but Evan doesn't seem worried about those. As long as his cloaking spell holds, we should be fine. At least, that's what I'm telling myself.

We reach a door with a plaque reading *Essence Storage*. Evan raises an eyebrow at me, and I shrug. He tries the door's handle, but it's locked, so instead, he casts an unlocking spell. There's a click, and Evan opens the door effortlessly. Inside, there are shelves upon shelves of jars, each coated in a brass-coloured mesh and containing a dully glowing golden mist. The room is vast and bitingly cold, with the shelves reaching all the way up to the ceiling. There must be hundreds – no, *thousands* of these things.

"What are they?" I whisper, and even my soft words carry across the space in front of us, bouncing along the shelves.

Evan's eyes are wide, and his lips are quivering. "I think . . . I think . . ."

I step closer to him.

"This is the magic of all the witches who have been converted," he says, voice thick with grief.

Evan reaches out toward the nearest jar, placing the tip of his finger on the mesh coating. At his touch, the mist inside glows brighter and swirls with sudden energy. He pulls his hand back, clutching at it as though he's been given an electric shock. The mist returns to the slow, dim state it was in before.

"Evan?"

"I could feel it. Like it was flowing into me." He looks up at the jars, scanning them all. "That mesh on the jars . . . it's the same material as the machine in the conversion room. The same material as the wands and the artefacts. It conducts magic."

"Right."

"Don't you see?" Evan's eyes are frantic, and his whispers are getting worryingly close to the volume of ordinary speech. "That must be how she did it."

"How who did what?"

"Lily."

And then it clicks. We know Lily had the artefact capable of holding open the door to the afterlife, and now we know how she used it. She wouldn't have needed any magic of her own because she had access to the jars.

"She used another witch's magic," I say, disgusted at the idea but knowing it must be true. "Magic that she stole."

"Magic that she claims is an abomination." I can hear the rage in Evan's voice, that same fury that fuelled his recklessness in the train station.

I take his hand, hoping to calm him.

"So let's defeat her," I say. "Let's find the keys and end this."

Evan hesitates, glaring at the jars. I know what he must be thinking. Somewhere on these shelves, unmarked and impossible to identify amongst the rest, is his grandmother's magic. Bottled and caged, filed away in the darkness. The very essence of the person he loved most in the world.

He clenches his jaw and turns away, leading me out of the room. On to whatever comes next.

We pass interrogation rooms and research labs as we continue down the curved corridor. At one point, it branches off in two directions, and I get the uneasy sense that we're completely unprepared. If I were home, I'd be navigating these corridors with ease. But this space is the creation of hateful humans, not gods and angels.

I share a glance with Evan, who shrugs before opting for the left-hand path. Barely a second passes after I step forwards, however, before Evan yanks me backwards and pins me against the wall. I bite back a yelp as I realise what's happening.

A man in a crisp black suit emblazoned with the witchfinder crest is walking towards us from the other direction. His hands are clasped behind his back, and he walks with the air of someone who believes they own everything around them. But he doesn't react to our presence. In fact, he doesn't seem to notice us at all. I can feel Evan trying to keep his breathing steady as we both remain completely still against the wall. The man's footsteps ricochet off our tiled surroundings, each one filling me with dread, but he soon passes us and leaves our sight completely.

"That was close," Evan whispers. "Let's be more careful."

I nod, not wanting to make any unnecessary noise, and take Evan's hand as we continue left.

We soon reach a set of stairs which descend in a curve, continuing the shape of the corridor. It's like we're caught in a tightly woven ball of thread and are getting closer to its centre. There's a nagging sense in the back of my mind that the further we move, the harder it's going to be to get back, but what else are we supposed to do? We've come this far.

I start us down the stairs, holding my breath a little more with each one, until I exhale at the bottom. Yet another corridor stretches out before us, with doors to more rooms scattered along it. There are more research labs, a couple of meeting rooms and one labelled *Witch Records*. But our target is up ahead. A sign is built into the wall at the top of another staircase, with an arrow pointing down. The caption reads *Artefact Storage*.

"I hope you're right about this," I say, too nervous to face Evan. I can feel the sweat on the palm of his hand.

"The keys will be there."

We descend once again and come to a much shorter corridor at the bottom. This one doesn't have the chance to curve before it ends in a pair of double doors. Evan unlocks them faster than either of the previous rooms, and we enter into another space filled with shelves. There aren't quite as many here, though, and the shelves don't reach all the way to the ceiling. Nor is this room as large, which comes as a relief. It'd take us days to find the keys in a room as big as the Essence Storage.

The shelves are filled with brass-coloured items of various shapes. Each is a palm-sized box, but the number of sides changes. Most are triangular or square, but there are some pentagons as well. Also, unlike the jars, each artefact displayed on these shelves is accompanied by a label. I step towards the nearest one and read, *Allows the user to levitate for a period of ten minutes.*

"I know this one," Evan says. He's a few rows away, holding up one of the triangular artefacts. "I saw it in Tamara's memory. It severs the connection between spirit and body."

"You mean . . ."

He nods, placing it back down and wiping his hands on his trousers. "It can kill people."

I shiver at the thought. I suppose such magic is the reason necromancers aren't viewed very favourably.

"You take that half, I'll take this?" Evan suggests, pointing at the two ends of the room.

I nod and start my way down the aisles, skim-reading each label I come across. There are artefacts capable of paralysing people, razing buildings to the ground, and causing huge explosions. But equally, there are ones capable of sustaining a person through hunger and thirst, healing severe wounds, and ensuring the safety of a person in labour. Magic, like humans, is capable of both good and bad.

"Any sign of the keys?" Evan calls in an elevated whisper.

"Not yet."

"I've found the teleportation artefact."

Before I can respond, a thud echoes through the room. The sound of the door closing. My eyes dart to the source, and my heart drops.

"What a shame you won't get to use it," says the figure now standing at the doorway. Lily Morgan, alone, holding a square artefact in one hand and a jar in the other. Her face twists into a sickening grin as she places the jar against the artefact's base. The mist glows bright, the artefact whirrs to life, and within seconds, the world goes black.

Chapter Twenty-Six
Evan

"You're lucky, really," says a voice.

My head is reeling, and my vision is blurry as I blink my eyes open. I try to move my arms, but I can't. Something is keeping them bound. My legs, too. Adrenaline rushes through me, and my vision clears, revealing an all-too-familiar machine above me.

"No," I say, voice weak. "No!"

"The conversion team don't do night shifts," the voice continues. "Still, they'll be here in a few hours."

I strain to bend my head towards the voice, though I already know who it is. I manage to make part of her face out across the room, along with her blonde hair.

"Let me go!"

Lily tuts and moves close enough that I can see her full face, along with the wand she's passing between her hands. My wand. "Now, you know full well I can't do that. After all, you've broken multiple laws in the past couple of days, haven't you?"

I spit in her face, briefly dispelling the authoritative façade she's given herself. She looks almost scared as she wipes herself clean.

"You're more guilty than any witch," I say. "I know what you've done."

She composes herself and smirks. "Was that a cloaking spell you were attempting earlier? It's effective enough when you're focused, I suppose, but I can't say I'm impressed. You really ought to have improved when my men saw through it."

"Your men?"

"I believe you met them on the train, though they spotted you a day earlier, running from a house you had no business being in."

The dead man's house. Of course they saw us. The straps holding me down feel tighter than ever as I realise how stupid I've been. I should never have assumed my spell worked.

I grit my teeth. "Why didn't they stop us then?"

Lily laughs. "You were hardly a threat, but as soon as they told me a pair of teenage boys had been snooping around that house, I made sure eyes were being kept on local points of interest. Once you blundered your way into that Manchester witch's house, I asked them to apprehend you."

"Her name is Tamara."

Lily shrugs, but I think there's an act to it. I don't believe for one second that she doesn't remember Tamara's name. She's put far too much work into this. She's thought it all through, meticulously. And now she has me trapped.

No, not just me.

"Where's Orpheus?" I ask, stomach churning with worry.

"Is that his name? Interesting. Well, he won't be coming to save you like he did on that train, if that's what you're hoping."

"Where is he?"

She regards me with her practiced expression. It's like she's wearing her own mother's face as a mask. She wants to be the hateful woman who commands the witchfinders with an iron fist, but I know she's nothing more than a fraud.

"Elsewhere," she says. "I have far more use for him than I do you."

"And yet here you are, taunting me. Is this what you do to every witch who ends up here? You try to make them feel weak because you know they're stronger than you could ever be?"

She scowls, the façade dropping again.

"It's true, isn't it?" I say, my words driven by the venom that built up at the sight of the jars. "Your mum's driven by hatred, but you? You're driven by jealousy. You see the power that witches have, and you want it for yourself."

I grip the surface of the chair, wondering if it's the exact same one Gran was forced into. I can feel her now, watching me, guiding me. Her magic may be trapped in this place, but her memory is always in my mind.

"I've always hated your mum," I say to Lily, "but at least she makes sense. Bigots like her have always existed, hating what they can't understand, destroying anything that's different from them. But then there's you, her pathetic hypocrite of a daughter. I bet she thinks you're worthless."

Lily's face turns red. "My mother loves me," she says, spitting her words. "She raised me alone, and everything I have done has been for her."

A memory stirs. The home of the man whose death opened the door that remains unlocked. The photo of him with Eloise and a child. A little girl.

"And what about your father?"

Lily looks lost for words.

"He saw through you, didn't he? He knew about the monsters you and your mother were. That's why you killed him."

With my wand still in one hand, she raises the other and slaps me across the face. It stings like hell, but I don't let her break me. I don't let her see the pain. She doesn't deserve the satisfaction. I listen, eyes closed, as she leaves the room, heels clicking with every step. It's only once I hear the door close that I let myself cry.

How could I be so stupid as to think this plan would actually work? To think Orpheus and I could just waltz in here, find the keys and teleport away without issue? Now here I am, trapped beneath a machine that can take away my magic, with no idea where Orpheus is. Lily said she has use for him. What did she mean by that? She must know what he is after her lackeys saw him transform on the train, but how could he be useful to her?

I try to twist myself free from the restraints, but with every movement, the straps dig deeper into me. There's no escaping this, not when so many witches have come before me. No one has ever escaped this fate once bound to it.

I have to hold on to hope, though. Orpheus and I may have come here alone, but Mary's coven know the truth about Lily. They'll be spreading the word right at this moment. The world is desperate for an answer about the immortality; they won't ignore one when it presents itself.

I close my eyes and picture Gran. The witchfinders took her happiness, her soul. They killed her. I won't let that be in vain. I will avenge her, even if it kills me.

Chapter Twenty-Seven
Orpheus

When I wake, I find myself in another white-tiled room, much smaller than any of the others. I'm sat in a chair in the corner, hands tied behind my back and legs tied to those of the chair. And I'm not alone. In the centre of the room is a bed with a single occupant: a frail-looking old woman who I recognise from news footage, even if she's far gaunter than in any of those images. It's Eloise Morgan, unconscious and hooked up to all sorts of machinery, including a steadily pulsing heart monitor. It's a familiar sight, one I've seen through many doors in the Halls of Styx.

There's a click, and the door to the room swings open. Lily walks in, face flushed, and looks at me.

"You're awake," she says. "Good."

"Where is Evan?"

She locks the door behind her, saying nothing, and I notice a wand in her hand. I get a dreadful feeling that it's Evan's.

"If you've hurt him, I'll—"

"You'll what?" she says, seemingly surprised by her own volume. She tucks the wand into the inside pocket of her blazer, where it clinks against something metallic. Then she runs a hand through her hair, taking a moment to compose herself.

"Where is he?" I ask again.

"He's alive." She pauses, taking a moment to look at her mother. "And safe. And he will remain that way provided you do as I ask."

I can tell her words are supposed to be intimidating, but there's a lilt of panic to them that prevents that from happening. I watch, curious, as she digs her nails into her palms. She may hold the power here, but it seems she's hanging onto it by a thread. I need to be careful. If she needs me to do something, then I can leverage that for information.

"And what exactly are you asking of me?"

She bites her lip, smooths the creases from her skirt, then faces me. "My mother is ill. Terminally so."

"I gathered."

Her face hardens.

"That's why you stole the keys, isn't it? To keep her alive."

"Evidently."

"How did you do it?"

She raises an eyebrow. "I know you and your friend met that witch in Manchester. No doubt you extracted information from her. You already know how I did it."

"We know you used the artefact, yes, but you must have known what you'd find on the other side of the door. You must have known the keys existed. You must have known about my mother. How?"

Her uncertainty transforms into a curious smile. "Mother? Now, that's interesting."

I silently scorn myself. So much for being careful.

"I did wonder who you were. I assumed you were just some angel servant sent to fetch the keys. But you're the son of Death herself? Fascinating. My research never mentioned a child."

"It can't have been very detailed research, then."

Lily chuckles. "On the contrary. Like you say, I did know about the keys, which is a great deal more than most witches know. There are a few necromancers here and there who understand a little, but the afterlife is mostly a mystery."

"So how did you find out?"

She considers me carefully, and I can see something sparkling in her eyes that I didn't expect: excitement. She is genuinely fascinated by my identity and proud of how much she knows, and therefore, she's eager to brag.

"The notebooks of a warlock who went missing nearly two decades ago," she says. "He was deeply interested in necromancy and even crafted a few artefacts, but he was especially enamoured with details of the afterlife."

My heart races as I realise who she's talking about. The man who built the artefact that could hold open the door to the Halls of Styx. The man who travelled through such a door and was never seen in the mortal world again. My father.

I can't help but recognise a part of myself in him through Lily's description. His notebooks were like my diaries. He was as obsessed with the afterlife as I am with the mortal world. An obsession that meant everything to him. A special interest.

"Thanks to him, I knew what I'd find on the other side of the door," Lily continues. "I had a second artefact that causes confusion and used it to distract your mother while I took the keys from her."

"And so you made the entire human race immortal, just to keep your mother alive." I look over at the frail, unconscious Eloise. "It doesn't look like it helped much."

Lily's face falls. "She's alive," she says, "but her illness hasn't stopped spreading. It's been over a day since she was last awake, but she was suffering for a long time before that."

I almost pity her. "What did you think would happen? She's supposed to be dead. You can't just undo that."

"Maybe not." She fixes me with an intense look that I can't quite fathom. There's a desperation in her eyes that I never expected to see. "But you can."

"What?"

"I have tried everything. I put her through every available treatment. I used every healing artefact. I made her *immortal*." She walks over to her mother and places a hand on her forehead. "But still, this is all I get."

"Science and magic can only do so much."

"Which is why I need you."

I stare blankly at her.

"You're an angel," she says. "You're from a world beyond science and magic. You must be able to heal her."

"Lily, I . . ."

"You're the son of Death, for God's sake." She storms over to me, eyes wild. "I know you can save her."

There is nothing I can do to save Eloise. Her life has come to its natural end, but her daughter has kept her alive beyond that. Her illness has continued to act beyond the point that should kill her, and now her very existence goes against every natural law. Not even an angel can heal that. But I know that to say no to Lily right now is the most dangerous thing I could possibly do.

"Tell me where Evan is, first," I say.

"You're in no position to bargain."

"I need proof that he's safe."

Lily glares at me, beads of sweat forming on her forehead. She turns to a computer screen on a table beside her mother's bed, taps on the keyboard and makes a few clicks with the mouse, then turns the screen to my field of view. It's across the room, but even from here, I can make out the image of Evan strapped to the chair in the conversion room.

"Save my mother, or your friend will have his magic taken away."

The sight makes me want to throw up.

"Okay," I say without hesitation. "I'll save her."

It's a relief to be free from the chair. I stand at the side of Eloise's bed, across from Lily. I move my hands over Eloise, mimicking the thread-gathering motions I've seen Evan perform.

"She's very weak," I say, pretending that I've somehow gleaned this information through angelic power.

"I'm aware." Lily views me through narrow eyes. She's suspicious, and right to be so given that I'm lying to her face. In her hands, she's holding the jar and artefact that she used before, ready to knock me out again if I try any funny business.

I have a plan. Well, half of a plan. Maybe less. If I shift into my angel form, I should be able to escape, but I only have seconds left to safely be in that form without completely falling apart. If I'm to risk that, I need to know where Mother's keys are first.

"To save her, I'm going to need a connection to the afterlife," I say.

"What do you mean?"

"Your mother's spirit is drifting between worlds. To tether her here completely, I'll need to draw power from an object from my mother's world. Like her keys." I keep my voice as flat as I can. If she sees through my lies, I don't know what I'll do.

Lily smirks. "Do you take me for a fool?"

"No."

"You think I'm just going to hand you the one thing you came here to find?"

I grit my teeth. This isn't going to work. Maybe it would be better to just transform and get back to Evan. We can escape this place and come up with a whole new plan.

Unless . . .

"Well, at the very least, I need a wand," I say instead.

"You're not a warlock."

"That doesn't mean I can't use their tools."

I can feel the cogs turning in Lily's mind as she glares at me. "Very well," she says, holding the jar awkwardly in the crook of her elbow while she reaches into her pocket and withdraws Evan's wand. And there's that sound again. The sound of clinking metal I heard earlier. Almost like a set of keys . . .

And I realise Lily would never keep such an important object anywhere other than on her person.

I hide a smile as Lily passes me the wand. "Thank you," I say, holding it over Eloise. "I'll begin." I start moving my hand and the wand in mock-witch fashion.

A phone starts ringing, painfully loud in this small room. Lily keeps staring through her narrow eyes, not yet moving to answer. She steps back slightly and positions herself near the desk with the computer on it. There, she sets down the jar, never once breaking eye contact, and uses her now-free hand to pull her phone from one of her outer pockets.

"Hello?" she says, holding the phone to her ear.

We're close enough that I can just about make out some of the words on the other end of the call.

"Online . . . everyone . . . saying that you . . ."

Lily's eyes widen with every word, and I realise what's happening. The coven have done as they promised. The truth is spreading.

Lily glares at me. "What have you—"

But I don't let her finish.

I tear the anchor from my neck and leap forward as the room fills with light and my wings sprout from my back. I collide with Lily, sending her to the floor, phone and artefact flying out of her hands and colliding with the walls. Lily falls unconscious as her head hits the ground, and I'm free to delve into the inner pocket of her blazer.

And I feel it: the ring of keys. The moment my fingers connect with the metal, I know I'm touching something from home. My other hand remains clasped around the wand, which feels like home too. A different sort of home. One that's new. One with Evan in it.

I rise up, lifting the keys and wand with me, and fly full speed at the door, sending it careening off its hinges along with chunks of the wall. I continue down the corridor, quickly orienting myself from the doors I recognise, and already feeling myself grow weaker. I have moments. Seconds.

But there's the door to the conversion room. I tear through it and feel my heart soar at the sight of Evan. He's strapped to the chair, but he's alive and unharmed.

"Orpheus!" he calls, straining his neck to see me.

"Evan," I move forward but fall to the floor, my wings useless already and my vision blurring. But I need to reach him. I need to free him.

"Orpheus!"

"It's okay," I say through slurred speech as I use the last of my energy to throw his wand towards him. I hope to all the gods that it is enough to keep him safe, even if it's too late for me.

The very last thing I see is the wand land in Evan's hand.

Chapter Twenty-Eight
Evan

"No!" I scream.

Orpheus' eyes fall closed, and dark rivulets spread rapidly across his skin. I watch as the cracks meet, and small fragments of his flesh begin to float away in ever-smaller pieces. He is turning to dust in front of me.

I grip my wand tightly, summoning the threads into view. They're almost impossible to make out through my tears, but multiple glow and vibrate as I focus on escape. With my hands bound, I can't reach them like I usually would. Still, I manoeuvre my wand the best I can, catching the threads with its hook. But it's not good enough. I can't form rows of stitches like this. I can't cast any spells at all.

"No!" I scream again. I call on all the power I have inside me. Every ounce of magical energy. Everything that makes me who I am and who the witchfinders despise. I grip my wand more tightly than ever before, forcing my power into its metal surface, forcing it out into the few threads caught by the hook. Begging for something. Anything.

I flinch as the room fills with white light. My arm seizes as though a bolt of electricity is flooding through it, and then it dissipates as quickly as it began. But my arm feels looser somehow. I look down and see that the strap that was fastened around my arm has fallen away, melted in half, leaving a sore pink burn across my wrist.

There's no time to stop and think about how I did that; I just use my newly free arm to tear open the strap on my opposite arm, along with the rest. I stumble off the chair, straight towards Orpheus, who is barely still here. I can't make out any of his features anymore. He has become a husk. The shape of his body remains, but there is no face, no wings, no clothes or skin or bones. Just a mound of dust, barely holding its shape.

A ring of keys lies on the floor where his hand once was, and beside that is the anchor. I grab this without hesitation and place it over what remains of Orpheus' neck.

"Please don't be gone," I say, though it comes out as barely more than a sob. "Please."

The anchor glows, which means it has to be doing something. Orpheus isn't gone. Not yet. Not as long as the anchor does its job. I won't even let myself consider the possibility that it's too late. Orpheus will not die for me. I won't let him. But if it took hours for him to return to me last time he began to fall apart, how long will it take this time?

I glare at the open door to the room. We need the teleportation artefact, but Orpheus is in no state to move right now. I'm going to have to get it myself.

"I'll be back," I whisper, knowing there's almost no chance Orpheus can hear me.

I leave the room, casting a locking spell on the door behind me. I can't risk anyone else finding Orpheus and removing the anchor. It's then that a blaring alarm fills the air, and I remember the cameras. I look up at the top of the nearest wall, right into the lens of a security camera. There's no cloaking spell covering me now.

I run full speed down the corridor, retracing the path Orpheus and I took God knows how much time ago. The alarm follows me as I move, summoning whichever workers are currently in the building. I pass a room whose door has been torn off its hinges, with shattered tiles strewn across the floor outside, but I don't have time to look in. I have only one destination: Artefact Storage.

At the top of the staircase, I see the man who walked past us earlier, but he barely has time to register me before I pass him at full speed. He pulls a walkie-talkie from his belt, however, so I know he's calling for reinforcements. I dread to think what that could mean. The witchfinders can't all be smarmy people in suits. Their security team could have guns for all I know.

The Artefact Storage doors are still unlocked, so I barrel my way in and head for the teleportation artefact on one of the rear shelves. But then I stop, because this is a room filled with powerful artefacts that could let me do all sorts of complex spells. When else will I have an opportunity like this? When else could I have access to this kind of magic? But no, there's no time. I can't browse these shelves like I'm shopping.

I can, however, grab one extra artefact along with the pentagonal teleportation box.

Beyond the door, I hear the shouts of people coming closer. The witchfinders, ready to put a stop to me right before I escape with the keys.

I pocket a triangular artefact and hold the teleportation one in my hands, summoning the spark of magic within me and picturing my destination. The artefact whirrs to life, metal prongs rising from each corner and weaving around each other to rapidly create rows of stitches in the threads. There's a lurch, a bright light, and I feel the ground give way beneath me.

It's smoother than before, when Mary's coven cast the spell, thanks to the expertise that went into crafting the artefact but also because the distance travelled isn't anywhere near as far. As the world comes back into focus, I find myself stood at the door to the Essence Storage room. The noise of the witchfinders is more distant now, though the alarm still blares. They'll all have run to Artefact Storage. I smirk, knowing I've got the better of them, and push open the door in front of me.

A rush of grief spreads through my chest as I stare at the shelves of magical essences. Thousands of jars containing the stolen magic of witches who were punished simply for staying true to who they were. A punishment no one should have to suffer. I will not leave this place while these fragments of witches' souls remain held in captivity.

I pull the extra artefact from my pocket, pointing it into the room, and channel my magic through it. But it's more than just that. I channel every ounce of shame I've ever felt in my life. I channel all the anger I've ever harboured towards my father. I channel the pain and grief I felt after Gran's conversion and death. I channel it all.

The metal warms as magic flows, and the mechanism whirrs into action. Its prongs stitch together threads in a more complicated pattern than I could ever hope to create. And then, with another pulse of my power, it sends a shockwave out into the room before me.

The label that was beneath this artefact when I saw it downstairs had only one word on it: destruction.

In an instant, every shelf collapses, and each jar shatters. The brass mesh keeping the magic contained crumbles to dust, and what was a dim golden mist glows brighter than ever before. I watch as the magical essences rise up, free from their cages, and vanish through the ceiling, Gran's somewhere amongst them. I don't know where they'll go now. Maybe I'll never know. But wherever it is, I hope it's far from here.

I would love to bask in this moment, but I know I can't, so I grip the teleportation artefact again and think of Orpheus.

Chapter Twenty-Nine
Orpheus

"Back so soon?" Charon leans against his wooden pole, causing its tip to sink slightly into the earth, piercing the grass and exposing the dirt beneath. This realm has changed since I was last here. While Charon and I still stand on a patch of green, the smoke that was in the far distance now surrounds us, billowing from angry flames that attack the infinite grass.

We're running out of time.

I shake my head. I've got no patience for Charon's games. "Is he safe?"

"Who?"

"Evan."

He studies me with ancient curiosity. "I'm not sure why you think I would know. Echoes are all I receive here; you know that."

I recall the last image I saw. Evan had his wand. That'll be enough to save him. It has to be. Evan will escape, and he'll deliver the keys to my mother. The world will be saved, and I will be gone. But at least Evan will be okay.

I turn my gaze to the sky, where Charon said beings float in their last moments of existence.

"Is it my time?" I ask. I thought I'd be sad in the end, but I feel strangely empty. Like the emotions I should be feeling are just too much, so my mind has opted for the absence of feeling instead.

Charon laughs, which is bizarre to hear from him. It sounds unnatural, almost eerie. I'm never quite sure whether I should be scared of him. I watch as he sweeps his pole across the space between us, creating ripples in the air just as he did the last time I was here. But this time, the ripples are far more aggressive, and they cascade over a seemingly infinite distance, blowing back the smoke and reducing the intensity of the flames. Voices fill the air, too, all combining into an indecipherable sea of noise.

Then something new arrives. Forming amongst the ripples is a layer of golden mist. It fills my vision, giving everything around me a golden hue.

"What is this?" I ask.

Charon doesn't reply, but he does bare his teeth in a wide, animalistic smile. He raises up his hands, holding the wooden pole aloft, and the golden mist comes together, conglomerating around him and sinking into his flesh (if you can call the body of an angel flesh).

The ripples vanish, and Charon stares at me, eyes now a glistening gold.

"No," he says. "It is not your time."

He steps forwards, throws the wooden pole to the ground beside him, and shoves me with both hands, sending me falling to the ground as well.

Chapter Thirty
Evan

Orpheus sits bolt upright, body fully restored to its human form once more. He gasps for breath, fingers grasping the ring of keys I left beside him, and looks up at me while I stand at the open door.

"Evan?" he sputters. "What happened?"

I run to him and scoop him into a hug, pulling him to his feet. "You're okay! Oh, thank God, you're okay!" It seems impossible for him to have healed so quickly, but then who am I to question the power of angels?

He hugs me back, despite the clear weakness in his body. "What's that alarm?"

I feel so overwhelmed I could cry. "We need to go," I say, releasing him and holding the teleportation artefact between us. I beam at him. Despite everything, we've succeeded.

There's a groan from the door, and I turn to witness a sight I hoped never to see again.

Lily Morgan stumbles into the room, barely able to stand. Her hair is stained with blood, and she looks at us with a hatred more palpable than I've ever seen from anyone before. In one hand, she holds the same jar she held earlier. The only one left. With the other, she holds an artefact that I wish I didn't recognise, but even from this distance, the carved image of a knife is clear.

I grab hold of Orpheus and begin sending my magic into the teleportation artefact, picturing the house where all of this began. Where Lily killed her father and held open the door to the afterlife.

Outside the room, frantic-looking witchfinders gather behind Lily. They watch in confused horror as she presses the jar to her artefact. Before the teleportation takes hold, a wave of energy moves through the air, colliding with me. My breath catches as I feel the connection between my body and spirit sever.

Chapter Thirty-One
Orpheus

"Evan!" I scream as the wind howls around us.

He's pressed against me, but I'm blinded by white light, and his grip no longer feels as safe as it used to. But we're escaping. We're teleporting away from the witchfinders, and both of us are here. We made it out. Whatever Lily just did didn't work. It can't have. Can it?

When the ground returns beneath me, Evan finally comes into focus. We're in the middle of a field. The air around is cold and crisp, and the only light comes from the moon high above. Evan's eyes reflect the silver glow as he blinks up at me.

"You're okay," I say, relief flooding my chest, but it doesn't last long.

"No," Evan says. His voice sounds hollow. "She killed me."

"But you're still..." And then I stop, because understanding comes crashing down around me. And it's like everything we've done has been for nothing. Evan is alive because the immortality still holds. As soon as I return the keys to my mother, he'll be dead.

I shake my head, refusing to believe that it's true but knowing deep down that it is.

"There must be a spell or something . . ." I start.

"There isn't." Evan's voice sounds hollow. "Re-connecting a spirit to its body is resurrection. That's never been done before. I'm only still here because no one can die right now."

"No." No. I refuse. Evan is not going to die. Not after everything. He can't. I won't let him.

"Orpheus," he says, bringing a hand to the side of my face. His soft skin caresses my cheek, warm despite the bitter cold. Despite his dwindling life. "I'm sorry. If I hadn't wasted time back there, then I—"

"You're not dying." I stand up and pull him to his feet. "You're forgetting who my mother is."

"But—"

"No, Evan. If anyone gets to decide who lives and who dies, it's Death herself. I wouldn't have found the keys without you. She owes you a debt."

There's no hope in Evan's eyes, but that's okay. He doesn't need it. I have enough for the both of us, and I know this will work. Mother will listen to me. She has to. I've done everything she asked.

I look around the vast field. "Where are we?"

Evan hesitates, his face clouded by doubt as he studies me. He sighs and looks over my shoulder. "My focus dropped when Lily attacked, but we can't be too far from the house." He points. "There are buildings over there."

"Let's check them out." I grasp Evan's hand tightly. "It's going to be okay; I promise."

The houses are similar to those around Lily's father's, but according to Evan, this isn't the same village. We're about a half-hour walk away from where we need to be. I'm still weak, but I should be able to manage it. I'm more concerned about Evan, even though he assures me there are no physical effects from what Lily did to him. Not until Mother has her keys again, that is.

Before we leave the village, Evan pauses at the sight of a phone box.

"What's wrong?" I ask.

"I know you said your mum can save me . . . but if she can't—"

"She can."

"But *if* she can't . . ." Evan has his hand to my chest, right above my heart. His eyes still sparkle in the moonlight. "I want to be able to say goodbye to Wren." He glances back at the phone box. "I'm going to call them and ask them to meet us at the house. Okay?"

I want to tell him there's no need. That saying goodbye would be pointless because he's not going anywhere. But I can hear in his voice how much he wants to do this, and even though he frames it as a question, I know it would be cruel to say no.

"Okay."

He smiles and walks over to the phone box, where he casts a spell to activate it without needing money. I'm reminded of the train ticket machine, though where that spell was cast out of anger, this one is out of sorrow.

"Hey, Wren," Evan says. "Yeah, I know it's early. Listen, I need you to meet me at 25 Woodwalk Street, Blackwell Hill. Yes, now. I know it's a weird request. I'll explain when you get there; just . . ." His voice cracks, and I have to turn away. No matter how upset he gets, I can't let myself feel that way too. I'm going to save him. "Please do this for me. Thank you."

He hangs up the phone and takes a moment before stepping out.

"The village is this way," he says, voice tinged with fake confidence.

As we walk along the road, I think back on my first morning in this world. I had no idea then that I was about to meet a boy I'd be willing to break the rules of mortality for. But now

I walk with him. All those diary entries about family, friends, partners, and spouses make a little more sense now than they did when I first wrote them. I think, perhaps, that love never really makes sense until you experience it. And I do love Evan. That much is clear to me.

It wasn't the keys or the fate of the world that mattered most to me when I was confronting Lily. It was Evan. Only Evan. And I would rather drift through Charon's realm into non-existence than let any harm come to him.

"What do you think will happen to the witchfinders?" Evan asks, staring ahead into the darkness.

"I don't know."

"The ones who came down because of the alarm . . . they saw Lily using magic."

I wouldn't know. I was busy watching Evan when the blast of energy hit him.

"She could lie about it, I suppose, but everyone will know the truth soon."

"They will," I agree. "Lily got a call when she was with me. The news has already started to spread."

"That's good." His voice is still hollow.

I picture Mother walking Evan through the Halls of Styx on his final journey. I imagine filling a diary with the story of his life. His hateful father, his loving grandmother, his best friend, his dream of a world where magic isn't so hated. It's an image I'd gladly accept were Evan old and at peace, ready to move on to whatever comes next. He deserves a long and happy life.

"Are you going to tell Wren what happened?" I ask.

Evan nods. "I think it's about time they know the truth about me. Even if they're angry that I've lied."

"They won't be angry. They'll understand."

Evan smiles sadly. "I hope so."

I wrap an arm around Evan's shoulders. It makes walking more difficult, but it feels like the right thing to do. It's something that feels so beautifully human: to find comfort in the physical touch of another. It's a reminder that you're not alone. That all you have to do is reach out, and there'll be someone there. A shoulder to cry on. A hand to hold. And through that contact, you know that the other person is alive.

"Will you take me on a date when all this is done?" I ask.

"A date?"

"That's what people do, isn't it? When they're . . . romantically involved."

Evan laughs, and it's the most beautiful sound in the world.

"Where would you want to go?" he asks.

I squeeze him, knowing that if he's indulging this fantasy, then he must have hope. Even if it's the tiniest fragment.

"The ocean," I reply. "I've always wanted to see it properly. I've caught glimpses through the doors, but it's not the same as properly being there."

"Well then, I'll take you to the seaside. We'll stroll on the beach and eat fish and chips and dodge seagull attacks."

"Do you promise?"

"What?" He slows to a stop, and I face him. Doubt is creeping into his eyes again.

"Once all this is over, do you promise to take me there?"

He thinks it over but nods. "Yes."

I return my arm to his shoulder and move us both along. "See? You've made a promise now. There'll be no dying for you today."

It's weaker than before, but he laughs again. It's cut short, however, when he spots something up ahead. "There it is," he says.

I look out and see the dim lights of the village of Blackwell Hill. The place where all of this began. I will not let it be where it ends.

Lily's father's house is just as silent as it was when I first entered it, and the darkness feels almost alive. Even when Evan switches the lights on, darkness remains in the nooks and crannies. It's as though a permanent haze seeps out of every surface. The shelves have been cleared of the trinkets and photographs that once adorned them. All that remains is the sad-looking sofas.

"Is it still there?" Evan asks when we enter the living room.

"Yes," I say, staring at the translucent green door that still stands in the room. All it will take is one turn of the handle and a step forward, and I'll be back home. Mother will be there, ready to receive the keys and bring death back to the mortal world.

There's a knock at the house's front door.

"That'll be Wren," Evan says, glancing over his shoulder. He moves but then pauses, turning back to me. "Do you really think you can convince your mum?" There's still no hope in his eyes.

"Yes," I say. And even though I believe what I'm saying, the sorrow surrounding Evan makes me step forward and kiss him.

When I move my face back, I feel Evan's tears lingering on my cheeks.

"That wasn't a goodbye," I say, both hands on his shoulders. "That was a promise."

Evan sniffs and forces a smile.

"Go and speak to Wren. I'll talk to my mother." I pull the keys from my pocket. "And I won't let her have these until she promises to save you. Okay?"

Evan wipes away his tears. "Okay."

With a final nod, I turn to face the translucent door once again. I reach out, grasp the handle, and open it.

Chapter Thirty-Two
Evan

I make sure my tears are completely gone before answering the door, but as soon as I see Wren's comically puzzled face, the floodgates open. I pull them into a tight hug and sob into their shoulder. I'm sure a million questions are flooding their mind right now, but instead of asking any of them, they just hug me back.

I feel like a pot of water that's been on the cusp of boiling for three days. And here's Wren – someone from the normal world, a world without witches and psychopomps and angels and gytrashes – tipping me over the edge with their mere presence.

When my breathing steadies and the tears aren't so visceral, I slowly let go of Wren and step back to face them properly.

"Well," they say, "I was going to ask why we're at this random house, but I think maybe you've got something bigger to tell me."

I laugh, and for a moment, it feels like an ordinary day. But then I feel the distant dizziness that's been present ever since Lily used that artefact on me, and I remember I'm on the cusp of death.

I take a deep breath. "You'd better come inside."

It feels wrong to be sitting on sofas that belong to someone who so recently died, but I figure since I'm now essentially an animated corpse, I've earned the right to ignore social customs. Wren sits beside me, the picture of concern. I glance over at the empty space where I know a door to the afterlife exists. Where just moments ago, Orpheus stepped out of this world and into his own.

"You're right," I say. "I do have something big to tell you." I look into Wren's eyes. "Quite a few things, in fact, so maybe . . . just let me get them all out? You're going to have a lot to say, and believe me, I'm ready to hear it all, but can you let me tell you everything first?"

Wren fidgets with their fingers. "Evan, you're kind of scaring me."

"I know, I know." I take a deep breath. "The thing is . . . I'm a warlock."

Wren's fingers freeze.

"I know that out of everyone in the world, you'd be the safest person to tell that to, but I never did because my Gran made me promise to keep it a secret."

Their eyes widen, and I find myself unable to look straight at them.

"She was a witch, too, you see, and she . . . well, she got converted. Because my dad forced her to. Because he's a witchfinder."

It's strange. I thought it'd be the hardest thing in the world to do this, but now that I've started, it's sort of easy in a way.

"And Orpheus . . . well, he's half-angel. And he's the son of the angel of death."

Wren stays silent.

"And he came to our world because Lily Morgan stole the keys to the afterlife from his mum, which is why no one's been able to die. I've been helping him get the keys back, and we succeeded, but . . ." My voice catches. "Well, see, Lily's been using the stolen magic of converted witches to power confiscated artefacts. One of those artefacts severs a person's spirit from their body, and before Orpheus and I got away, she used it on me."

I look back at the spot where the invisible door is.

"Orpheus has gone to talk to his mum, and he's going to try and persuade her to save me, but . . . but if she says no, then I'll . . ."

Wren puts a hand on mine. "You'll die?"

At long last, I face them. The shock has left their face; only concern remains.

"Yes," I say, feeling the tears start to return, "I'll die."

Wren scoops me into another hug and lets me cry against them once more.

"You're not mad at me?" I say through sobs.

"Mad at you? Never." They sit back. "This angel boyfriend of yours had better be as magical as he sounds, because there's no way in hell you're dying today."

I shake my head, laughing lightly. "He's not my boyfriend."

They raise their eyebrows. "I thought you were done with the lies?"

I shove them playfully. "I just told you I'm dying. This is not the argument we're supposed to be having."

They shove me back. "You're not dying. If you expect me to believe the frankly ridiculous story you just told me, you can bet I'm also going to believe that you're going to live."

I bite my tongue. I know they're only being positive to keep me from losing hope, but I can't pretend it isn't working ever so slightly.

"And honestly?" They pause, considering their next words. "I'd be lying if I said I hadn't started to suspect the whole warlock thing."

I thought there wasn't anything left to shock me. "Really?"

"I don't know . . . there were these little hints over the years. The way you spoke about your dad and his work, things you said about your Gran. I was never sure, and I hadn't suspected for a while, but then you were suddenly all interested in witchy stuff the other day. I figured you'd tell me when you were ready."

There are plenty of things still weighing me down, but I really do feel lighter.

"I'm sorry I lied."

Wren shakes their head. "There's nothing to apologise for. You made a promise to your Gran, and I know how much she meant to you. I'm just glad you felt able to tell me eventually.

"Now," they say, tilting their head in a way I know means they're desperate for gossip, "I know you're leaving some juicy details out, so tell me again from the beginning. What happened?"

Chapter Thirty-Three
Orpheus

The Halls of Styx aren't the way I left them. The ethereal glow is dimmer than I've ever seen, and there are cracks running through every surface, emanating from the door I've just stepped through. There's a chill in the air and a distant howling from a wind that shouldn't exist.

"Mother!" I call.

There's no answer. Instead, there's a loud crunch as though from great stones colliding with each other, and everything shudders. I stumble but regain my balance. Charon was right about the Halls crumbling. Mother needs the keys to be able to restore things, but she's going to need to listen to me first.

I make my way along the corridor, turning when it feels right. The internal map I know so well is coming back to me, even if it feels more fragmented than before. Instinct will lead me to Mother. That's just how things work here. I'm not in the mortal world anymore.

There's another painfully loud noise as a crack snakes along the ceiling above me. I quicken my pace while also trying not to fall as everything around me continues to shudder.

Soon enough, I find myself at the edge of the central forest. The fake cloudy sky above is dark grey, and the trees before me have lost all their leaves. Through their sparse, bare branches, I can see the cabin I've called home for so long. Half of its roof has caved inwards, and Mother stands in front of it, her back to me, wings spread as she holds her hands aloft. I watch as planks of wood rise and slot together above her. She's trying to repair the roof.

"Mother!" I call again.

Immediately, her arms drop, and she turns around. The moment she spots me, she flies over, faster than I've ever seen. Twigs snap from the trees and fall to the dying grass below as she brushes past them.

"Orpheus!" Her eyes are frantic. Long gone is the emotionless face I'm used to seeing. "Do you have the keys?"

I grasp them tightly in my pocket. "Yes."

Joy rises in her face.

"But I can't give them to you."

And it disappears just as quickly.

"Not until you make me a promise."

She stares at me with a perplexion that has never been directed my way before. "Orpheus, don't be ridiculous. Hand the keys to me."

"No."

"Look around! This is not the time for playing games!"

"I'm not playing games. I only found the keys because I had the help of a warlock, and because he helped me, he is now dying. I won't give you the keys unless you promise to save him."

There's a fury igniting in Mother's eyes, and I know I'm treading on dangerous ground. But this needs to be done.

"What are you talking about?" she says through gritted teeth.

"There's a boy named Evan. He's a warlock, and he helped me find the keys. A spell was cast on him that severs his spirit from his body. As soon as you go back to reaping souls, he will die. Unless you save him."

Another thunderous crunch echoes around us, and the distant howling grows louder. Mother studies my face like it's entirely new. In a way, I suppose it is. I'm not the person I was when she last saw me. That person had never been to the mortal world. He'd never experienced human life. He'd only ever heard about it through the stories of the dead. But now I know what humanity truly is. I know how beautiful and terrible it can be in equal measure. And I love it.

"Orpheus, there are rules."

"Rules can be broken. You've broken them before. You let dad live here when he wasn't supposed to!"

"That was different."

"No, it wasn't. You broke the rules because you loved him. Well, I love Evan. It's exactly the same."

Mother shakes her head. The ground shudders, and a nearby tree falls over, turning to dust as it topples.

"I learned about Father while I was on Earth."

Mother's eyes falter.

"I know that he was a warlock. It was because of his notes and an artefact he made that someone knew how to steal the keys."

I wonder if she's picturing my father now. If she's remembering how she twisted the rules for him. Can she see her feelings for him reflected in my feelings for Evan? Can she remember the pain I'm feeling? The pain I know she felt when she lost him, no matter how much she tries to pretend to be emotionless?

"This is the only thing I'll ever ask of you," I say. "I swear it. The only thing. Just please, please save Evan."

Chapter Thirty-Four
Evan

"You're right," says Wren, face filled with glee as they scroll through their phone. "It's already spreading, and most people here aren't even awake yet. Other countries are going wild, though." They look at me, beaming. "This could genuinely change things. The witchfinders are screwed. Also, not that it matters, but I can't believe you met Chantelle Adeyemi."

I smile back, but it's half-hearted. I'd love to see the downfall of the witchfinders, but I don't think I'll be alive for it.

A noise from the corner of the room grabs both our attention. It's Orpheus, stood in a doorway that was invisible before. I leap off the sofa, catching a glimpse of a dimly lit wall behind him as he steps through before the door swings shut and vanishes from sight again.

"Woah," says Wren.

I'd laugh, but there's something in Orpheus' face that stops me. Before he went through the door, he was the personification of hope. But now?

"It didn't work, did it?" I ask.

"Actually, it did." He smiles, but it's even weaker than mine has been. "There's a way to save you."

My heart skips a beat, but my face doesn't know what to do. Why doesn't he sound happy? This is good, isn't it? This is what we wanted.

"How?"

Orpheus steps towards me. "We need to keep your spirit and body fused together. Two things stored in one singular form." His hand rises to the anchor, grasping the quietly ticking circular pendant. "Luckily, we've got something that can do that."

"Okay," I say, hope rising, "but why aren't you . . ." I trail off, realisation falling like a heavy rain that soaks me to the bone.

"But this is the only anchor in existence," he adds.

And now his sadness becomes mine. Because yes, I will live, but Orpheus can't stay in this world without the anchor. If he gives it to me, he'll have to go back to the Halls of Styx forever.

"You don't have to do this," I say through the new lump rising in my throat.

Orpheus almost laughs, but there are tears forming in his eyes at the same time. "I made a promise. I'm not going to let you die."

I step forward and reach my hand up to his face, wiping away one of his tears.

Wren says, "I'll leave you two to talk," and I hear them close the living room door as they exit.

"This isn't fair," I say, sniffing as I look up into Orpheus' beautiful face. The face I'd hoped I'd be able to see every day from now on. "You were supposed to stay here. We were supposed to go on that date. I promised. You made me promise!"

The more he cries, the redder the whites of his eyes get, making the blue of his irises even more intense. The blue of the ocean we'll never see together.

"Can't your mum make another anchor?" I ask, though I already know what the answer will be.

He shakes his head. "It was made by the gods. It's not the sort of thing they do twice. They won't be happy about me giving it to you." He glances behind him, in the direction of the invisible door. "Mother only gave me a few minutes. She needs to start doing her job again."

I wrap my arms around him and bury my face into his chest. "I don't want you to go."

I feel his arms wrap around me too. His voice is thick with emotion when he says, "Nor do I."

It feels crazy to admit after knowing him for such a short amount of time, but I've truly never felt safer than when I'm in Orpheus' arms. Everything in me tells me that this feeling is right, that we belong together like this. Wren could see it, too. They've seen it for longer than I have.

I move back so that I can look Orpheus in the face again, and despite my shaking breath, it's with absolute certainty that I say the words, "I love you."

"I love you too."

There are so many conversations I want to have with him. So many places I want him to see. So much life to live and adventures to have. But for me to stay alive, none of that can happen.

"Will I ever see you again?" I ask, my hands finding his.

He nods. "As long as you keep the anchor on, you'll stay alive. But when you're old and grey, when you've lived a good, long life and you're at peace, you can take it off. Your door will open, and I'll be there."

My heart shatters at the thought of not seeing him for so many years.

"But you need to promise me you won't take it off any sooner," he adds. "Promise me you'll live a full life. I want you to see the world, spend time with friends, fall in love again." He runs a hand through my hair, smiling through the tears. "Promise me."

It takes everything in me to be able to speak rather than break down. "I promise."

Orpheus keeps one hand in mine as he turns and opens the invisible door again, revealing a rectangular hole in the air. He steps through it, then turns back to me for the final time.

He cups my face and brings it to his, kissing me through the doorway. Kissing me at the boundary between worlds. I close my eyes and pretend for a moment that we're just two ordinary boys in love. That we've got the rest of our lives ahead of us to spend together. That love really does conquer all.

But then I feel a cold chain slide over my neck, and when I open my eyes, I find Orpheus transforming on his side of the door. He has returned to his angel form, with his wings spread behind him and a warm glow emitting from his skin. He really is the most beautiful person I've ever seen.

The anchor isn't around his neck anymore; it's around mine. I can feel its power already. That distant dizzy feeling is gone, and there's a gentle, calming energy radiating through my chest.

Orpheus smiles at me one last time. He opens his mouth to say something, but he stops himself. And I understand completely. To say goodbye would feel too final. Too hopeless. There isn't time to say all we want to say. So this is it.

I smile back at him, and before either of us loses our composure completely, the door swings closed, and he's gone forever.

One Week Later

Chapter Thirty-Five
Orpheus

The Halls of Styx are almost fully repaired, though I still spot the occasional crack on the walls. Mother seals them when she gets the chance, but she's had a lot of reaping to catch up with. I don't join her at the doors anymore. I'm sure I will eventually, but for now, it's still too painful a reminder. The idea of catching a glimpse of the human world and not seeing Evan there hurts too much.

Instead, I spend time in my cabin. Mother offered to repair it, but I took on the job myself. Now that I know this will be my home forever, I figured I should learn some of Mother's powers. It turns out even a half-angel can craft elements of reality, at least in this realm. The cabin wasn't so hard to fix – I just had to hold the desired image in mind and guide it with my hands. Of course, it brought back the memory of Evan casting his spells. I found myself picturing him beside me, holding his wand aloft and stitching together the fabric of the universe to build a home for us to share.

I didn't restore the forest to its original design. The green leaves didn't feel right after my days in the human world. Instead, I gave them the orange hue that so often surrounded me and Evan. Autumn feels fitting. The state between the warmth of summer and the cold of winter. A liminal space between beginnings and endings. It's where I feel I belong.

Mother doesn't say much on the rare occasion that she sees me, but there's an odd look in her eye when she does. It's a look more complex than the apathy she usually wears, and I think, perhaps, that she understands how I'm feeling. There's empathy there, behind her mask. I saw it when she explained how the anchor could save Evan. I saw it when I came back through the door after seeing Evan for the last time. Before she locked the door, she held my gaze and said words I never expected to hear.

"I'm sorry."

I didn't reply to her. I couldn't. All I wanted in that moment was to be with Evan, and since that wasn't possible, I wanted to be alone. My chest was filled with heartache and resentment. Resentment at the world, which I couldn't help but direct towards my mother. Even though I know that none of it is her fault.

I made sure to tell her what happened when I saw Charon and how he believed she'd lose her position as the psychopomp. But the gods haven't deposed her, at least not yet, and she's been having frequent meetings with them, so I think she's safe. She seemed more concerned about my second brush with Charon, and what the golden energy that filled his realm could have been, but as far as I'm concerned, that's a problem for the gods to deal with.

Mother has passed the cabin a few times over the week, sometimes asking if I want to join her as she heads to another door, sometimes merely observing me through the windows. Just yesterday, she watched as I ate a stack of pancakes, conjured from the memory of those I had in Wren's home. I thought about inviting her in and offering her a taste, but I wasn't ready. Not yet.

Today, I'm reading through old diaries. Well, not truly reading. I'm searching for a specific entry which might not even exist. One from approximately three years ago in mortal time. I've been searching almost every day since I returned home. I set another diary down after turning the last page and pick up the next one. Inside, I find an entry about a man named Edward and sigh as I begin to think that this is likely a fruitless venture, but then I turn the page to the next entry.

And here is what I've been hoping for.

Today, I met a woman named Sylvia. She seemed weary when I spoke to her and didn't have much to say. At least, not at first. She told me she was a witch, and that she had loved being one. She told me she had a son, who she wished hadn't turned out the way he did. She told me she had felt ready for death, in the end, and she seemed like she didn't want to say much more. But then her eyes lit up when she told me about her grandson, a boy named Evan, who was the greatest person she had ever known. She loved him more than words could possibly say, and he had given her hope, right through to her final moments. She knew that he would make her proud, even when she wasn't around anymore.

I run my finger across the entry, feeling my eyes fill with tears as I read the words over again. The memory of this encounter is so distant now, but I can just about picture Sylvia's face, and in it, I see Evan. I see his eyes. I see his smile. I hold the diary tight against my chest and find solace in the knowledge that Evan knew how much his Gran loved him.

Hours later, I sit in front of my favourite door, running my fingers across the cracked ocean blue wood just like old times.

"Orpheus?" Mother says.

I look up to see her in her blonde, white-gowned form, with that same odd look in her eyes that she's had all week.

"Yes?"

She walks towards me and, much to my surprise, sits down on the floor by my side.

"Mother?" I ask, perplexed.

"I miss your father all the time." Her voice is unlike I've ever heard it. Emotional. Full. *Human*.

I don't reply. I'm not sure how to. But I look in her eyes and see the sadness in them laid bare. I think she's been preparing these words all week.

"And I choose not to talk about him because I know that it would hurt." She pauses. "And I'm right. It does hurt." She reaches out and places a hand on mine. "I want you to know that I understand how you feel."

These are words I wasn't expecting. A topic I never thought she'd confront. I find myself feeling guilty. Here I am, mourning the loss of a boy I knew for just over two days, while my mother lost the father of her child.

I shake my head. "Mother, I'm sorry; I know I've been selfish. I—"

"No, Orpheus. We all grieve in our own ways. You should never be sorry for that."

I frown and look at the door. "How do you bear it?"

She rises from the ground, standing tall above me, wings spread. "You accept that they're never truly gone so long as you remember them. Your paths have crossed, and now you are both irrevocably changed. That's a connection that stays with you forever." She turns away and makes her way down the corridor, but she calls back one last message, "Why do you think you love that door so much?"

Chapter Thirty-Six
Evan

When the funeral ends, I feel empty. I thought it would bring me relief, that putting my dad behind me at long last would be like a transition into a new sense of freedom. But that's not what happens. Instead, I feel numb. Attendance is low, just as I expected for a man with such intense hatred inside him, so when Mum and I leave the crematorium, we don't have to speak to many people. What I don't expect, however, is the large crowd outside.

Camera flashes and loud strings of questions explode towards me the moment the doors open. Wren steps in front of me to block the paparazzi's view, and I take the chance to rush Mum over to the nearby car, her eyes still red and teary.

"I'm sorry, Mum," I say, closing the door once we're in. "I didn't think they'd be here."

My TV interview is scheduled for later this afternoon. I knew agreeing to it would bring undesired attention, but I didn't anticipate it being quite this invasive. Still, I know it's something I have to do. Ever since the news spread about what happened last week, people have been desperate to hear from the warlock who was at the centre of it all. It's only thanks to me going public that Dad's funeral got pushed up to today. The waitlist has been huge since the mass deaths that followed the restoration of mortality.

"Are you okay?" asks Wren as they take the front passenger seat.

"Not really," I reply. I turn to the driver. "Can you take us home, please?"

I check my phone as the car starts to move. There are texts from a few of Mary's coven, plus Charlotte, all wishing me luck for the interview. Some of them have already braved the cameras. Just yesterday, Mary, Jacob and Chantelle were on a talk show discussing witch rights and their hopes for the future. Of course, there were some anti-witch "activists" on too, but they looked far less comfortable. Apparently, the show tried to get some witchfinders on but weren't able to find any willing volunteers. What with their leader dead and Lily Morgan under intense investigation, the witchfinders can barely even call themselves an organization at the minute.

I've had my own share of being investigated too. In the aftermath of last week, the police had plenty of questions for me. I did perform illegal magic, after all, something which might still get me into trouble. But what with the fact that I helped stop the immortality and expose the witchfinders, for now, my trial is being postponed, and I'm not being held in custody. And hey, if Wren's optimism is to be believed, maybe my TV appearance today will help get some laws changed.

There's a buzz from my phone, and I open it to see a text from Charlotte, letting me know that her coven are showing signs that they might wake up soon. That's some good news, at least.

And how's Tamara? I text.

Better, Charlotte replies.

I smile, picturing the two of them together. It was one of the first things I learned about after contacting Charlotte in the days following the restoration of mortality: Tamara had shown up out of the blue, asking Charlotte if they could talk. She's been flitting in and out of lucidity ever since, and if rumours are to be believed, then I think I had something to do with it.

It seems that some witches who underwent conversion and are still alive have been getting their magic back over the last week. Breaking those jars in the Witchfinder HQ may have cost me time that meant Lily was able to catch up to me before I escaped, but at least it's led to this. I just wish Gran was still around to see it.

"Your gran would have been proud, you know?" says Wren. They're sat on my bed, watching as I adjust my tie for the millionth time.

"Hm?"

"She'd have loved seeing you do this. Taking a stand. Going public. Taking down the witchfinders."

I smile, looking at myself in the mirror. It feels wrong to only be switching my tie before heading out for the interview, but I only own one suit, so people are just going to have to deal with the fact that everything but the tie is the same as it was at the funeral. The TV people did offer to change the day when they found out the funeral was happening, but I told them it doesn't matter. My dad is gone now; I'm not going to let him have any further impact on my life.

"It might not make that much difference," I say. "Other witches have already said all the things I'm going to cover. Especially Chantelle."

"Yeah, but people will listen to you. You're the one who saved the world."

I roll my eyes. I didn't save the world. At least, not on my own. If it hadn't been for Orpheus, I'd have suffered through the immortality with everyone else until the world crumbled. He should be here with me now, preparing for this TV appearance together.

I put a hand to my chest, feeling the anchor beneath my tie, the small metal instrument that's keeping me alive. It's the one part of my story I've kept secret from everyone except Wren. To the world, I am an unscathed hero. They don't know quite how perilously close my life came to its end. They'll never know the sacrifice Orpheus made to keep me alive.

I feel a familiar pang as I take one last look in the mirror. The longing for Orpheus to be here with me. For it to be his face looking back at me rather than my own. In the moments after he closed the door, I thought of so many things I wanted to say to him. Words that can't be spoken until I see him again, many decades from now.

"The car's here," says Wren. "Are you ready?"

I take a deep breath as I wait backstage. The camera crew are preparing, and the show's hosts are already sat on their sofa, waiting to welcome me. I feel like a ball of anxiety, even despite the many supportive texts from other witches plus Wren's unwavering optimism. Still, I know this is what I have to do. The events of last Sunday were the starting point. The first domino in a long, long line. This is just another domino.

From the corner of my eye, I spot my new companion. It has followed me ever since the moment death came back to the world. I suppose it's been there for my entire life, really. Everyone has one, after all.

Ever since my fate was sealed as someone on the very edge of life, clinging on thanks to the anchor, I've been able to see it. It's always nearby, drifting along whenever I travel. I'm sure many would see it as a harbinger, or a morbid reminder of how close death is at every turn. But not me. For me, it's a new source of strength.

The blue door, with its worn-out surface and shining brass handle. The door that stands between me and the afterlife. The door that one day, many years from now when

I take off the anchor, will open, and I will step through with a smile on my face. The door whose colour matches the eyes that I see every night in my dreams. The door behind which I choose to believe Orpheus is standing right now, cheering me on as I prepare for the next step in the life he granted me.

The door which remains closed so that all those in front of me can open.

About the Author

Based in West Yorkshire, England, Christopher Hartland is the author of Against the Stars. He's a queer, autistic writer with a particular love for sci-fi, fantasy, and romance. Despite going on to complete a physics degree, "author" was always his answer to the childhood question of "what do you want to be when you grow up?" When not writing, you can find him nerding out over musical theatre, playing Dungeons and Dragons, or endlessly rewatching Doctor Who.

Acknowledgements

It's a daunting thing to write a second book, especially in a new genre, so I must first thank the readers of *Against the Stars*. I'll never get over seeing people expressing how much they enjoyed my writing, and it kept me thoroughly motivated through the writing of *Our Immortal Bind*. If you're reading this after *Against the Stars*, thank you for coming back, and if this is the first book of mine that you're reading then thank you for diving in!

One of the most important lessons in this book is Evan's realisation that he does in fact need a coven. While I am by no means a warlock, I am no stranger to the power that comes from the friends around me. I must therefore thank Onyx and Morel, who I lived with throughout the writing of this book, and who I am always able to bounce creative ideas off. You two are my equivalent of a coven and always will be. Zeriel forever!

Thanks must also go to Everett O'Donoghue, who read some of the very early drafts of the beginning of this book. I can always count on you to give me brutally (and beautifully) honest feedback. Also, with this book having such an autism focus I have to thank you once again for being the one who set me on the path to my diagnosis.

It takes far more than just an author to create a book – it's a whole team. Thank you to Thomas Shah and Melody Jaikes for your magical editing work, to Reuben Davies-Hoare for all the business and sales matters that I could never hope to understand, to Lewis Hughes for the marketing, and of course to Joshua Dean Perry for believing in this book and all the wondrous work you've done to bring it to life.

One of my favourite parts of the publishing process is seeing the cover, and what a cover this book has! Huge thanks to SJ Gautreaux for taking my words and turning them into beautiful art. Orpheus, Evan and every other detail look utterly perfect.

Last, but by no means least, I must thank Connie Ibberson for giving me my own love story while I worked on this one.

ALSO BY CHRISTOPHER HARTLAND...

AVAILABLE NOW WHEREVER BOOKS ARE SOLD
FOR MORE SPOOKY QUEER STORIES SIGN UP FOR OUR
NEWSLETTER AND FOLLOW US ON SOCIAL MEDIA

WWW.TINYGHOSTPRESS.COM
@TINYGHOSTPRESS

MORE BOOKS FROM TINY GHOST PRESS

AVAILABLE NOW WHEREVER BOOKS ARE SOLD

FOR MORE SPOOKY QUEER STORIES SIGN UP FOR OUR
NEWSLETTER AND FOLLOW US ON SOCIAL MEDIA

WWW.TINYGHOSTPRESS.COM

@TINYGHOSTPRESS

www.ingramcontent.com/pod-product-compliance
Lightning Source LLC
LaVergne TN
LVHW032004070526
838202LV00058B/6291